"I want to have a baby, Mac!"

Elizabeth could see the shock of the confession washing over him in waves.

"A baby? Elizabeth, I'm forty-six years old. I have two grown children."

"Well, I don't! Mac, do you know how much I've longed for a baby?" As she tried to explain, her voice held a strange intensity. "For as long as I can remember."

"I'm sorry. I wish you'd told me." He shook his head helplessly. "I didn't know."

"You do now."

There was a tense moment of silence. Then a regretful look slipped over Mac's features. "Elizabeth," he said, "I *can't* have any more children."

ABOUT THE AUTHOR

"Writing *Thy Heart in Mine* got me in touch with my own family history," says Cara West of her fourth Superromance novel. "My grandmother's father left Tennessee for Texas after the Civil War. I still have some of my grandmother's books, with the notes she wrote in the margins. I also have family letters dating back to the 1830s. Perhaps that's why the character of Sarah Elizabeth became so real to me." Cara lives in Austin. Her next Superromance novel , Lone Star Drifter,will be published next year.

Books by Cara West

HARLEQUIN SUPERROMANCE

Don't miss any of our special offers. Write to us at the following address for information on our newest releases.

Harlequin Reader Service
P.O. Box 1397, Buffalo, NY 14240
Canadian address: P.O. Box 603,
Fort Erie, Ont. L2A 5X3

Thy Heart in Mine

CARA WEST

Harlequin Books

TORONTO • NEW YORK • LONDON
AMSTERDAM • PARIS • SYDNEY • HAMBURG
STOCKHOLM • ATHENS • TOKYO • MILAN

Published October 1991

ISBN 0-373-70471-2

THY HEART IN MINE

To Joye and Lowell,
who grace my life with wit and wisdom....
With a special thanks to Joye,
who nurtures my prose....

PROLOGUE

THE OLD WOMAN sat at her writing desk near the window of her room. Springtime had come to Austin, and for a long moment she stared out on the shaded porch and beyond, to the grounds of the Confederate Widows' Home. But her senses were failing, and it was hard to distinguish the sights and sounds of the season. In vague frustration, she turned away from the window and ran a gnarled hand over the desk's mahogany surface and scrollwork detail, lingering over the texture of the wood beneath her fingers.

This piece of furniture was one of the few possessions she'd brought when she'd come to live in this room, in this place. She could remember the day her mother had chosen it for her out of a mail-order catalogue, a gift for the bride in her new home.

Her mother had been dead almost forty years now. Her father, longer. She'd outlived three brothers, their wives and most of their children. There were few people left to remember her. Yet there was so much to remember.

The past was hard to separate from the present. Days slipped away and became blurs in her mind. Voices crowded near, causing confusion.

It was time to die. At ninety-seven, she'd outlived her usefulness. And she was tired.

Feeling a sudden chill, the woman tugged at the shawl draped over her shoulders. Her body protested the simple movement.

It was time.

And yet she'd failed to find the peace that should come after a long, productive life.

No peace. No rest.

With an agitated flutter, her fingers tugged open the desk's top drawer. She found the volume she searched for, turned to the inside front cover and read the words she'd inscribed there.

Diary of Sarah Elizabeth LeBow, Volume IV

Fumbling through the pages, she found a blank one near the back. Carefully, she flipped the leaf of her daily calendar, her anchor to reality. After noting the day, she took her pen and wrote, "April 11, 1959."

Only then did she realize the significance of the date.

Seventy-nine years ago today she'd been married. The beginning of it all.

The pen fell to the desk, and she closed the diary with tremulous fingers.

She could write no more. There was nothing left to say.

Opening the drawer once again, she took out the other three volumes. The clippings. His letters. The letter.

A life was contained within these few precious mementos.

Would strangers read the diaries when she'd gone? Would they understand? Would they carelessly discard her memories?

Panic seized the woman's frail mind. She began to look around, her eyes searching frantically.

But there was no place to hide her treasures.

Then, with the mental acuteness that came from desperation, she remembered the floorboard near her bed, the one that creaked each time she trod on it.

She needed something to pry the board loose. Her look returned to the desk, and she spied the letter opener, heavy and ornate.

Her wedding gift from Johnny.

She took the brass implement and bent to her knees. With a long-forgotten strength, she worked at the pine plank until a space had been exposed between the floor and foundation. She gathered the papers and diaries, wrapped them in her shawl and stuffed the bundle into the nook she'd created.

The task accomplished, relief rushed over her.

Relief and exhaustion.

Still on her knees, she leaned against the bed for a moment, then pulled herself onto it and lay, closing her eyes. Her fingers clutched the brass letter opener.

So tired.

She must sleep awhile.

CHAPTER ONE

April 11, 1880

This afternoon I am to be Married. The Sun has barely peeked over the Horizon, yet it has already promised a Lovely Day. I feel as though it is bestowing a Blessing on the Union between myself and Mr. LeBow.

I confess I am somewhat apprehensive. Mr. LeBow is much older than I, and my feelings for him are more fond than ardent. But he is an old friend of Papa's—they fought in the Tragic War together. His cotton farm prospers, and Mama says that he will provide well for me and our children. Despite his forty-seven years, he is a Handsome, Virile Gentleman. And Mama says that at almost nineteen I am a grown woman, ready for Marriage. She expects me to dispense with childish frivolities.

You may notice Mama has a Great Deal to say about a Great Many Things. She feels that a Lady who has been sent at some expense to the Normal Academy for Females in Huntsville, Texas, should maintain her Education. At her suggestion, I intend to keep a daily Journal in order to record the events of the farm and to express my private thoughts. A writing desk has been ordered for just such a purpose to go in my new parlor. Not that Mama feels I should have thoughts that are private from my husband. However, in this one Particular, I do not think I shall do exactly as Mama says.

Indeed, I could not divulge to anyone the Terrible Quarrel I witnessed between Mr. LeBow and his son, Johnny. Mama had informed me of their earlier estrangement, which came about when Mr. LeBow asked Johnny to stay and work the farm. Johnny refused and left Bastrop to attend Columbia University in New York City. His ambitions have been quite the subject of Speculation in our small community.

Unfortunately, I fear our coming nuptials precipitated the current Disagreement. Johnny feels I am too young to marry his father. He informed us both that we were an ill-matched pair. I do not believe his words to be the Truth. However, they wounded me deeply, and I felt they were an Insult to my future Husband.

When the Quarrel became violent, I confess I grew frightened. I had not known two people could fly at each other so harshly. Fortunately, we shall not be seeing Johnny often. When he is graduated, he intends to live in Austin, our Capital City, and become a Reporter for the Newspaper there. A frivolous profession, as Mama says.

I only hope Johnny will not play the Ancient Mariner and cast a pall on the Ceremony with his Gloomy Visage.

Mama has sewn for me the loveliest gown. . . .

ELIZABETH WAITE glanced at her watch for the hundredth time and counted off the minutes.

She was suffering from nerves.

Sheer nerves.

Not unreasonable under the circumstances, but entirely uncalled-for. She'd been executive director of Austin's Capital Coalition for the Elderly less than a month. This January meeting would constitute her formal introduction to the other board members. Not even the most antsy among them expected miracles so soon.

This afternoon, she wouldn't be asked to conjure loaves and fishes to feed the multitudes, or rather, a two-hundred-thousand-dollar grant to pay off the mortgage on the building they'd recently moved into. The board prayed for that miraculous feat by June.

No, this afternoon Elizabeth had only to present herself as a compassionate, articulate, energetic, efficient, creative, assertive director who could lead the fledgling group of agencies out of the wilderness of inadequate funding and into the promised land of perpetual endowment.

On second thought, maybe she should be a little nervous.

"Here're the handouts you asked me to copy." Hope, Elizabeth's secretary, interrupted her thoughts. "Ready for your debut?" Hope settled into a chair as she asked the question.

"No. I'm working on a panic attack. How do I look?" Elizabeth stood and turned for Hope's inspection. "This suit was bought on sale especially for the occasion."

"You look cool, collected and elegant. The panic doesn't show."

"You're sure I don't look skinny?"

"Slim. Fashionably slim," Hope said firmly. "And the rose color flatters your complexion."

"It had better," Elizabeth said, grateful for the compliment. "Even on sale, this suit cost the earth."

"A sound investment."

Elizabeth grinned. "I thank you for your flattering words and bow to your professional judgment."

Hope Kersey had been a haute couture model in former days. Even in her late sixties, she kept her girlish figure and modeled in local shows, now that the clothing industry had awakened to the fact that women over fifty retained their sense of fashion.

"Just performing my duty," Hope said. "Third paragraph of my job description. Boost the morale of the director at least once a day."

"And for that, also, I am eternally grateful." Elizabeth bowed once more. "I don't know what I'd do without you."

Hope not only added glamour to the CCE offices, she was also the most efficient assistant Elizabeth had ever been blessed with. Elizabeth gave thanks daily that she'd decided retirement was dull.

Hope wasn't through with her pep talk, apparently. "You know, you shouldn't worry about this meeting. Everyone who's met you has been impressed. Especially after Louis."

By now, Elizabeth was aware of Hope's views on Louis Dennis, the previous director.

Still, she felt an obscure need to defend a fellow professional. "Louis was in over his head. It took courage to admit that."

"You're not issuing a veiled threat?"

Hope's mild anxiety was comforting.

"No. I don't plan to jump ship, even if it founders." Which they both knew was a distinct possibility. "Although sometimes I wish I were twins."

"You've just got a touch of stage fright." Hope's thoughts had returned to the meeting ahead.

"I've never worked with a volunteer board. My lack of experience in this area was the hiring committee's major concern."

But Mary had overridden that concern.

Mary Clark Reynolds, one of the founders of CCE and its original board president. Who, even though she'd resigned to make a place for her son, was the guiding light and power source of the coalition.

After the Louis Dennis disaster, she'd handpicked Elizabeth to be his successor.

Elizabeth's real fear was that she might not live up to Mary's expectations.

Or she wouldn't live up to her own.

Her thoughts scattered when she heard Hope offer, "I have a remedy for stage fright that works when I model."

"Oh?"

"Yeah. I imagine the audience with nothing on but their underwear."

Sudden pictures of board members flashed into Elizabeth's mind. Portly and fiftyish Jerry Tansy. Herb Briscoe, dapper at seventy-three. Carol Summers, the new president and youngest member, a walking advertisement for Neiman Marcus and the Junior League.

An incongruous trio, fully clothed.

Elizabeth's lips twitched at the images Hope's words had conjured. When the women's looks met, they broke into giggles.

Finally Elizabeth sputtered, "Just the thought of Jerry Tansy stripped to his skivvies boggles my mind."

"See what I mean? It's working already."

"What you see is hysteria. Stay and listen while I go over my speech."

THIRTY MINUTES LATER, Elizabeth sat beside Carol Summers in the second floor conference room, trying to pay attention to Herb Briscoe's treasurer's report. He'd already dissected it with Elizabeth this morning, and her mind drifted to the upcoming performance.

She felt her stomach knotting, and she clutched her hands together tightly, focusing intently on Herb's bow tie.

Boxer shorts. Pressed boxer shorts with neat creases, fresh from the laundry—Herb was a widower. With a pattern of little red hearts, to match his crimson tie and socks. Herb went in for matched accessories.

Elizabeth's lips curved slightly. He caught her smile and returned one of encouragement.

After a disconcerted moment she looked away. Her gaze came to rest on Jerry Tansy, whose tastes ran to gold nugget cuff links and pinky rings. Elizabeth had an awful suspicion he also had a penchant for bikini underwear in exotic hues. She bit her lips, fighting amusement.

When Carol asked a question, she drew Elizabeth's attention.

Silk. Nothing but silk would adorn Carol's sleek body. Lane Summers, her husband, could afford such trifles. He was a partner in a successful electronics firm.

Elizabeth glanced down at her hands. They lay relaxed in her lap. Hope's ploy had worked.

For the first time, Elizabeth allowed herself to scrutinize an unknown quantity—the man who'd arrived late and now leaned back in his chair near the fringe of the group.

A tall man in his mid to late forties, he had a muscular build and a broad back and shoulders. His size lent him an air of authority. He seemed to dominate the immediate area.

With salt-and-pepper hair, thick eyebrows and a rakish mustache, his features were too craggy to be called handsome. But he was undeniably attractive, and he radiated power.

Jockey briefs. White cotton jockey briefs. Stretched smooth over tapering hips and tight buttocks.

For some reason, the image reminded Elizabeth of her own cotton bra and panties.

The man caught her look. His brow arched inquiringly. A small smile tugged at his lips.

Elizabeth felt a wave of color creep up her neck.

She jerked around to stare at Carol unseeingly.

This was *not* what Hope had had in mind to calm her nerves.

In the midst of Elizabeth's embarrassment, Carol's introduction took a moment to penetrate her brain.

"…the moment we've been waiting for. Many of you have already met Elizabeth. The rest of you must come by after the meeting—with your name tags in place. But for now, it's my great pleasure to formally present the new executive director of the Capital Coalition for the Elderly, Ms. Elizabeth Waite."

Hoping her knees would support her, Elizabeth stood to a smattering of applause.

"Since this is the first time I've appeared before the entire board," she began, managing a smile and a steady tone, "I wanted to take the opportunity to thank you for the confidence you've shown in hiring me."

Elizabeth felt her hands shaking and folded them securely. "It's truly an honor and a privilege to be a part of such an innovative project. This group represents an affiliation of concerned agencies that understand the need for cooperation. Now, with the purchase of this wonderful old building, an Austin landmark—"

"And falling down around our ears," came Jerry Tansy's sotto voce remark.

"But a part of Texas history," Elizabeth countered, smiling. "I think it's fitting we should be housed in what used to be the Confederate Widows' Home. Many of the people we serve are widows and widowers, often indigent or on modest fixed incomes.

"This building has been mistreated and neglected, like many of our elders. We want to restore it to its former charm. Just as we hope to aid our clients in maintaining full and functional lives."

"I hear we have ghosts. The ladies who lived here." This came from a member Elizabeth had yet to meet.

"Well, if we do," Elizabeth said, "I haven't seen them. Although, I have to admit, I wouldn't know a ghost if it tapped me on the shoulder."

Her answer drew laughter.

"I do feel," she said more soberly, "that if any of the gentle ladies haunt their old home, they'd approve of the way we're putting it to use.

"Which leads me to what I wanted to talk about briefly—the challenges I see before us. I felt you'd want to hear about the plans I've made, so I could get your input. Soon, I hope to meet with each of you to get your perspective on the job ahead.

"Certainly, our first Spring Fund-raising Gala is of vital importance. Although the board has responsibility for this event, I wanted to say I'll be glad to help in any way I can."

"Is this on top of your twelve-hour days?" Herb asked. He turned to the people seated around the room. "We can't overwork Elizabeth or we'll lose her." Herb, one of the most knowledgeable board members, was also one of its shrewdest. He knew more than most the stresses and strains of her job.

Elizabeth nodded, acknowledging his comment, and said, "That brings me to my primary duties."

This was the part of the speech Elizabeth had planned most carefully. She wanted to show the board they'd hired a competent professional who could act on events rather than just react to them, someone who shared the board's vision for what the future held.

"Our most pressing need is to pay off the mortgage. I've already contacted various foundations to find out which ones have money that can be used this way."

"If we ever get the note paid off," Herb reminded them, "Mac can work up a cost estimate for the renovations."

All eyes turned to the man Elizabeth had just mentally undressed.

Mac. Mac Reynolds, Mary's son. Elizabeth should have guessed as much.

"I've already come up with an estimate," Reynolds said, his voice incisive. "After we hear from Ms. Waite, I'll hand out the figures."

He gave her a slight nod, effectively placing the meeting back into her hands. Elizabeth was torn between gratitude and irritation.

"I know we're all anxious to see your estimate, Mr. Reynolds," she said, suppressing both emotions. "So I'll be as brief as I can."

Taking a deep breath, she continued with the major points of her prepared remarks, emphasizing the goals she'd set for interagency cooperation, the additional services she hoped to lure to the building and the programs she herself hoped to develop for both the well and frail elderly.

When Elizabeth saw encouraging nods around the room, she knew she'd captured everyone's attention.

Even Reynolds leaned forward, rewarding her with a penetrating look.

"Will these programs pay for themselves?" someone asked. "December's financials were awful."

"Yes, they will." Elizabeth paused, knowing finances were on everyone's mind. "I believe Herb intends to present a revised annual budget at February's meeting, which would be a good time for us to explore other fund-raising options, such as an Arts and Crafts Fair.

"Until then, I just want to say that the coming year will be challenging and exciting, and I can't tell you how happy I am to be here to help meet that challenge. I am as committed as you are to the coalition's success. Thank you."

She sat down to the vigorous clapping of hands. It wasn't her all-time best performance. But at least she'd put on a creditable show.

Carol seemed to agree. She stood, still clapping. "Now you know why the committee was so excited about Elizabeth. I think we've found the perfect person for the job."

It was obvious everyone was pleased—and would continue to be so—until the honeymoon ended.

"Mac," Carol said, "I believe you have some figures to share with us."

He stood and distributed the handouts. "I'm sorry I was late. I had to stop by my office to pick these up. Luckily, I didn't miss our leader's stirring call to arms."

Elizabeth glanced at him sharply. Was he making fun of her?

No.

More likely he was just a man who found humor in most situations. Still, she was discomfited with the notion that he'd read her intentions so clearly.

She made a point of rewarding his quip with an appreciative smile.

"Mac." This was Herb, who was studying the columns. "I'm surprised the bottom line is so low."

"Most of the construction materials will be donated," Mac explained.

"By Reynolds Industries?" Herb guessed dryly.

Mac nodded and grinned. "Why do you think Mother put me on the board?"

His rhetorical question drew spontaneous cheers.

As well it might. The company's donation would run to thousands of dollars. Elizabeth made a mental note to be particularly accommodating and available to Mr. Reynolds. In a purely professional capacity, of course.

"If you have the time, I'd like us to meet for a moment after the meeting, Ms. Waite."

Elizabeth almost started when Reynolds's request so nearly mirrored her thoughts. "Certainly," she agreed. "And everyone, please, call me Elizabeth."

After Mac sat down, Carol asked, "Does anyone else have new or old business to discuss?"

Elizabeth could tell by Carol's voice she was nervous as she asked this question.

There were any number of items the board needed to take up, as well as disagreements to be aired. Even minor territorial skirmishes between certain of the agencies. And Elizabeth knew Carol was finding it hard to fill Mary's shoes.

But it seemed the board was as anxious as Elizabeth to present a good first impression.

THY HEART IN MINE

No one spoke up and the meeting was adjourned. Afterward, Carol squeezed Elizabeth's hand with satisfaction before allowing various members to surge around their new leader.

Elizabeth took introductions, answered questions and tried to memorize names of people she didn't know. In the periphery of her vision, she saw Herb and Carol give each other the high sign, then draw Mac into conversation.

After ten minutes or so, Elizabeth saw him look her way and glance at his watch. Mustn't keep the great man waiting. She excused herself and went over to the trio.

"So what do you think of Mary's taste in directors?" Herb asked with a wink, to Elizabeth's chagrin.

"My mother's taste is impeccable." Mac sent Herb an amused look.

Carol seemed to think his answer highly entertaining. The nuances of the exchange were lost on Elizabeth.

She took refuge in conventionalities. "I'm grateful Mary recommended me. I just hope I can justify her faith. Your mother is something of an idol of mine. I respect her enormously and have for years."

"I'm sorry to hear it," Mac said disconcertingly. "That means Mother has you exactly where she wants you."

Elizabeth blinked, not sure she'd understood him correctly. "I beg your pardon?"

"Carol, I'm surprised," Mac said, turning Carol's way. "I thought by now you'd have taught our lamb the facts of life."

"It was impossible to prepare Elizabeth for the Reynolds family."

"True," Mac murmured. "So I guess it's my duty." His eyes met Elizabeth's. "Mother is completely amoral when it comes to pet causes. She'll use fair means or foul to accomplish her goals. And admiring disciples make willing slaves.''

"I see." And Elizabeth did. However, she didn't appreciate being called a lamb. She also didn't like his gently mocking attitude. "Tell me, how should Carol have prepared me for you, Mr. Reynolds?" A challenge lurked beneath her pleasant tone.

Mac's brow shot up at the feistiness cloaked by her polite facade. "I think," he said thoughtfully, after a moment, "it would work best if I made my own introductions."

"So how did you come to be on the board? Are you one of Mary's disciples or a willing slave?"

"Neither. I'm pressed into service when the occasion demands. She's equally unscrupulous with her own kith and kin."

Discreet laughter seemed Elizabeth's wisest recourse. She'd already taken this conversation down a risky path.

"I believe you wanted to see me." She changed the subject with a smile. "Would you like to come to my office?"

With a nod, Mac acknowledged her efforts to seek sheltered waters. She led the way down the stairs in silence. Following her, he noted with detached appreciation her straight shoulders, slender back and well-turned rear.

Elizabeth's thoughts were more disturbed. She couldn't seem to safely converse with this man or ignore the irony of his verbal thrusts.

Yet she mustn't give in to the temptation to spar.

So what if he thought she was an earnest drudge? He could have a worse opinion, she decided fatalistically.

When Hope greeted Mac with the ease of a long-lost friend, however, Elizabeth felt mild envy. She doubted her own ability to be so comfortable with him.

"What did you need to discuss with me?" she asked moments later, settling behind her desk, obscurely comforted by the physical barrier. Relaxing a little, she gestured toward a chair, inviting him to sit.

Mac ignored the offer, choosing to stand by the window. He turned to her. "I think we ought to start improvements as soon as possible."

"You mean now?" He'd startled her and she blurted out the obvious. "We can't do that until I find money to pay off the loan."

"How long should that take?" he asked briskly.

"Well, I don't know. Every foundation has a different deadline. And once I find the two or three that are receptive to our request, I'll have to write grants geared toward their differing guidelines." She said the next in a conciliatory tone. "In the nonprofit world, Mr. Reynolds, two hundred thousand dollars is a lot of money."

"Mac," he ordered.

"Mac," she repeated obediently.

"Without the complete payment, CCE should never have contracted to move into this building."

Elizabeth might have guessed the setup bothered him.

"As far as I can tell," he went on brusquely, "this organization was conceived in a fit of idealism. I'm not sure there was a realist in the entire bunch."

In other words, its founders were a group of fuzzyheaded do-gooders. Mac hadn't said the words, but Elizabeth could bet he'd thought them.

"Mr. Reynolds—Mac—Capital Coalition for the Elderly is an extremely important project, a prototype for agencies in other cities. Do you realize the red tape elderly persons have to go through to get help? The number of bureaucracies they have to deal with?'' A fervent note crept into her voice.

Mac heard it and wondered if Elizabeth knew how attractive she was in passionate defense of a cause.

Apparently not, because she went on intently. ''Our clients get lost in the maze and don't know where to turn. Neither do the families who care for them—when they have families. All too often these people live alone and isolated, in substandard housing. With inadequate medical attention . . .''

Elizabeth realized suddenly she'd mounted her soap-box. Mac was studying her oddly, as if something about her had caught his regard.

Was he even listening to the words she spoke?

She felt a spurt of anger and immediately suppressed it. Taking a deep breath, she finished firmly, ''The coalition is making an attempt to address the problems our elderly face. That's why it's so important we succeed.''

He stared at her for a moment longer, then asked abruptly, ''How do you plan to do that if you can't pay the bills? The heating system in this place is fifty years old. And with the present air-conditioning, you won't make it through the summer.''

''Yes, I see what you're saying,'' she said thoughtfully. ''However, we're required to hire an architect and have a plan approved by the historical society before we start renovations. That could take time.''

''How much time? Does the society plan on paying your utilities this August? Someone's going to have to, because with our current revenues, we don't have the money.''

"I believe," Elizabeth reminded him formally, "that fund-raising will be discussed at the next board meeting."

"But will anything get done? I know all about decision by committee. By the time the board takes action, you all could be out on the street."

Elizabeth stared at him, momentarily speechless. Didn't he think she knew all this? Didn't he realize she took these problems home every evening? Didn't he have an inkling they kept her awake at night?

He must have caught a hint of her feelings, because his expression softened and his next words were kind. "I don't mean to corner you."

Didn't he?

"But as a businessman, I believe in paying as you go and attacking a problem to find a solution."

Taking over, he meant.

Mac sighed as if he could read her thoughts. "I'll try to get hold of the two hundred thousand. There are a few arms I can twist."

Elizabeth stopped herself from instinctively objecting to his offer. If Mac couldn't find the money, she'd have to beg elsewhere.

"And I'll get Lawrence Manley to look the place over."

Elizabeth swallowed hard. "Won't he be expensive?" Manley was a local architect known for his meticulous restorations.

Mac sent her a look tinged with irony and went on without answering. "At which point I'll get approval to begin the job. I wanted to fill you in on my plans. And ask you to back them."

"That's very thoughtful," Elizabeth murmured, not above an irony of her own. "I am, of course, in favor of any measures that will contribute to our financial health. However, as you say, everything we've discussed today will need board approval.''

"I suspect I'll get it." For the first time Mac unleashed a smile that was positively dazzling. "Don't you?"

"Yes," she agreed, nodding meekly. "I'm sure you will."

THE WINTER SUNSHINE was bright yet dappled with shadows as it streamed in Elizabeth's window.

Elizabeth didn't notice. Mac had just left and she was lost in thought.

One shadow in particular seemed to change and take form as it glided along the outside wall, slipping past each office as though searching...searching....

So tired...so alone. Yet there was no peace....

At the corner window, looking into a room that was bare of furniture, the shadow grew until it blocked the sun, casting gloom over the dingy walls and linoleum floor.

The treasures of a lifetime.

Words written long ago. Would no one find and read and understand them...and finally put that life to rest?

CHAPTER TWO

July 17, 1881

It is near midnight, and I am very Weary. Sleep has been a rare Commodity these last several days. Yet I feel within me the need to be alone with my thoughts and to try to comprehend the Terrible Event which has befallen us.

Mr. LeBow lies near Death even as I write. Only days ago, he was hale and hearty. As you know, he is easily inclined to Anger, so I was not unduly distressed when he came in from the fields, flushed and shouting. Before I could ascertain the cause of his Agitation, he fell to the floor in a fit of Apoplexy. Within moments, he lay unconscious at my feet.

I contained my Horror as well as I was able and sent for Dr. Peters and Mama. While I awaited their arrival, I did what I could for Mr. LeBow. He was unresponsive to my ministrations. When Dr. Peters arrived, he did not believe Mr. LeBow would live out the night. God has spared my Husband, however, and we pray for His continued Mercy.

The day after Mr. LeBow fell into a stupor, I telegraphed Johnny and informed him of his father's Condition. He rode over from Austin and was here by nightfall. Now he, Mama and I keep constant Vigil, not knowing when the Appointed Hour will come, when our Fears are to be transformed to Sorrow.

*Johnny is with his father now. Mama will take over
the watch at sunrise so that I may have a refreshing
Sleep. I thank God for Johnny and Mama. They do not
get along in the ordinary way of things. However, they
have put aside their Differences in this Anxious Hour.*

*I hardly know what I am doing from moment to mo-
ment, so filled am I with Dread and Confusion....*

"WHAT'S WRONG?" Hope asked when she came into
Elizabeth's office several minutes after Mac had gone.

"I think I've been run over by a steamroller."

"You mean, a Mack truck?"

Elizabeth grimaced.

Hope hung her head. "I'm sorry. The words just
slipped out of my mouth. So," she said, her contrition
short-lived, "which question do I ask first? How the
board meeting went? Or what this conference with Mac
was about?"

"The meeting went well. Although you failed to
mention the dangers of disrobing your audience."

Although Hope looked intrigued by the comment,
Elizabeth decided elaboration was dangerous. Instead,
she went on, "I'm not sure I'm going to survive our Mr.
Reynolds, however."

"He can be overwhelming. But we're lucky to have
him."

"I know that, believe me, and I'm properly grateful.
Still, I can't help feeling he's been coerced. How much
pressure did Mary put on him to join the board?"

Hope shrugged. "Who knows? Mary's good at getting her way. Although I can't see Mac being coerced
into anything."

"No," Elizabeth said dryly. "And obviously he could
be a tremendous help. I'm just not sure he sees the va-

lidity of what we're doing. We've probably canceled each other's vote the last five elections."

"Mac might be fiscally conservative." Hope came to his defense. "He still cares about people. And I haven't seen a hint of racism, sexism or ageism in his attitude."

"I wouldn't expect there to be in one of Mary's children."

"Yes. And while all the other Reynolds, including his two brothers, became doctors, lawyers and Indian chiefs, Mac took over the family business. From all accounts he's done a hell of a job since his father died."

"Is he married?" Elizabeth asked casually.

"Divorced. With two grown kids. I heard he took them to raise when they hit adolescence. His ex-wife's on her third husband."

"I'm surprised he hasn't remarried, as well."

"Don't imagine it's for lack of candidates. He is, as you may have noticed, a very attractive man."

Elizabeth heard the suggestive note in Hope's voice and decided she didn't like the tenor of the discussion. "Did I tell you he's offered to scrounge around for the loan payment?"

"No, you did not mention it. What great news!" Something in Elizabeth's expression made Hope ask suspiciously, "You didn't object, did you?"

"Oh, no. Beggars can't be choosers. The good of the coalition comes before personal feelings."

Hope studied her boss for a moment. "Why do I get the feeling you don't like Mac very much?"

"Like? I'm not sure that's a term I'd use with the man. He reminds me of an elemental force. You're either swept along by him, or you sit tight and ride out the storm, or you get the hell out of his way."

"Elizabeth—" Hope looked at her soberly "—don't alienate Mac. He makes a better friend than enemy."

Elizabeth had the feeling she might have trouble with him in either role.

"MR. REYNOLDS—Mrs. Reynolds is on line one."

Mac picked up the receiver. "Mother?"

"How did it go?"

"I'm fine. Thank you for asking. And how are you?"

"Don't be difficult. How did Elizabeth acquit herself?"

"Can I expect a call like this every month? If you want to know what's happening, you should have stayed on the board."

"No," Mary murmured. "They need you more right now. Besides, Carol consults with me on important matters."

"Then why not phone her? Or Herb? Which reminds me, when are you going to have mercy on that man?"

Mary wasn't about to be sidetracked by idle conversation. "Carol and Herb are already in Elizabeth's corner. I wanted a more objective opinion. What's your impression of her?"

"As a director? She's a vast improvement over Louis Dennis."

"And?"

"She seems knowledgeable and committed."

"Damned with faint praise. What did you think of her as a person?"

A suspicion popped into his mind. "Is it necessary for me to have an opinion of her personally?"

"You'll be working with her closely."

Closely?

"Mother, you're not doing what I think you're doing?"

"Don't be ridiculous. You and Karen have been divorced ten years. If you haven't found another woman to suit you by this time, I doubt you ever will. Although at forty-six, you're not getting any younger." Mary sighed elaborately. "I'd hate for a son of mine to have a lonely middle age."

"I feel the same." Mac's voice oozed sincerity. "At seventy-five, Mother, you're not getting any younger. I'd welcome Herb as a stepfather."

He heard a soft harrumph on the other end of the line.

After a long pause, Mary spoke again, her tone changed. "You will be kind to Elizabeth and help her any way you can?"

It was his turn to sigh. "If you see me as a threat to your protégée, why did you ask me to get involved?"

"Don't put me off, please. Just listen. I think it's important for Elizabeth to do well in this job."

"I'm surprised, Mother. I didn't picture her as one of your salvage operations."

"She's not." Mary fairly snapped the words out. "I'd never place the coalition in the care of someone I didn't trust. She comes highly recommended from a job with the state Human Services Department. It's just that life hasn't been kind to her."

Visions of a tragic past came unbidden to Mac's mind. Odd he should get such a mental picture. As odd as his ability to recall Elizabeth's face in detail. She'd never be called conventionally pretty. Yet there was beauty in the high cheekbones and straight brows, and vulnerability in the wide-set brown eyes, despite her level look.

"You know," Mary said, "she's nearly forty and never married."

"I didn't know." Mac kept his voice noncommittal.

"And not for any of the reasons you're thinking."

He laughed. "What makes you so sure you can read my mind?"

"Men are all alike," she said sweepingly. "Twisted and perverted."

"I've never heard you complain before."

She pointedly ignored the comment. "I'm just saying Elizabeth's a perfectly normal, healthy feminine female, if a little repressed. I can't blame her."

Mac suspected he'd be sorry he asked, but he bowed to Mary's manipulation. "Why hasn't she married?"

"She took care of her parents for eight long years. When she was twenty-seven and engaged to be married, her mother developed terminal cancer. Her father—you remember Dr. Waite—was devastated, and Elizabeth moved home to care for them both. Unfortunately, the engagement didn't last long after that. Then, within weeks of her mother's funeral, Dr. Waite was diagnosed as having Alzheimer's disease. Elizabeth nursed him until he died four years ago. Now she lives all alone in that barn of a house."

"Didn't she have family to help her?"

"Only a brother who lived near Brownsville and came up to visit maybe twice a year. Elizabeth bore the brunt of the care giving. She's still recovering. So, be helpful, son. She needs you as an ally, not an enemy."

Thinking back to their exchanges, Mac smiled crookedly. He wasn't sure Elizabeth would permit him either role.

"I don't plan to oppose her," he assured Mary gently. "And she has no intention of opposing me, either."

Later, as Mac let himself in the front door of his West Lake Hills home, he breathed a sigh of weary satisfaction. It had been a long day but a productive one. The board meeting had had its moments. He'd worked through the snafu in a building materials delivery and finalized a supply contract with the new electronics consortium moving to town. He also stood to recoup some of his losses in a deal with a real estate company that had declared bankruptcy. So many of them had.

Pundits were calling the past few years the Great Austin Depression. Even though Mac had exercised good business sense during the previous boom, many of the companies he'd dealt with had risked heavily during those heady years of frenetic activity only to lose their shirts when the bottom fell out of the local market. The failures had produced a ripple effect, and Mac's shirt had on occasion been somewhat threadbare. Yet he'd weathered the boom and bust, and Reynolds Industries had survived, as well—leaner, more efficient and ready for the predicted upturn.

Mac had decided, however, that hustling to preserve and enlarge a fortune held only so much allure. He was ready to explore another side of life.

After ten anxious years of being a single parent, he'd also decided a furlough was due. Not that he begrudged a minute of those years. The three of them had pulled through the rough times, which was what was important.

Tracy he'd never been seriously worried about. She was the tough one, and she'd weathered Karen's emotional desertion amazingly well. She'd sailed through high school and college, and now at twenty-three, she was married and pregnant—much to her delight. Mac felt sure she had no intention of repeating her parents' mistakes.

Two years younger than Tracy, Evan had been a different matter. The divorce had confused and disillusioned him badly. When he'd lashed out at his parents, Karen had thrown up her hands and essentially abdicated. Mac had seen the adolescent danger signs and braced himself.

After Karen's second marriage failed and she'd turned to the globe-trotting life of the rich and restless, Evan had turned his anger inward and become self-destructive.

He'd gotten into drugs, almost flunked out of school and had ended up in a drug rehabilitation center. Evan was a survivor, however, like his sister. With professional guidance, he'd worked through his anger. Mac had hung in there for him, and the family had made it to the other side.

Evan would graduate this spring from the University of Texas with a degree in psychology, and he'd been accepted into graduate school in the fall. Eventually he planned to go into private practice working with troubled adolescents.

As Mac's thoughts wandered, he made a trip to the refrigerator. Patting his hard-earned flat stomach—only ten pounds to go—he chose a diet soft drink and went to sit on the deck overlooking the pool. Steam from the heated water rose gently in the wintry air. Maybe later he'd swim a few laps.

The evening was mild for the end of January, and his view of the hill country spectacular. Leaning back in the lounger, Mac was content to stare into space and contemplate the restlessness he felt stirring inside. Mac knew himself well enough to be aware of the symptoms.

He would never have called himself a lonely man. Still, with Evan soon to be leaving the nest, he'd rattle around this sprawling house. Perhaps he ought to design and build a new one.

God knows, as an eligible bachelor, he had more invitations than he could handle, but the social scene left him increasingly bored. There were too many Karens nursing their white wine while floating through the chattering crowds, and too few Elizabeths stopping to listen and engage in real conversation.

Now that was an interesting comparison. Mac admitted to himself the woman had made an impression. Not that he'd ever let Mary know.

Mary. Certainly, he could fill his days with her numerous causes—as long as he was willing to obey her every instruction.

Was Mary right? Had he doomed himself to a solitary life?

"Hey, Dad, where are you?" Evan's voice echoed through the expanse of rooms.

"Out by the pool."

Evan appeared at the sliding doors that led to the deck. "I'm starving. Did Doris leave something?" Doris was their cook and housekeeper.

"I think I smelled pot roast."

Evan started in search of supper, then turned and came outside. "Listen, Dad. You mind if I throw a party this Saturday? Sort of a 'beginning of the last semester' bash?"

"As long as Doris doesn't come back to a mess on Monday, and you don't drive me out of my home."

When Evan had entered college, Mac had offered to help him find a place of his own. Evan had chosen instead to "bach" it with his father. Mac suspected it was because of the turmoil of those earlier years.

"I'll organize a cleanup brigade at the end of the evening. And Dad," Evan said with a grin, "the guys said to invite you. You're such a party animal. Hell, you can even bring a date."

"Thanks." Mac cast a jaundiced glance his son's way. "I think I'll pass."

"You're slowing up. The years are showing. I can see you now playing checkers in the park."

"Better checkers than college high jinks. By the way, there's a cold front predicted. It might put a damper on outside activities."

"See what I mean?"

Mac arched an eyebrow.

"It's been my observation," Evan said solemnly, "that when old folks get together, they talk about the weather."

This was a challenge Mac couldn't ignore. "It's been my observation that when young studs get together, all they talk about is getting laid."

"Unfair! Unfair!" Evan looked wounded. "My friends and my discussions have a philosophical bent."

"Yeah. Like how getting laid relates to the meaning of life."

"There's also the psychological aspect to consider. How the frequency of sexual encounters relates to the mental health of the college male."

"Now I know what I missed in business school. It didn't offer a course linking sex with market fluctuations."

"Poor old Dad. Over-the-hill and still a babe in the woods."

Since Mac wasn't about to fill his son in on the finer points of his love life, he contented himself with growling, "Shut up, young whippersnapper, or I'll beat you with my cane."

He made a point of tottering from the chair. Evan retaliated by offering a solicitous hand, and a minor scuffle ensued, threatening the placid surface of the pool.

The ring of the phone interrupted their horseplay. Mac went to answer it.

"Dad, is that you?" Tracy asked.

"Who did you expect?"

"Well, you do look a little like Sean Connery with hair. Although I've noticed a certain thinning on the crown."

"I'm surrounded," he said sorrowfully, "by impudent children."

"Why? Is Evan giving you a hard time again?"

"Let's just say he's decided I've entered my declining years."

"Don't pay him any attention. Twenty-one year-olds can't imagine life after thirty-five." Tracy spoke from her own vast experience. "But you'll have to admit," she went on judiciously, "you're not getting any younger."

Mac felt a spurt of genuine anger. "Why the hell is everyone suddenly concerned with my age?"

"Oh, ho. Methinks I hit a nerve. Has Grannie been at you?"

Mac mumbled something, feeling uncommonly foolish.

"Not to worry," Tracy said kindly. "You're still the sexiest father in the state of Texas, and you have to beat the women off with a stick."

"Only in Texas?" Mac asked plaintively.

"Humph," Tracy muttered, giving a fair imitation of Mary. "I refuse to pander to your male vanity. I called because we'd like you to come to the house this Saturday. I'm having what is known as an intimate soiree. Evan can come if he promises to behave."

"Evan's planning a party here. You may have just saved my sanity."

Tracy laughed, then paused for a second. "You can bring Belinda, if you like."

Mac knew what the invitation cost Tracy. She made no bones of the fact she didn't care for his sometime companion and bed partner. She felt their relationship was casual, meaningless and drifting. And although it wasn't any of her business, Tracy was right.

"I'll come alone," Mac offered easily, "to provide you with an extra male."

"Okay, but be warned. Grannie's coming with Herb and an unattached woman friend. This new director she's so high on. Grannie says I'll like her and can pick up pointers."

Tracy was already following in Mary's footsteps and had been instrumental in organizing one of the year's most successful charity drives, for the Heart Association.

"Consider me duly warned. Actually, I've already met the lady. I'm on her board." Mac's voice held reluctant amusement. "I have a feeling your grandmother's making plans. Saturday night should prove very interesting. Especially when Elizabeth realizes Mary intends to take over her life."

IT WAS SEVEN in the evening. Elizabeth had worked late again, and her shoulders sagged as she parked in the driveway to her parents' home.

Her home, she reminded herself doggedly. Until real estate prices rebounded and she could sensibly sell it.

After sitting for a moment, too tired to move, she dragged her briefcase from the passenger seat and located the house key on her crowded key chain.

Elizabeth Waite, executive director. A more apt title would be executive gatekeeper.

She was guardian to every door at CCE. She had a master key to the various offices, one for the copier and the drink machine, and a small brass latchkey for her donated desk. She even possessed the combination to the vintage safe that up till now had been depressingly empty.

Stopping her mindless cataloging, Elizabeth went inside. Jezebel, Tom and Cleopatra met her with yowls of hunger.

Three cats and a spinster. Catchy name for a movie.

"Fatigue," she muttered, "has finally unhinged me. I know—" she leaned down to pet her housemates "—you don't give a hoot about my mental condition as long as I'm able to open the cans."

Jess answered with a prolonged rub along Elizabeth's ankles. Tom tried to scale her expensive new suit. Cleo, the oldest and no longer the wanton temptress the name implied, was content to lean her head into Elizabeth's stroking palm.

"I'm sorry I said that," she spoke contritely. "You all love me dearly. Almost as much as you love tuna fish."

Greetings over, Elizabeth negotiated a tangle of tails as she headed through the shuttered rooms toward the old-fashioned kitchen. Along the way, she turned on every light switch. Electric bill be damned. Tonight, she couldn't stand the gloom.

Bowing to intense pressure, she served the Three Stooges, then brewed a pot of herbal tea, filled a cup and drank thirstily.

She should eat supper herself soon. If only it was as simple as feeding the cats. She hadn't been to the store in a week. The pantry was bare, and all the freezer offered was a chicken potpie and some leftover meat loaf. Both sounded unappetizing. She'd force herself to make a tuna salad after another cup of tea.

Elizabeth had always been tall and rangy. Losing weight left her feeling gaunt. With five pounds gone in the past three weeks, her work clothes sagged, her waist was waspy and her hipbones prominent.

And her face. Elizabeth knew without benefit of a mirror that the hollows in her cheeks had become more pronounced.

When she'd been twenty-five, her slimness had lent her an air of coltish elegance. She could still manage elegance on occasion. Hadn't Hope said so this afternoon?

At thirty-nine, she could also look haggard.

Middle-aged and haggard.

With that cheery thought, Elizabeth scavenged the refrigerator, poured the last of the milk, drank it determinedly and put an egg on to boil for the tuna salad.

When she sat back down, Tom jumped into her lap, and Elizabeth absently stroked him as her thoughts circled.

She was trying too hard to prove herself. To show the board and Mary they'd made the right choice. She wanted to ride to CCE's rescue and save it single-handedly.

That last bit of fantasy brought Elizabeth up sharp.

Is that why she resented Mac Reynolds's offer? Was she afraid he would steal her thunder? If so, she'd better clean up her act, or she'd be a far worse director than Louis Dennis.

Perhaps she was, anyway.

Why not admit the fear that drove her?

Burnout.

The down side of social work. It came from frustrating years of battling inept bureaucracies and public indifference on behalf of an endless stream of lost souls and victims.

One day a client would come along with yet another tragic story, and the caring and concern for that person would be gone, replaced by numbness, despair and a sense of inadequacy. The temptation would be overpowering to just walk away.

But there was no place for Elizabeth to go. She had to find meaning and hope in her work. It was all that sustained her.

She had no current illusions about saving the world. During her early twenties she'd spent two years in VISTA, the domestic Peace Corps. The experience had cured Elizabeth of such grandiose notions.

At the time, however, she'd discovered satisfaction from small successes like helping elderly tenants do battle with a landlord over much-needed repairs.

It was then Elizabeth had discovered the joys of working with older clients. She'd grown to appreciate their wisdom and perspective, and they'd taught her lessons in how to enjoy the pleasures of each day.

Soon after, she'd entered graduate school, earned her master's in social work and gone back into the world eager to make a difference.

Steven, a fellow social worker, had come into her life a year and a half later.

His had been a cautious and somewhat earnest courtship. Elizabeth, looking back, could scarcely remember their laughing together.

Still, when he proposed, Elizabeth accepted, knowing he might not be the great love of her life. She wanted marriage and children. Steven would be a caring father, and she was ready to make a commitment.

Then came the tragedy of her mother's illness.

The relationship with Steven, which Elizabeth had seen as solid if unexciting, had proved too fragile to survive the crisis.

A crisis that eventually consumed her life.

She hadn't even held a job the last two years of her father's illness. His condition had demanded too much care and attention. They'd both become prisoners to a vicious disease.

She'd lived with the agony of her parents' suffering and struggled with guilt, a constant companion to her anger and bitterness.

Those feelings still haunted her.

Ghosts.

She'd lied today, saying she'd never met one. She was surrounded by ghostly reminders.

Of a beautiful mother filled with laughter and passion who'd borne up bravely as she'd wasted away.

Of a physician father who'd been supremely self-confident, occasionally brusque and always generous. Who'd been stunned by his inability to save his wife. And then had lost all capacity to think or act as his world deteriorated into chaotic memories.

There were other ghosts roaming this cavernous house.

Of the children Elizabeth would never have.

Of lost youth. A tepid lover.

She might be lonely, but she was never alone.

Three pairs of eyes—two blue, one green—studying her from the middle of the table, brought Elizabeth back to her surroundings.

"I'm not only unhinged," she announced to her audience, "I'm sinking into self-pity. Ignore the depression. Despite evidence to the contrary, your food source enjoyed a successful day. They loved me at the meeting." Well, almost.

But if she couldn't brag to her cats, who could she brag to?

"I'll eat," she went on for her listeners' benefit, "soak in a tub of hot bubbles and start a novel I've been saving that doesn't have an iota of redeeming social value."

The phone's ringing halted the prescribed activity.

"Elizabeth, this is Mary. I'm sorry to bother you at home."

"Don't apologize. It's no bother." Which was true enough.

"I just wanted to tell you I heard great things about the meeting today."

"You did?" Elizabeth asked as she grinned and winked at the cats.

"Yes. Herb and Carol sang your praises."

"They've been so helpful. I don't know what I'd do without them."

"And Mac, my son, was impressed, as well."

"He was?" This was a surprising development. Elizabeth hadn't expected to receive his endorsement.

"He told me he's looking forward to working with you."

"He is?" Elizabeth realized her response lacked a certain brilliance. "I certainly look forward to his valuable input. He has a great deal to offer the coalition."

She steered the conversation in a slightly different direction. "I'm really excited about the year ahead."

"Not discouraged by all the problems?"

Mary's question rattled Elizabeth, especially in light of her earlier thoughts. After a second she gathered herself and carefully said, "Only a little daunted by my own inadequacies."

"Everyone feels like that at one time or another. Believe me, you're doing an excellent job."

"Thank you. Those words of praise are special coming from you."

"And I meant every one of them." Mary changed gears abruptly. "Don't forget Saturday."

"Saturday?" Elizabeth was momentarily lost.

"The party."

"Oh, the party. Listen, it was nice of you to ask, but I'm not sure I should come. I'd feel like a fifth wheel," she said, trying to beg off, having no idea what she'd be letting herself in for.

"Don't be silly." Mary brushed aside her excuses. "Tracy's calling to invite you tomorrow. She's Mac's daughter, a perfectly lovely grandchild. So anxious to meet you."

"She is?" For the life of her, Elizabeth couldn't imagine why.

"Yes. I've sung your praises to her also."

Also?

"Oh. Well—" Elizabeth said with a chuckle "—I hope I live up to your advance billing."

"Don't worry, Elizabeth. I'm sure you will."

After Elizabeth hung up, she was interested to note her depression had lifted. To be replaced by unease.

What on earth did Mary have in mind for her?

IT WAS DEEPEST NIGHT at the coalition offices. Too dark for shadows. Yet shadows seemed to creep from the old building itself. One hovered on the upstairs balcony.

Hovered...wavered....

So tired...so cold....

Yet now there was another who knew the prison of loneliness.

Someone to help.

Someone who could ease the ache of a woman's heart.

CHAPTER THREE

August 18, 1884

We have received no measurable rainfall for weeks. Our cotton is suffering from a Weevil Infestation, and I fear the crop will fetch a poor price at the Exchange in Galveston. Although my brothers come as often as they can to supervise the field hands, I fear the day is approaching when I will no longer be able to maintain the Farm.

I attempt to keep such Morbid Speculations from Mr. LeBow. However, I feel certain he is aware of our Precarious Plight. It is oftentimes hard to know what he is thinking. His words come slowly and are slurred to the ear. Yet much of his Mental Acuity remains intact.

The stifling heat we are enduring causes him discomfort, and this increases his irritability. My position is difficult on those occasions, since Dr. Peters has cautioned that I must not allow him to become distressed. When Johnny presented Mr. LeBow with a Rolling Chair so that he could sit on the porch during the cool of morning, I had hoped his new Mobility would lift my Husband's Spirits. That has not been entirely the case, however. I sometimes believe the device only reminds him of how his Disabling Condition has imprisoned him these last three years.

I correspond with Johnny to share news of his father, and he comes to the Farm on a regular basis. I am grateful Johnny is guided by his Filial Obligations, as his vis-

its can prove difficult for everyone concerned. I fear the Animosity between father and son continues unabated. Johnny is somewhat zealous in his Concern for my Welfare, and I believe that for Mr. LeBow, Johnny's presence is a bitter reminder of his own lost Vigor.

Although I do as much as I can to anticipate his needs, I am also the object of Mr. LeBow's Frustration. I understand that he rails, not against me, but against the Tragedy that has befallen him. Still, I fight the Demons of Self-Pity and Despair, and I Pray daily for Patience, Courage and Good Humor.

I must cease writing for now. Mr. LeBow's bell is scolding me for my inattention....

"HELLO, MRS. MORELAND. How are you doing?" Elizabeth leaned near so the woman could see her face.

"What's that, dear?" Mrs. Moreland was ninety and almost completely deaf.

"I said, how are you doing?"

A wide grin broke out on the wizened features. "How sweet of you to ask. I'm doing just fine. Got the same aches and pains. Not a one of 'em has left me. But my oh my, isn't it a beautiful day?"

It was a sunny February morning. But even if Austin's weather turned dreary, the elderly lady would make a similar comment. Her conversations with Elizabeth seldom varied in content or tone.

Mrs. Moreland's good humor was an inspiration to the Adult Day Care Center staff. She'd lost her husband at sixty-five and lived the next twenty years with sprightly independence. But now her mind and body were fragile, and the son she lived with brought her to the center on his way to work each morning so she wouldn't come to harm.

Elizabeth patted Mrs. Moreland's arm and continued across the room, greeting other clients.

"Hello, Mr. Beasley."

"Hello, Miss Elizabeth. I thought you promised to call me Joe."

"And I thought you promised to drop the 'Miss.' You make me sound like an old maid aunt."

They both grinned. This had become an established routine. Joe was eighty-four and black. He'd been a gardener most of his life.

Joe's mind was sharp but his joints were arthritic, and his granddaughter, a lawyer, wasn't about to leave him alone during the day.

"Thank you for reviving our hanging baskets." Elizabeth glanced around at the flourishing flowers. "The bright colors make this place look festive."

"They do, don't they?" Joe surveyed his handiwork with great satisfaction. "Nothing like real plants to spruce up a room. Don't need a fancy decorator."

"That's fortunate since we can't afford one. When do you plan to start your garden?"

Joe had staked out a portion of the side lawn for a vegetable plot.

"I'll begin tilling in a couple of weeks. And plant in March."

"As long as you don't overwork those knees of yours."

"Better to work 'em a little than to let 'em set. Can't give in to rheumatism, or it'll get you for sure."

Elizabeth nodded her understanding, then caught sight of Mrs. Cooper huddled in one of the chairs that lined the wall. Giving Joe another smile, Elizabeth went toward her.

A sad but all-too-common case, Mrs. Cooper. She was only seventy-one, but she had Alzheimer's disease and no family to care for her. And she'd been living in a boarding house run by a couple who'd neglected and abused her. Concerned neighbors had called the police. They'd taken Mrs. Cooper to the hospital, then brought her to the Emergency Shelter attached to the center. Now the day care staff had to find a permanent place for her to live. Alzheimer's patients weren't usually eligible for nursing home benefits. Elizabeth made a note to herself to talk to someone with the Guardianship Program.

"Mrs. Cooper. Do you remember me?" Elizabeth sat down in the adjoining chair.

Mrs. Cooper stared at her with vacant eyes. The last stages of Alzheimer's. Elizabeth had faced that look daily for two interminable years.

Gently she took Mrs. Cooper's hand and noted the fading bruises along the forearm. "We're glad to have you with us."

A flicker of emotion came into watery blue eyes. "Have you seen Charlie?"

"Charlie?"

"My husband, Charlie. He was supposed to come for me." The woman's voice grew agitated. "We can't be late."

Elizabeth knew Mrs. Cooper's husband had been dead for years. "No, I haven't seen Charlie," she said soothingly. "But I'm sure he'll be here."

Life faded from Mrs. Cooper's eyes. She seemed to shrink within herself.

Elizabeth sighed and rose from the chair.

She made a point of touring the building every day, and dropping by the wing that housed the center was usually a high point of her rounds.

Seeing the elderly clients sharing in games and activities reminded her of why the coalition existed—to support programs that served the Mrs. Morelands, Joes and Mrs. Coopers of the world. Still, cases like Mrs. Cooper always distressed her. They brought back memories and fed her sense of frustration.

"Elizabeth...?" Betsy, the center social worker, hailed her from across the room.

"Yes?"

"Wait up a minute." Betsy hurried over and they walked into the hall. "I wanted to tell you how excited we are about the Alzheimer's Association joining CCE. Several of our families have been asking about it."

"I'm just pleased we could help the group stay afloat. Support is so important to families under stress."

"Isn't that why the coalition exists? To foster this kind of organization?"

Elizabeth nodded. "That's the premise I'm operating under."

Betsy laid a hand on her arm. "I want you to know my staff and I are very glad to have you."

"Thanks, I needed that."

"Don't we all? A warm fuzzy a day keeps the analyst away."

"Which is why my next stop's the nursery. I'm due a morning hug."

Moments later, Elizabeth arrived at the Infant Care Center. Offering day care for babies as well as older people was one of Mary's innovative ideas. She hoped to involve the elders in caring for the toddlers as part of an Adoptive Grandparents Program.

Implementing the plan, however, had proved difficult. The activities would have to be carefully coordinated, and getting the support of the children's parents was essential.

Nevertheless, Elizabeth was determined to see the idea a reality. She'd met twice with both staffs to work out logistics, and a meeting with the parents was scheduled next week. The rocking chairs that graced the first and second story porches would serve their purpose by the end of the month.

At the nursery, she was greeted by squeals and a lively rendition of "Farmer in the Dell" issuing forth from the stereo.

"How's the diaper set today?" she asked a child care worker.

"We've had an amazingly peaceful morning. Jeremy's pulled Lisa's hair only once so far."

Elizabeth gravitated toward one of the playpens.

"Are you being a gentleman for a change?" she asked one-year-old Jeremy, who cooed with pleasure at her familiar face. Visiting the babies was a bittersweet experience for Elizabeth. One she wouldn't miss.

She picked Jeremy up and dangled him playfully. "Don't you know tweaking Lisa's curls is no way to gain her affection?"

Jeremy gurgled, reached out chubby fingers and tugged at a strand of Elizabeth's hair.

She laughed. "So much for today's etiquette lesson." When she kissed Jeremy on the cheek, he promptly latched on to her nose with a dribbly mouth.

"Argh," she mumbled, to his delight. It took her a moment to disengage herself. "As much as I'd like to stay and receive your attentions, it's time to get back. I've probably had ten calls, all of them important."

Jeremy watched her departure with a wistful look.

Hope's harried expression greeted her return to the office. "Your phone's been ringing like mad."

"Of course."

"Here're your messages. The urgent ones I've indicated."

Elizabeth reached for the slips of paper, and Hope hesitated a moment. "Before you start returning calls, Suzanne came looking for you a while ago. She seemed upset."

Suzanne was the director of Respite Care for the Elderly, an in-home custodial care agency, which took up where the Adult Day Care Center left off. She was one of the sharpest agency heads CCE boasted. If something had disturbed her, Elizabeth needed to know what it was.

"I'll talk to her first," she said, putting aside the messages.

She dialed the respite care number and waited for Suzanne's assistant to connect them.

"I need to talk to you, if you have the time," Suzanne said as soon as she heard Elizabeth's greeting.

"Come now, if you'd like."

Five minutes later Suzanne appeared at her door.

"What's the matter?" Elizabeth asked as soon as she saw the woman's face.

"I'm afraid this isn't a social visit."

Elizabeth smiled. "People with problems are also admitted. Have a seat."

Suzanne edged toward a chair. "It's just that you've been here less than a month. I don't want to be the first person to rough you up."

"I'm tough. I can take it. Besides, I don't think you'll inflict terminal damage. If you have a concern, I'm sure it's legitimate, and I'd like to hear it now rather than months down the road."

Suzanne took a deep breath and started to speak.

Before she could begin, however, the door opened and Mac Reynolds walked in.

Elizabeth's office, euphemistically termed cozy, suddenly became claustrophobic with the addition of this particular third party. Her first contretemps with a disgruntled director, and she was faced with her most unsettling board member.

"I'm sorry," Mac said easily. "I waved to Hope down the hall, but I didn't think to ask if you were in a conference. Did you get the message I planned to drop by?"

"I hadn't gotten a chance to go over my calls, but I should be free in twenty minutes. Can you wait that long?"

Mac looked down at his watch with vague impatience.

At that point Suzanne spoke and Elizabeth braced herself. "Wait, please. Aren't you Mac Reynolds?"

"Yes. And you are?"

"Suzanne Tomlin, director of Respite Care for the Elderly."

They shook hands as Elizabeth berated herself for not handling the introductions.

"From everything I hear, yours is a much needed service," he offered smoothly.

"Yes, it is." Suzanne's tone was militant. "And if you don't mind, I'd like you to stay and hear what I have to say."

Elizabeth gave Suzanne her due. No one would ever call the lady fainthearted.

To Mac's credit, he immediately took the chair to one side of the desk. "No, of course, I don't mind. I want to learn more about the care you provide."

As he spoke, Elizabeth's expression remained calm and attentive. It took some effort. Just as it took effort to ignore Mac's presence.

She was relieved when Suzanne turned back her way. "I have concerns about the direction the coalition's heading. When I heard about the activities you were developing, I had to say something. Art classes. Senior aerobics. A crafts fair. I'm not saying these aren't wonderful ideas. But should the coalition be expending its energy this way?"

She paused for a moment, then plowed on determinedly. "What about my clients and their families? The frail elderly whom I serve with my in-home companions? These people are infirm, incontinent, often bedbound. They can't take advantage of weekly art classes. Or a daily exercise session. I need support for the respite care we offer."

"I know you do," Elizabeth returned quietly. "My first priority is the work of the current member agencies. Right now, Mac and I are working to clear the mortgage. When that's done, the coalition's monthly outlay should be greatly reduced, and agency costs will consist of a share of the security, maintenance and utility expenses."

"It's a start," Suzanne said slowly. "My overhead is killing me."

"I know. I've looked over the financials you sent me."

"You have? Already?" Suzanne seemed somewhat mollified.

Still, Elizabeth knew her work was unfinished. "Reducing monthly expenses is only a start. As a new service entity, we need community visibility, which will bring in clients for every agency here.''

"Yes," Suzanne protested, "but what good will it do to inform people of our care, when we can't offer them affordable service?''

"Raising our visibility should also bring us community support. We both know support translates into money. That's why I want to develop programs for the well elderly.''

"I hear what you're saying. And you have a point.''

"You'd just like to see some results for a change.''

"I guess I'm impatient.''

"I get impatient, too. Then I remind myself the coalition's been in existence less than a year. It needs nurturing. By the board, the member agencies, me, the community.''

"I know. And I feel guilty about complaining.''

"No." Elizabeth shook her head adamantly. "That's the last thing in the world I want you to feel. Suzanne, I know the stresses you face.''

Something about her words caused Suzanne to blurt out, "This morning was awful. One of our best workers came to tell me a woman she sits with had died. We needed to be caring for that lady every day, but the daughter who lived with her couldn't afford us. She's retired herself and in poor health. Now our sitter-companion feels guilty because the death occurred on one of the days she wasn't scheduled to be there. Perhaps she could have prevented it. In situations like this, we need to offer low cost or free hours. But we can't right now, because we don't have the money.''

"I'm working on raising funds for subsidized care. In fact, I'm in the process of writing a grant using your agency, the Adult Day Care Center and the Guardianship Program as examples of what we do. I hope to come through with specified funds."

"You make me feel better." Suzanne's grin had a sheepish quality. "If I hadn't just had the session with my sitter, I wouldn't have felt the need to come charging down here."

"I want you to feel free to come to me anytime. Working with the agencies is the most important part of my job."

"Well, anyway, I'm happy to meet you, Mr. Reynolds."

"Mac. And I'm glad to meet you, too. I've learned a lot in the last fifteen minutes."

There was a small silence after Suzanne left the room. For the first time, Elizabeth turned her attention to her male visitor. His face held a look she found hard to read.

His words were plain enough, however. "You handled the situation very well."

She waved a hand dismissively. "I didn't handle anything. I just sympathized with Suzanne's plight. We're all in this together."

"Still, I'm impressed."

"Don't be," she said, mildly embarrassed. "It's what I get paid for."

"Elizabeth...." Mac's expression grew whimsical. "You should have learned by now how to take a compliment. Say 'thank you' graciously without protesting."

Now she was flustered as well as embarrassed. Because, somehow, in the past few moments, some element of their relationship had mysteriously altered.

"Thank you graciously," she muttered, at a loss.

"You're welcome," he said with a bland smile.

She searched for similar protective coloring. "I really am sorry about not getting back to you. When Hope told me Suzanne was upset, I felt I needed to talk with her first."

"A wise decision."

"Thank you." She paused, waiting for him to continue.

Instead, Mac seemed content to study her face.

Ordinary scrutiny she could have handled. The way he watched her, however, seemed to speak of forbidden speculations and provocative inquiries.

There was a definite gleam in his dark brown eyes.

It unnerved her completely.

Dear heavens, she was blushing!

"Yes, well, uh..." She stood hastily, realized the gesture was uncalled-for and sat back down. "I...what can I do for you? I mean—" her face was hot "—why did you come? Do you need something from me? I mean—"

"I know what you mean," he interrupted gently. "And this is the first time I've seen you in disarray. It's very charming."

"Disarray is never charming," she corrected severely.

"No?" Mac lifted a brow and grinned.

Elizabeth noted with horror an adorable dimple to one side of his mouth.

He murmured, "Dishevelment can be."

There was a distinct pause.

Then he checked his watch and became all business. "Actually I dropped by to tell you I talked with Manley. He's willing to do the architectural honors and asked me to get hold of the blueprints, if possible."

"We don't have them." Now that Mac's manner was impersonal, hers could be, too. "At least, not to my knowledge. I suppose there are records at the county courthouse. Or the state archives.''

''We won't know till we look.''

''I'll begin checking.'' Relaxing, she embraced the new subject of discussion. ''I've been fascinated by this place from the very beginning. There's an atmosphere of the past about it. Did you know there were boarders here until the late 1950s?''

''A hundred years after the Civil War?''

''Apparently the surviving women were widows of men much older than themselves. I wonder what those women's lives were like?''

Once again his look grew intent. ''You make it sound as if there were stories this building could tell.''

Elizabeth's own look grew unconsciously abstracted. ''I think there may be. I always feel welcomed when I walk in the door. Yet sometimes when I come early or stay late, I feel...it's hard to describe...a sense of melancholy.'' She stopped abruptly. ''I sound like a hopeless romantic, don't I? I assure you I'm normally a levelheaded person.'' She meant the last as a subtle counter to her earlier foolishness.

He took it as such. ''I've seen your practical side. You don't need to remind me. It's the hopeless romantic who's beginning to interest me.''

She grinned weakly, her heart suddenly thumping madly.

''Speaking of which,'' he said easily, ''I understand you're going to Tracy's party.''

''Yes. Mary invited me. Your daughter was kind enough to confirm the invitation. I'm not sure if I can make it, though.''

''I'm invited, too. I'll come by and get you. We can talk about Manley's suggestions on the drive over.''

Elizabeth noted the way he overrode her objections, but with the dangerous undertones of this conversation, she was safer going along with the arbitrary arrangements.

"What time will you come by?" she asked politely.

"How does seven-thirty suit you?"

Like a trip to the dentist. "That sounds fine," she agreed pleasantly. "Let me give you my address."

"While I'm here I'll look around the building to get a feel for what's original and what's been added," he said as she presented him a scrap of paper with her address printed on it. "Would you care to join me?"

"Well...I..." She fumbled with the pile of messages before her.

"I understand," Mac said smoothly, then stood in a lithe movement and seemed to take over every available space.

Without giving warning, he bent over her shoulder and spread the squares of paper, finding the one with his name on it. "This you can throw away." Turning his head so their faces were barely a foot apart, he grinned at her. "Perhaps next time we'll tour the building together."

"Yes, of course," Elizabeth murmured, her pulse hammering ferociously. She was finding it all she could do not to lean away. "So, I'll expect you Saturday evening."

"If not before. You know, Elizabeth," he commented thoughtfully, "I find this role of board member much different than I expected. You have yourself to thank for that."

THE REST OF THE DAY proved routine. After Mac left, Hope phoned out for sandwiches, and lunch was spent scheduling the coming week. The next two hours Elizabeth returned phone calls.

Director's ear, the researchers would label the chronic condition she envisioned. Like tennis elbow or jogger's knee.

It was past three before she had a chance to tackle the grant in progress.

At five-thirty, Hope stuck her head in the door. "Let's go home. You don't get paid overtime."

"I know, I know. But I'm on a roll." She grimaced at the typewriter she was using. "I'd sell my soul for a computer right now."

"That won't be necessary," Hope assured her solemnly. "Just don't miss lunch with Jerry Tansy next Wednesday. He's making noises he can get us a couple of computers at cost."

"I wouldn't think of skipping a free meal."

"You'll have earned it after an hour with Jerry."

Elizabeth laughed and waved her away, but instead of leaving, Hope came into the room and looked over her shoulder. "That's not the final draft?" Hope asked suspiciously.

"Oh, no, you get to catch my spelling mistakes. I'm just roughing out the narrative section. I'll be out of here within the hour."

"Consider that a promise," Hope said, and left reluctantly.

Elizabeth knew Hope worried about her staying alone in the building, located in one of Austin's oldest and most eclectic areas. Little old ladies in modest bungalows shared back fences with yuppies eager for bargain homes to restore. And college students flocked to newly built apartments and converted duplexes.

The neighborhood at its best was a gracious reminder of an earlier era. At its worst it provided grim statistics of an escalating crime rate. CCE had suffered a rash of burglaries, and Elizabeth had no intention of offering herself as a victim.

Thirty minutes later she'd put the finishing touches on a narrative she modestly admitted was an eloquent and stirring plea for help.

By now, dusk had settled outside the window.

Elizabeth gathered her things, locked her door and walked into the hall.

She was met by silence.

No lingering sounds of staff or children. Or from the overnight shelter, separated in its wing off the main building.

Apparently, she was alone.

Billy, their maintenance man, checked the doors every evening, but Elizabeth decided to take a five-minute survey. If there were stragglers, she'd urge them home.

All the downstairs offices were locked and dark.

Elizabeth climbed the stairs to the second floor and walked the length of the hall to the north turret.

Funny, that door should be locked, as well. Inside was equipment for presentations. She'd make a note to talk to Billy tomorrow.

Elizabeth switched on the lights as she stepped through the door and glanced around the pentagonal room.

There was no evidence it had been disturbed.

Relieved, she stood for a moment studying her surroundings. They were spacious and served by three sets of windows.

The room was structurally untouched by the years the building had housed government offices. Elizabeth had a sudden vision of gentle ladies arranged in a circle, chatting and quilting as they enjoyed fresh breezes that wafted in.

Or perhaps they congregated on the upstairs veranda to occasionally wave at a passing neighbor.

She went to the side door that served the porch. The empty rocking chairs seemed to beckon her. Trailing her hand along the railing, she peered down into the yard below.

It had an air of gloom in the deepening evening.

Elizabeth felt a sudden chill. She must leave soon.

Still, just for a moment, she sank into one of the wicker chairs. She kept promising herself she'd come here during the day for a peaceful break. She never seemed to find the time, however.

"You should make time."

Elizabeth started and realized she'd spoken aloud. Spooked by the sound of her own voice. And reduced to talking to herself, as well.

"Not a good sign."

She rocked gently back and forth before slowing to a stop.

The creaking movement had intruded on the penetrating silence. For a long moment she sat quietly taking in the atmosphere. It seemed to wrap around her like the cloak of night.

Then, with a prescience she'd never known before, Elizabeth sensed she was no longer alone.

She looked toward the south turret. There was no one in sight.

She turned her head...and saw a female figure twenty feet away framed by the doorway she'd just come through.

For a split second, Elizabeth thought someone had wandered upstairs from the shelter, or like herself was staff who'd stayed to work late.

She could delude herself only the briefest instant.

For the figure lacked substance.

It was not of this world.

Wavering in the darkening gloom, it—she—could have been a fading sepia print photographed at the turn of the century.

She stared at Elizabeth with intent regard.

Elizabeth stared back transfixed. "H-hello...w-who are you?" she managed to croak, still searching for a rational explanation.

Her visitor remained silent, yet Elizabeth could have sworn she was trying to speak.

Elizabeth blinked...and blinked again. Could this possibly be a hallucination?

But she couldn't take refuge in temporary madness, for when she opened her eyes there was still a ghost standing before her.

She felt no terror...or horror...or menace.

Only...immeasurable sorrow. Grief so intense it washed over her in waves.

"How can I help you? What do you want?"

The ghost raised a hand in supplication.

Elizabeth reached out in an answering gesture.

Their looks met for a final moment.

Then the apparition slowly faded away.

CHAPTER FOUR

December 5, 1885

The day is overcast and cold. An icy Rain has fallen since early morning. If the temperature continues to plummet, by tomorrow the world will be covered with a clear, glassy Mantle. It could be the earliest Ice Storm in memory, and the almanac is predicting a severe Winter. I, too, feel as if a dreary Cloak, invisible to the beholder, has settled about me, suffocating my Heart.

The LeBow Family Farm has been sold. Yesterday, the land, buildings, livestock and implements were auctioned off to pay debts amassed since Mr. LeBow's illness. Even with the help of my brothers, I could no longer manage the farm alone and care for my Husband day and night as I must. Truth to tell, I was weary of being a burden to my Family, understanding as I do how great a Trial that can be.

I was able to keep some furniture for the small house in Bastrop in which my Husband and I have settled, but several Family Heirlooms have fallen into strangers' hands. I saved what I could for Johnny.

Should I have responded differently to the offer he made to come back and work the Homestead? Could I have sentenced him to the constant strain of his father's hostility? Should I have grasped greedily and selfishly at his outstretched hands, seeing Pity and Regret in his eyes, knowing the Burdens I shoulder would then weigh on yet another? I will never know the answers to these gnawing questions. I only know that, finally, I could not tear Johnny from the Work he loves.

For so many reasons....

"HAVE YOU BEEN deserted?"

Elizabeth looked up from her chair to find Tracy, her hostess, leaning over solicitously.

"Heavens, no," Elizabeth said. "Mac was engrossed in a discussion of the timber industry. I realized I had nothing of interest to add, so I wandered off to sample the hors d'oeuvres."

Besides which, Elizabeth thought, if she'd stayed, she'd have put her foot in her mouth, being more concerned about endangered species and the preservation of forests than the fluctuating supply of building materials.

Tracy looked chagrined, however. "How like Dad to talk business at a party."

"Don't be too hard on him," Elizabeth said quickly. "He was cornered and couldn't extricate himself gracefully. It gave me a chance to look at your music box collection." She indicated the tall glass case beside her. "They're lovely."

"Would you like to listen to them?"

"Oh, no. I've just enjoyed looking. Several are unlike any I've ever seen before."

"Yes. This is the first one Grannie brought me—from Peru." Tracy pointed out a small carved box inlaid with various grains of wood. "That one's from Tibet. Next to it is a Japanese version. They each play a folk tune from the respective country."

"Did Mary bring them all to you?" Elizabeth asked with some surprise.

"Not all of them, but she does get around. No senior citizen cruises for her. More likely nature hikes in the Galápagos Islands. I have a hard time keeping up with her."

"I know what you mean."

Tracy turned back to the display. "Dad found several for me. Allen and I discovered these two in an antique shop in Geneva on our honeymoon in Switzerland. But I'm afraid I'll have to put them away soon. Allen's in the process of toddler-proofing the house."

So Elizabeth hadn't been mistaken about the swell of Tracy's abdomen.

For a brief moment, she felt a flare of intense longing. It was a familiar sensation. She managed to damp it out and offer a congratulatory smile.

"When are you due?"

"In three and a half months. I can hardly wait. Allen's in a panic."

"And Mac?" Elizabeth couldn't help asking. "How does he feel about becoming a grandfather?"

Tracy grinned. "Until a few days ago, I'd have said he was taking it in stride. Now I'm not so sure. Male vanity is strange and wondrous to ponder."

As much as Elizabeth would have liked Tracy to elaborate, she felt uneasy discussing Mac with his daughter. Besides, she was all too aware of her ignorance on the subject of males.

She smiled and looked around her, choosing a safer topic. "Your house is beautiful."

"Thank you. Daddy built it for us as a wedding present. Of course, we decorated and furnished it ourselves. I love this antique display case especially."

Tracy ran her hand down its pecan wood trim. "We found it in Houston on a buying expedition. I'll hate seeing it go into storage. Do antiques interest you?"

"In a small way. I inherited several pieces from my mother."

"You must come over for lunch one day," Tracy decided. "I'll show you some of my better finds and we'll take out the music boxes. I promise not one plays 'The Blue Danube.'"

Elizabeth nodded noncommittally, leery of deeper involvement with the Reynolds family.

But Tracy wasn't to be put off. She'd just begun to suggest dates and times, when Elizabeth was reprieved by the arrival of a pregnant fellow guest who was eager to compare notes with Tracy.

As soon as Elizabeth was on her own, she stood, her smile in place, and negotiated purposefully around the clusters of guests as though she had a definite destination.

She never did well at these sorts of gatherings. And everyone here was a stranger except Mary, Herb, Mac and now Tracy.

Interesting that Tracy hadn't once mentioned her mother when they'd discussed contributors to her collection. Of course, theirs had been the lightest kind of party conversation. Still, it was sweet of Tracy to spend time and effort with a guest who'd been foisted on her.

Despite Elizabeth's air of purpose, she wasn't sure what she was looking for or how she'd know if she found it. When she walked past the doors to the patio, however, she knew she'd discovered a temporary haven.

The air was brisk, discouraging guests from stepping outside, but Elizabeth's wool dress was high necked and long sleeved. She could spend fifteen minutes in peace before the chill got to her. In the meantime, she'd figure out a socially acceptable way to leave early in a cab.

From the moment he'd picked her up, Mac had been an attentive escort. Perhaps too attentive for her peace of mind. Yet nothing he'd said or done had been anything but friendly.

It was just that every time she'd seen him this week, which was more often than she'd expected, Elizabeth had felt as if she were riding a whirlwind. And every sweep of that wind managed to rearrange her insides.

She must resign herself to the fact that Mac was a charismatic male who casually and unconsciously created flutters in female breasts. She'd become immune to him—eventually.

On the way to Tracy's, they'd discussed the preliminary report Manley had made after inspecting the building. How like Mac to have the architect of his choice on site within days. He had a kind of focused efficiency that must serve him well in his business. Elizabeth wondered if he conducted his personal life the same way.

She and Hope had been busy, too, contacting the state archives and the Austin History Center. She even had Hope researching newspaper files, thinking they might contain an article describing the old home's look and layout as well as a list of the women who'd lived there.

Of course, Elizabeth had a hidden motive for this flurry of activity. A well-hidden motive.

After all, how did you tell someone you've met a ghost? How did you look a man like Mac in the eye and say, "You know the feeling I have when I come to work early in the morning? Now I know where it comes from. One of our old occupants is seeking help from the grave."

Elizabeth smiled ruefully. So far, the sighting had not been repeated. Of course, that might be partly due to the fact that she hadn't had the nerve to return to the upstairs veranda.

Putting aside her disquieting thoughts, she looked around and realized the patio ran the length of the house, was sectioned off into areas of activity and extended down the hillside in tiers. Only the top level, where she stood, was floodlit. Below was a fenced-in pool, the deck and water shadowy in the encroaching darkness.

Impulsively she descended the cedar steps and was rewarded with the sight of a screened-in gazebo nestled under an overhang of oaks. The location was private but selected to catch stray hillside breezes. When she discovered the door had a simple latch, Elizabeth opened it and went in.

She could imagine what it would be like on a long summer evening, and for just a moment, she pictured herself peacefully stretched on a recliner, momentarily freed from the cares and responsibilities she shouldered. Water from the pool beaded on her skin, and she nursed a frosty glass of iced mint tea.

Now a gust of winter wind rustled the evergreen live oak leaves, slipped through the screen and nipped at her skirt. The night was colder than she'd realized. Turning to leave, she saw her way blocked by a pair of lovers standing on the cedar platform up the hillside from the pool.

They'd obviously left the party for a private moment.

Elizabeth had no voyeuristic tendencies that she was aware of, but she hated to embarrass the couple by her interruption.

Surely after a moment or two...

She tried to look away. But something about the scene compelled her attention.

The protective way the man seemed to shield the woman from the cold. Their murmuring voices more tender than passionate. His hand as it reached out to touch her hair.

The silhouettes merged in a silent kiss. After the kiss ended, the woman laid her head against the man's chest as he held her closely.

A voice from above broke the couple apart.

"I thought I'd find you here." It was Mac who spoke.

And the voice that answered him belonged to Mary. Elizabeth's mouth sagged open as she finally realized who the lovers were.

"Why were you looking for us?" Mary sounded cool and collected.

"Tracy sent me. She has someone she wants you and Herb to meet, and I didn't think her newly adult sense of propriety could handle her Grannie smooching with a boyfriend under the stars."

Herb's tones were chagrined as he said, "I guess you think we're behaving like a couple of kids. But I've been out of town since Tuesday. This is the first real chance Mary and I have had to be alone."

Mac laughed and put his hand on Herb's shoulder. "You don't have to explain to me. I'm all for young love and private moments. As Mary's son, I do feel obliged to say I hope you make an honest woman of her."

"What do you think I've been trying to do for the last—"

"That's enough," Mary interrupted firmly. "Both of you. This is neither the time nor the place to discuss my private life."

"But Mother," Mac said smoothly, "that's just the point. It's not so private. Anyone with half an eye can see that you and Herb can't keep your hands off each other."

Elizabeth, listening to this unlikely discussion with fascination, admitted she hadn't noticed the mutual attraction. By now, however, she'd decided her powers of observation were woefully impaired.

But who would have thought that Herb and Mary...?

With Mac's teasing, Mary's voice rose. "Mac—you know I don't approve of cross-generational sex discussions."

"Is that a promise you won't hound me about my love life?"

Mac had done the impossible. He'd reduced Mary to silence.

Pleased with his success, he turned to Herb. "Are you sure Mother's worth it? She's bossy and nosy and plays hard to get."

Herb chuckled. As Elizabeth's eyes widened, he patted Mary's rump with affectionate familiarity. "I know. But she has her moments."

Mac's laughter rang out into the night.

Mary's sputter was evident even from where Elizabeth was standing.

"You, my son, can keep your opinions to yourself. And you, Herb Briscoe, keep your hands where they belong."

"But Mary," Herb said plaintively, "I thought that's what I was doing."

His comeback was apparently the final straw. Without another word, Mary, her back regal, stalked up the stairs. Both men watched the departure in silent admiration.

"I'd better follow and repair the damage," Herb said. Still, he stood for a minute longer and asked quietly, "Why won't she marry me?"

"I'm not sure," Mac answered after a long moment. "I know Dad's death hit her very hard."

"But that's been twenty years. When Laura died, I wasn't sure I could go on. But time did blunt the pain, and slowly I learned to accept life on the terms it had given me. Laura and I had a good marriage. I guess that's why I think Mary and I could, too."

"Mary's not a substitute for Laura, is she?"

"Lord, no. Laura was shy and retiring. She centered her life on the children, grandkids and me. I'm only a scribbled entry in Mary's crowded appointment book."

"Does that rankle?"

"No. I accept her for who she is. Hell, I admire her enormously. I wouldn't want to change a hair on that queenly head. We both lead full, satisfying lives. I just feel they could be fuller and more satisfying if we were together."

"For what it's worth," Mac said, "Mother hadn't looked at a man twice before you came along."

"Somehow, your words don't reassure me. They just confirm my suspicions that Mary's satisfied with her trips and projects."

"This relationship with you has shaken her up."

Herb laughed shortly. "I sure as hell hope so." He glanced at the man standing beside him. "I'm in love, Mac. It's a scary feeling. Especially at my age."

"At any age."

"Yeah." Herb headed up the stairs. "Are you coming?"

"In a minute."

Great, Elizabeth thought as she watched Herb leave. By now she was acutely aware of the chill night air. Her dress might be wool, but the weave was sheer. She was beginning to shiver.

And the rock of Gibraltar loomed between her and warmth.

She'd been a fool to wander down here. A fool not to make herself known as soon as she'd spied Herb and Mary. A brief moment of embarrassment was better than this furtive feeling of guilt.

Mac looked around slowly as though he were searching for something, before the direction of his gaze settled her way. Without any further hesitation, he took the steps in two easy strides.

Elizabeth's heart began to thump heavily.

When Mac opened the door and walked in, he found her backed against the screening.

"What are you doing hiding in the gazebo?"

"I'm not hiding." Her voice came out rushed and quivery. She resented his light tone. She resented the smile she could just make out. Most of all, she resented him catching her in a position not at all becoming an executive director. "How did you know I was here?"

"After you ran away from me—"

"I beg your pardon?" She sought refuge in indignation. "I just didn't think you or your friend would appreciate my comments on forest preserves."

"After you ran away," he began again, ignoring her feeble attempt at provocation, "I saw you talking to Tracy before you went outside. When I was sent to find Herb and Mary, you were nowhere to be seen."

"Well, I wasn't playing hide-and-seek. I just went exploring. Before I knew it, I'd become an unwilling witness to a . . . a tender scene. I wasn't sure what to do at that point. I didn't want to embarrass anyone.''

"Yourself, you mean. You wouldn't have embarrassed Herb and Mary.''

"But I didn't know it was Herb and Mary. I just assumed, I mean…'' Damn, why did he always fluster her so! "You see, I never imagined Mary and Herb . . .''

"Why? Don't you believe in sex after sixty?''

"Well, of course, I do. It—it's an individual thing. And I'm hardly qualified—''

"Why? Did you take a vow of celibacy when you broke off your engagement?''

"How did you know about my engagement?''

"Mother provided me with a brief history.''

"Ancient history. Why on earth would she drag that out?''

"Perhaps she thought it would help me see you as a person. Or make me a sympathetic ally.''

"I don't need sympathy.''

"I agree. I'd say it was well down the list of what you need. Let's get back to your nonexistent love life.''

"What makes you think it's nonexistent?'' she asked with bravado.

"Are you seeing someone?'' he countered quickly.

"Well . . . no. Not at the moment.'' Elizabeth took a deep breath to steady herself. "But as Mary might say, I don't think this is a proper discussion for professional colleagues.''

Mac's soft chuckle wrapped itself around her, heating her skin despite the cold. "That's where you're wrong. Mary would be the first to approve of this conversation.''

Before Elizabeth could question his puzzling statement, Mac went on, "But I'm more interested in what you see as 'proper' between us. Hope's a colleague. Haven't the two of you ever discussed love and the opposite sex?''

Elizabeth made a frustrated sound. ''Well, of course. Once or twice. Hope's different. She's a woman.''

''So?''

''And I'm a woman.''

''You'll be happy to know I noticed immediately.''

''And you're a man,'' she finished lamely.

''I'm glad to hear you noticed that, too.''

How could she have failed to!

''You're not getting my point,'' Elizabeth said as calmly as she could.

''And what was that?'' he asked pleasantly.

''Hope is…'' She floundered, not sure exactly how she meant to continue.

''Safe?'' he suggested.

Elizabeth took another deep breath. She looked down to find her hands clenched together.

''Thank you. I think 'safe' is an excellent description of Hope's and my relationship.''

''Which implies it would be dangerous for us to compare notes on our dreams and fantasies.''

''I can't think,'' Elizabeth said huskily, ''of anything I'd less rather do.''

''Because of the mutual attraction we're feeling?''

''There is no mutual attraction.'' Elizabeth's hurried denial held an imploring note.

He refused its plea to say quietly, ''Like hell there isn't.''

''There *can't* be.''

Mac laughed suddenly. ''Elizabeth, don't you know the word *can't* constitutes a challenge?''

"No." Her voice cracked on the single syllable. She shook her head helplessly, reached out a hand to touch him and jerked it back. "Please, Mac. Don't make me a challenge. I have a difficult job to do, which takes energy and commitment. I need your friendship and support. Please don't consider me a possible conquest."

For the first time since this unlikely scene had begun, a hard tone crept into Mac's voice. "Is that what you think? That I'm so shallow I'd look at a woman as a conquest? That I'd notch my bedpost with each new adventure?"

"I think," she said quietly, "you're a very attractive man who's used to women wanting him."

"And do you know how I see you, Elizabeth?" His voice was tender.

"No," she managed to croak.

"As an intelligent, sexy, vibrant woman, who's been without love too long."

If he'd said anything else she could have coped with it. Anything at all.

But those particular words spoken with a hint of kindness were Elizabeth's undoing.

Tears sprang into her eyes, and she was very much afraid there were more to follow. She turned away blindly, hoping the darkness would hide them.

"Elizabeth...?"

She could feel the heat of his body close behind her. His voice was little more than a whisper beside her ear.

"I've already told you I don't want your pity," she muttered.

"You won't get it, either." Before she knew what was happening, he'd twisted her around so they were facing each other once more. "I don't deal in that kind of debased currency."

As he spoke, his hands still cupped her shoulders. The intensity of her response set off a shudder that rippled through her.

"You're cold." Mac reached up to brush his thumb against her cheek. "And you're crying." Without another word he drew her into his arms.

A small distressed sound came up from her throat.

Or was it a murmur of pleasure?

All Elizabeth knew was that she couldn't break away. Without conscious thought she sought the heat of Mac's body.

He opened his suit coat and drew her arms around him. After a moment his fingers began a journey up and down the path of her spine.

"You're a strong woman, Elizabeth. I respect you too much to ever offer pity."

"I don't feel very strong right now," she gasped, her senses swimming.

"Umm, right now I'd say you felt delightful." Both his hands lingered down the contours of her back.

She stiffened instinctively.

"Just relax," he said, as if soothing a child.

"How can I?" she asked distractedly. "I find myself in an impossible situation."

He settled her body along the length of his. "It feels pretty damned possible to me. In fact, I'd say probable." By this time, his lips had found the slope of her neck, and he brushed her skin ever so delicately.

She quivered like a violin string bowed by a master.

"Mac," she breathed, clutching the material of his shirt, "you have to stop. You mustn't seduce me."

There was a moment of silence... before he agreed calmly, "You're right, Elizabeth."

Dropping his hands, he stepped back and broke her hold on his waist. "A casual seduction would be a disservice to both of us."

Now all that connected them was the frustration he'd created. The look on his face was enigmatic as he watched her in the semidarkness.

"Wha...?" It took her a moment to catch her breath. "What was that all about?"

"I don't want you to ever feel I've taken advantage." The cad!

"You mean—" her voice rose "—I'm going to lie awake for the next week struggling with guilt and not even get a kiss out of it?"

"Would you like a kiss?" he asked blandly.

"Well, I had assumed..." She looked away.

"Or two?"

"No," she said hurriedly, "one will do."

"And how would you like it?" He caught her chin and tilted it so she was forced to meet his look. "Sweetly tentative and filled with promise? Restless and urgent to match our mood? Desperately passionate as we face the tragedy the Fates—"

"Just—just a nice ordinary kiss," she instructed, speaking each word distinctly. "To get it out of our systems."

"I see." A corner of his mouth curved upward. "Can I add hands and arms?"

"Just do it, dammit."

"I've always been a sucker," he murmured, "for assertive women."

Still, he took his time before obeying her order. As they stood staring at each other, the tension between them became a palpable force.

Finally, he reached out to cup her neck and draw her slowly closer. Her pulse beneath his palm set up an instant clamor.

His other hand skimmed along her cheek, smoothed back her hair, then journeyed randomly along her shoulder, down her back and around until it found a home in the vicinity of her waist. His thumb began to brush back and forth against her lower rib cage.

"Am I doing all right so far?" he asked huskily.

"Yes...." Elizabeth's breaths were becoming increasingly shallow.

By now her breasts had made tentative contact with his coat. Her nipples puckered in anticipation.

"Come inside and wrap your arms around me."

Her hands stroked up the fine cotton of his shirt, under his lapels and around to his broad, solid back. Without volition, she rubbed her aching breasts against him, seeking the heat of his body.

"Damn," he muttered. "Who's seducing whom?"

"Shut up," she said shortly, arching her face to his, seeking his mouth.

The kiss they shared held promise and urgency and desperate passion. When it ended, Elizabeth wrenched herself away and stumbled blindly to the door.

"You do understand," she mumbled as she caught hold of the latch, "this can't happen again."

There was silence. Except for the sounds of their labored breathing.

"Mac...?" She turned.

He stood exactly where she'd left him, the oddest smile around his mouth.

"Mac, are you listening?"

"I did hear you say you believed in sex after sixty?"

She shook her head helplessly. "What does that have to do...?"

"Because I don't intend to give up something this good in only fourteen years."

CHAPTER FIVE

March 25, 1889

Mama came calling at our house today. I do enjoy her weekly visits. With my care-giving duties, I seldom leave home on frivolous outings, and she always brings news of Family and friends. I wish, however, that in recounting the news, she would not be so judgmental of minor Transgressors. I realize, as one of the founders of our First Baptist Church, she feels her moral position in the Community keenly. I, too, have seen the evils of an intemperate life and how they have degraded our fledgling society. It has been a difficult struggle to bring Law and Refinement to this unruly land.

If only people could look into Mama's heart and understand that her actions are undertaken with the sincerest of motives. I am afraid Johnny does not see her in such a sympathetic light. Truth to tell, he has never forgiven her for pressing the suit between Mr. LeBow and me. I tell him there is nothing to forgive. My situation has taught me Fortitude and Patience. I wish I could say such a thing to Mama, for I believe she has suffered needless pangs of remorse.

I cannot agree, however, with her disapproving attitude toward Johnny, although I understand its origin. I suspect his views of God and man would challenge her Theology. I suspect that Mama feels so, too.

But let me go on to a happier topic! I have received a letter from him just this week. Enclosed with it was his

Democratic Statesman *article on the inauguration of our twenty-third President. It was as though I myself were in our great nation's Capital seeing this historic moment through Johnny's eyes, so vivid was his description. I was amused, however, for although his piece was factual and unbiased, his letter was filled with lively invective. Johnny is a staunch Democrat and supporter of Mr. Cleveland, and he was dismayed that Mr. Harrison could be elected with a minority of the votes. Our new President is certainly not popular in Texas. He fought with General Sherman, and feelings still run deep about the late Tragic War.*

At the end of Johnny's letter, he waxed eloquent on the need for reform of our Electoral College. As you might have guessed, Johnny is a man of strong convictions. In that regard, he is very like his Father.

Perhaps I am biased, but I believe Johnny's powers of observation and command of our language raise him far above the ordinary reporter.

His newspaper must think so, too. More and more they have assigned him to record the momentous events of our times. Later this year he will be sailing to France for the Paris Exhibition. He tells me of the newest Wonder of the World that has been constructed there, a nine-hundred-foot wrought-iron tower named for its designer. I cannot imagine such a structure. The main street of Bastrop sports only two-story buildings. Johnny has promised to provide me with pictures of the Tower when he returns.

Where Johnny journeys, I journey also. He brings the world and lays it in my hands. I have dined on Escargot and walked the cobbled streets of Havana. I have breathed rarefied air from the summit of Pikes Peak. I WILL NOT obey Mama's strictures to discourage his letters or the books he sends me. If I did so, I would surely come to harbor great resentment at her interference.

Again, I shall not linger on Mama's and my differences.

Johnny has sent me a work entitled The Adventures of Huckleberry Finn. *Although I have read only a few chapters, the novel both disturbs and amuses me.*

I shall have to read it thoughtfully. The author, Mark Twain, is one of Johnny's favorites. He will expect a lively discussion when next we meet....

"GREAT NEWS," Hope announced as she came into Elizabeth's office. "The state archives have located the building's original plans. They've even been able to copy them for us."

Elizabeth, in the midst of wading through the latest CCE financials, looked up and attempted a smile.

Hope stopped to survey her thoroughly. "What's wrong?"

"The usual. Every time I go over one of these printouts, I feel like I'm in over my head."

"That's what the treasurer of the board is for. Call Herb if you have questions."

"No. Herb's one of our hardest working board members. I don't want to abuse him. Mac's right—social work education doesn't prepare you for some of life's mundane realities. A course in basic accounting should be a requirement for every would-be administrator."

Although it didn't take a C.P.A. to realize the center was operating in the red. They'd already stripped expenses down to the bare essentials. But somehow there had to be an infusion of new money soon.

Hope looked suspicious. "Are you sure there isn't something specific that's upset you?" She sat down and reached across the desk for the printout.

Elizabeth tapped her hand lightly and slipped the statement into its folder. "There's always something. But we can't do anything about it today."

She rose and walked to her window, drawn by the sounds of children playing. "Spring's coming," she said inconsequentially. "It must be sixty-five degrees outside. According to the paper, the peach trees along Town Lake are budding. They'll be in full bloom by March the first."

"Are you coming down with a case of spring fever?"

"Perhaps."

"You have shadows under your eyes. You don't look like you're sleeping well."

Elizabeth might have known Hope's eagle eye would pick out the traces of fatigue.

"Elizabeth..." Hope's summoning tone made her turn from the view. "You can't let this job get to you. By now, you've seen all the problems to be tackled. But what you may not realize is what a difference you've made. The Arts and Crafts Fair is shaping up nicely. Our day care clients are on the porches rocking our babies. The newsletter's coming out on a regular basis. You're doing a wonderful job, and you just can't lie awake worrying about it."

If only CCE problems were all that Elizabeth wrestled with at night!

She smiled at her friend and assistant. "I lie awake worrying about what I'd do without you."

Hope laughed. "Well, get some sleep because I'm not leaving."

"Make that a promise. If you decided to retire again, I'd probably run screaming out the nearest exit."

"Only if you promise to get out of the office for the day. You need fresh air and sunshine. Walk, do not scream, as you head for the door, and enjoy the drive to the capitol complex. The archives librarian is expecting one of us to run by. After that you can swing by the Austin History Center. They've unearthed some interesting information."

"Yes, Mother," Elizabeth said meekly.

She retrieved her purse out of the desk drawer, walked through Hope's office without a backward glance, hurried down the hall for fear someone might corner her and only stopped to unlock her car where it was parked across the street.

She stood for a moment taking a deep breath of the balmy air, feeling as though she'd been freed from a prison. Yet when she gazed over the roof of her Honda compact toward the place she'd just left, it didn't look like a jail.

Bright sunlight warmed the sandstone exterior. Three and four-year-olds were swarming the newly built playground equipment. In one of the wicker chairs on the upstairs veranda, a solitary figure slowly rocked back and forth.

Elizabeth's heart got caught in her throat. She had trouble breathing.

Then she sighed. It was Mrs. Moreland benignly surveying the yard's activities. Elizabeth started to wave before remembering that the elderly lady's eyesight was no more acute than her hearing.

With another sigh, Elizabeth got in her car and drove away.

Jumpy. She was definitely jumpy. And Hope didn't begin to know all the reasons.

Elizabeth considered herself a moderately well-educated, clearheaded woman. To keep abreast of world events, she read the paper and a weekly newsmagazine. She subscribed to a scientific journal and kept up-to-date on technological breakthroughs. A book of essays by a noted biologist currently resided on her bed stand. She was very much a product of the twentieth century.

Neither would she ever have called herself fanciful. No salt over the shoulder or aversions to ladders. Jezebel, her cat, was black from whiskers to tail.

In short, Elizabeth Ann Waite was highly skeptical of so-called paranormal phenomena. Yet the ghost she'd met hadn't seemed to care a hoot about her doubts.

At times her sense of the absurd had surfaced about the strange experience. Maybe she ought to write a memo to the CCE board.

You will be interested to learn that our historic building is indeed haunted. Verification comes from a personal sighting by your calm, cool and collected executive director. In light of this development, I recommend we seek the advice of a professional medium who could lead a séance to ascertain the apparition's needs. I also ask the board to authorize a nominal fee to pay for this consultant. We could recover the monies with daily tours, pointing out the places our ghost has been sighted. Such tours would greatly enhance our community visibility.

Elizabeth might as well resign as confess to what she'd seen.

Or thought she saw.

That's what Elizabeth kept telling herself. It was the gloom, the solitude, the atmosphere of the building, the stress of the job that had produced the female figure.

The first couple of days afterward, Elizabeth had felt truly haunted. The woman even called to her one night in a dream. Now the incident was assuming more and more an unreal quality. Except for the woman's face. Elizabeth could still see it in exquisite detail. The beseeching eyes, made more earnest by the imploring hand.

Maybe the entire episode had begun in her imagination. But something in the building or about it, some memory that permeated its stone, some incidental fact that had burrowed into Elizabeth's subconscious, some sense beyond measuring had prompted her hallucination. And Elizabeth had enough faith in her sanity to try to find out what it was.

Which was why she'd bowed to Hope's directive to play truant and drive by the History Center.

Oh, come on, Elizabeth. Be honest. That's not the only reason you're out enjoying the springtime.

Mac was due by the office later to pick up material Carol had left for him. Tomorrow the Spring Gala Committee, which included Mac, began discussions on the event that could prove crucial to CCE's future.

The gala was the board's first big chance to raise money through a charitable affair. Unfortunately, it would have to compete with fund-raising functions more entrenched on Austin's social calendar.

Since tomorrow constituted the first planning session, Elizabeth was obligated to make an appearance. She wasn't looking forward to the proceedings. Especially since this would be the first time she'd seen Mac since the disastrous night he'd kissed her.

Now, Elizabeth....

Okay, okay, since she'd kissed him.

And made a thorough fool of herself. The repressed spinster, unable to keep her hands off an attractive male.

Only she wasn't repressed. Just absurdly fastidious.

After her father's death, when she'd been so lonely and vulnerable and more than a little crazy, she'd been tempted, more than once, to go out and jump into bed with a man at the first opportunity, even though she knew a casual mating constituted a poor substitute for loving intimacy.

Except the first opportunity had been slow in coming. Straight, sane, unattached male social workers over thirty were an endangered species, but the only fauna available in the life she led. She wasn't about to seek out a partner in a singles' bar.

Then an opportunity of sorts had presented itself while she was working for the state. Only he wasn't terribly sane. He'd just gone through a messy divorce, and from certain hints he'd given her, Elizabeth suspected he was suffering from a case of performance anxiety.

With neither the training nor inclination to become a sexual therapist, Elizabeth had passed on the offer. And that was the last time she'd discussed sex with a man.

Until Mac.

She winced at the thought.

Avoiding him was both immature and impractical. But she kept hoping that somehow, some way, the memory of the kiss they'd shared would fade, along with the emotional tension that had led to it.

When hell freezes over....

Elizabeth muttered an expletive and pulled into a parking space outside the archives and library.

As Hope had said, she was expected. Fifteen minutes later, she walked outside with copies of the plans. Looking around, she spied an empty bench on the capitol grounds and headed toward it, wanting the chance to examine the drawings for herself.

They were simple enough to read and contained small surprises, the first being that the structure housing CCE was only part of the original complex. The other major building, which had long since been razed, was a hospital established especially for the widows. It reminded Elizabeth that the women who'd come to live there were aging or enfeebled.

Elizabeth could imagine the last twenty or so years of the home's existence, when there'd been no influx of occupants. The population must have slowly dwindled, until at the last only a handful of ladies waited to die.

How sad. And how poignant that the minuscule office she inhabited had once contained the remnants of a person's life. The structure still standing had not been greatly changed internally. The patterns of hallways, north and south turrets, and the tiny dormitory rooms, each with a window, remained much the same.

For the first time, she caught a glimpse of what these women had sacrificed when they'd been forced by circumstance to give themselves over to the charity of others.

She blinked back tears, rolled up the architectural drawings and walked to her car.

In another ten minutes Elizabeth arrived at the Austin History Center, where she was greeted by Jane Dorsey, the docent at the desk.

"Mrs. Kersey called and told us you were coming," Jane said as they exchanged introductions. "We've located several items you might find useful."

"Anything you've found will be helpful. We know very little about the home's history."

"Did you know it was originally built by the Daughters of the Confederacy in 1908?"

"I did notice the date on the architectural plans."

"The state of Texas didn't take it over until 1911. Every southern state maintained a home. Ours was considered one of the finest. We also had a Confederate Veterans' Home, which has long since been demolished."

Elizabeth had this sudden vision of a couple forced to live apart when they needed each other most. Was that the kind of story her ghost had to tell?

"...many years they were both considered—"

"I'm sorry," Elizabeth interrupted her. "I was thinking about the ladies. What were you saying?"

Jane smiled her understanding. "I know. I thought of them, too, when I began researching for you. I was saying that for many years both homes were considered architectural landmarks of Austin. Now very few people even remember they existed. It's so easy for a city to fritter away its heritage. Fortunately, we still have pictures."

"Of our building?" Elizabeth asked hopefully.

"Yes, I thought you'd be pleased. Come with me."

The two women made their way to one of the offices, where Jane had gathered a small but impressive collection of memorabilia.

"Here's one of them."

Elizabeth eagerly took the photograph from her.

Yes, the facade and entrance were still recognizable. She was charmed with the north turret in the foreground of the photograph. It was topped with stone battlements. They lent a fairy castle quality to the original edifice.

The grounds were more spacious in the picture she held. Later street improvements had taken their toll. And through the trees she could just make out a building, which must have been the home's infirmary. The addition that housed the Adult Day Care Center now stood on its site.

Not such a dreary spot to live out one's days. Elizabeth was comforted.

"Did you find any descriptions of the widows who lived there? Any lists of names?"

"Not really. We do know that in the 1930s an average of eighty ladies were in residence. Later, of course, the number declined. I do have a piece on the women in an Oral History Collection done in the forties."

Jane located the material and handed it to Elizabeth, saying, "Several of them described their early lives."

Elizabeth sat down in the chair Jane offered and began to read.

Four women had provided vignettes of their lives during the latter part of the nineteenth century. All had come of pioneer families who'd journeyed to Texas to tame the land. Each had been raised on a farm, and their recollections of hardship and fortitude opened doors to a vanished past.

Annie Armstrong had been widowed during the war, married again, borne eight children, outlived her second husband and several of her offspring. At the time of the interview she was still hale and hearty and close to a hundred. Elizabeth could tell from the tone of her anecdotes that she was a feisty old lady. Hard to picture Annie calling from the grave.

Katherine Hickman, on the other hand, had married a Confederate officer soon after the war, moved off the farm and into Austin, where her husband gained prominence in the state senate. Apparently Katherine herself had been active in local society.

She'd told tales of a city very conscious of its status as a state capital. A city yearning for cosmopolitan ways and demanding a newspaper that covered the events of the world. Nevertheless a small town where everybody knew everyone else's business. A wild and woolly frontier outpost where gunfights were common and gambling dens and brothels flourished. With a main thoroughfare grandly called Congress Avenue, which wasn't even paved until 1905. Katherine's account of those days was cozy and gossipy.

Sarah Elizabeth LeBow, another of the ladies, had been sent off at sixteen to matriculate at an institute of higher learning, a rare endeavor for a rural female of that era. She'd told stories of her father, a prosperous and progressive farmer, who'd rotated his crops before it was common practice.

When she'd married, it was also to a veteran much older than herself, and after he died, she'd become one of the first public school teachers in Bastrop, Texas. Elizabeth sensed pride and dignity in Sarah Elizabeth's recounting. She found herself pleased they shared a name.

The last woman, Margaret Connor, had been the second wife of a veteran who'd died shortly after the war ended. She'd raised his six children and maintained the family spread until the 1930s, when drought and the depression had driven the farm into bankruptcy.

When all of her stepchildren and their kin migrated to California, she'd chosen to enter the home, saying she wasn't about to leave her native state. Margaret had broken her hip not long before the interview. Elizabeth could sense she was telling her story in preparation for death.

Could Margaret be the woman Elizabeth had seen? Could any of these women? She realized for the first time the difficulty of her task. Yet the task still compelled her. She sensed there was something she was expected to do.

"Are there any photographs with these histories?"

"Only of Katherine Hickman." Jane picked up a slender book. "This is some of her poetry, which I believe she wrote while she was at the home."

Elizabeth took the poems and read them over. They were simply composed, religious in tone and illustrative of a life at peace. Elizabeth didn't think Katherine had any need to haunt her old quarters.

Then Jane gave her the faded photograph of a smiling, bosomy lady, and she knew her instincts had been right. This was not the figure who roamed the second story.

"These are lovely." Elizabeth gestured to the poetry. "Could we have copies? Some of our clients might enjoy reading them."

"Of course," Jane said. "We can copy any item you want."

"We've heard," Elizabeth said tentatively, "that the building is haunted. Do you know where that bit of folklore originated?"

"No. I do have an article from the *Austin American* dated 1925 regarding deteriorating conditions in the home at that time. Here, you can look at it. Apparently this article and others caused a stink in the legislature.

Some people claimed there was actual mistreatment. Maybe that's when the gossip started.

"From what I can tell, however, the residents' care improved, and no problems recurred during later years. That didn't stop the rumors from flying when the home was closed and converted into an office building. You haven't had a sighting, have you?" Jane asked with a gleam in her eyes.

"Not exactly," Elizabeth hedged. "But there's no denying the building has a certain aura."

"I know. I sensed it when I made a tour several years ago, right before they boarded the place up. I'm so glad your group has bought it. If there's any way the History Center can be of further help in your restorations, don't hesitate to call."

"If we only knew more about the people who lived there."

"I have just the lady you need to talk to."

"Oh?" Elizabeth looked hopeful.

"Yes. Her name is Cassie Taylor. She's a native Austinite, and her grandmother Cassandra Carter lived in the home almost until the day it closed. Cassie visited all the time and knew several of the ladies. She has all kinds of stories she likes to tell."

Jane went on to explain, "We met because Cassie's an amateur historian with a set of photographs and papers that she's willed to the center. The collection includes a scrapbook of her grandmother's, assembled while Cassandra lived at the home."

Elizabeth's heartbeat quickened. "I'd enjoy meeting Mrs. Taylor. Could you give me her number?"

"I'll phone and vouch for you, if you'd like. Cassie's rather formal and prefers an introduction. She doesn't go out much, so you'll have to visit her at home. But once you get to know her, she's utterly delightful.''

"I'd like that very much," Elizabeth said as calmly as she could.

While Jane called, Elizabeth tried not to get her hopes up. Jane was simply arranging a visit with an elderly woman who had memories to share.

Still, it was hard to keep the eagerness out of her voice when Jane handed her the phone and she spoke to Cassie, setting up a visit for the very next morning.

As she walked out of the History Center a little while later, laden with photocopied documents and pictures, Elizabeth felt better than she had all day.

She'd needed this afternoon. And it had ended successfully. They had the drawings for Manley, and she'd found someone to talk to about the ladies.

When Elizabeth remembered how starchy Cassie had sounded on the telephone, she smiled to herself. She'd probably have to pass inspection before Cassie opened up.

Starting down the steps to the sidewalk, she glanced up the street where her car was parked.

Mac stood beside it, watching her approach. There was a definite gleam of challenge in his deep brown eyes.

CHAPTER SIX

May 25, 1891

My thirtieth birthday. A date that calls for celebration, yet I find I am distracted with morbid Fancies. I look into the mirror and am astonished by what I see. A woman of indeterminate years, whose skin is pale, smooth and unlined. The contours of that woman's face are growing pronounced, and youth and life seem to be draining from it, just as complexion fades when denied the Sun's healthy rays.

The woman I see reflected has a slender waist. Her bosom is firm. Her figure does not bear the weight of repeated childbearing.

Can I possibly be this person? I ask myself.

I feel ancient with cares and repressed longings. Should not these cares and longings have etched themselves upon my brow? Yet the emptiness I feel inside is met by the empty expression of the image that stares back at me, and I must tear myself away from the dreadful reflection.

Mr. LeBow has taken a turn for the worse. He is bedbound, incontinent and unable to feed himself, his speech incomprehensible even to me. Dr. Peters says this could be the beginning of the end, although my husband's Constitution has proved tenaciously resilient. I wake to each day determined to see its end without harboring Fears about tomorrow. Oftentimes this is my *most difficult task, far greater than those Mr. LeBow's Condition demands of me.*

A birthday package from Johnny arrived this morning. Inside, I found a box of chocolates from Lamme's Candies, Austin's premier Confectionery. I was immensely cheered and greedily sought out the strawberry creams as though I were a girl again.

With the chocolates came a volume of sonnets by Elizabeth Barrett Browning. In the inscription Johnny wrote, he said he'd chosen these poems because their author and I shared more than a name. He felt her words would speak to me.

They speak to me too well! I began to cry as I read them and had to put away the volume in order to compose myself.

Johnny can sometimes be unconsciously cruel in his determination on Plain Speaking and Honesty. Why won't he understand that my path is difficult enough...?

But no purpose is served by this Digression.

I must find a way to thank him while disguising my emotions. I both dread and yearn for his upcoming visit.

Is it possible for me truly to go on in this manner...?

WHEN ELIZABETH SAW Mac casually leaning against her car, as if his appearing like this were an everyday occurrence, she almost stumbled down the steep stone steps. As it was, she clutched the iron railing and stared at him stupidly.

A full minute passed before she had the strength to move. Mac waited patiently, his look never leaving her.

All Elizabeth could think as she slowly approached was, how dare he spoil her lovely afternoon.

"You tracked me down," she said, her truculence showing.

"It wasn't difficult," he replied calmly.

"I don't imagine it was with Hope's assistance. But why bother?" she asked, still feeling belligerent.

"Because," he said shortly, "I was tired of being treated like a case of the plague."

"I have not treated you . . ." Her voice rose in contradiction before fading away.

A moment passed.

She began again. "I'm sorry if any actions of mine caused you to feel that way."

"No, you're not."

"Yes, I am. I never intended—"

"Yes, you did."

"No, I didn't!" Elizabeth gasped and clapped a hand to her mouth.

She'd just yelled at one of the most influential members of her board. Her eyes closed briefly in prayerful supplication. When she opened them, she found Mac grinning down at her.

"Come on," he said easily, opening her door. "I'll follow you home to drop off your car. Then we'll go get dinner."

She nodded mutely and slid behind the wheel, still horrified by her outburst, realizing belatedly that her mortification had prevented her from rejecting his offer.

In the ten-minute trip to her house, Elizabeth couldn't think of a thing to say to address the incident.

Mac apparently planned to ignore it—for the time being, at least. He parked his BMW sedan behind her Honda when she pulled into the driveway. And without waiting for an invitation, he followed her to the door.

Elizabeth stifled a protest and went inside, meaning to hurry out as soon as she'd put down her briefcase with the material she'd collected. Instead, she was besieged by the Three Stooges.

"What do you feed these animals?" Mac asked over their howling. "Starvation rations?"

"Don't be silly," she said lightly, bending to pet them. "They just miss their mommy. It gets lonely in this big old house during the day."

Mac looked around the gloomy living room, and Elizabeth could guess what he was thinking. But this time, she was determined not to bristle. "This was my parents' home. When the market improves, I plan to sell it. All I need is a town house, really."

Their gazes met. The memory of the gazebo flashed between them. The words he'd spoken...

... *well down the list of what you need.*

Elizabeth looked away. "W-why don't I feed them? Since I'm already here." She glanced around for the cats.

Having received their greeting, the trio had strolled over to inspect the stranger in their midst.

Cleo, in particular, having felt a stirring in her heart, was now purring loudly and rubbing hard against Mac's leg.

"Oh, Cleopatra," Elizabeth murmured, "have you no shame?"

"She seems a creature of taste and refinement." Mac glanced up smiling from where he'd crouched to reward Cleo's affections. "Her mistress could take lessons from her in the art of seduction. I notice Cleopatra doesn't kiss and run."

"You're not going to let it be, are you?" she asked abruptly.

"No."

"Then I expect we'd better talk."

"That's why I'm here." Mac paused for a moment as he stood to face her. "Also to tell you I think we've got the money to pay off the mortgage."

Elizabeth's face was transformed. "Oh, Mac! Why didn't you tell me? I've been so worried. How did you do it?" Too pleased to care about the consequences, she threw her arms around his neck.

He returned the favor with interest, and Elizabeth found herself snugly ensconced in his embrace. She tried to break away. He wouldn't let her.

Instead, his laughter brushed against her hair. "You didn't give me a chance to tell you," he reminded her softly. "You seemed in the mood for a shouting match."

"Which you drove me to."

"Now why would I want to do such a thing?"

"I don't know." Her voice was muffled against his shoulder. "I think you enjoy ruffling my feathers."

"I'd like to ruffle more than that."

This time she did succeed in placing distance between them. Looking everywhere but into his eyes, she called to the cats. "Jess, Tom, Cleo, it's suppertime."

Although his name hadn't been mentioned, Mac followed everyone into the kitchen and watched as Elizabeth opened cans and emptied their contents onto a plate.

After a moment of seeming concentration on her pets' greedy appetites, she turned to him, a bright smile firmly in place. "I believe you mentioned dinner? Once we're there, you'll have to tell me all about how you've saved us from foreclosure."

He smiled faintly. "I'd be glad to. What good are valiant rescues if you can't savor them?"

An hour later, in the restaurant, when Elizabeth did press him for details over chicken *fajitas,* however, he seemed surprisingly reticent. She was left with the impression he'd called in an old debt.

"Just how did you effect this feat of magic?" she asked, her intuition working. "Did you call in a favor from someone whose hide you'd saved?"

She blinked once and then again. And stared at him openly.

"You're blushing," she said, astounded.

Sure enough, pink tinged the tips of Mac's ears.

"Is this the hard-nosed, conservative businessman I've come to know and love?"

"An encouraging admission."

Elizabeth ignored his comment. "Come on, confess," she pressed him. "How did you get the two hundred thousand?"

"I have a college friend," he explained, looking vaguely uncomfortable, "who started a computer software firm. When he had a cash flow problem, I refinanced his loans. Later one of his programs became a bestseller. Last week, I went hat in hand reminding him of old times."

"You'd bailed him out, hadn't you—earlier?"

Mac shrugged. "He made good the loan eventually."

She shook her head slowly. "I can't decide whether you're an old softy or just a fair approximation of Mary."

"I am not old," he growled.

Her eyes widened. "Tracy told me you were getting touchy about becoming a grandfather."

He leaned forward, a definite gleam in his eyes. "Did she? And what else did you two talk about?"

"N-nothing." Elizabeth leaned back, suddenly aware she was playing with fire. "You have a lovely daughter."

"Yes, I do. I also have a son you'll enjoy meeting. He graduates from U.T. this spring and starts work on an advanced degree in clinical psychology. But I don't want to talk about either of my children right now."

Elizabeth cleared her throat. "What would you like to talk about?"

"I thought we'd agreed to discuss the nature of our involvement."

"I feel," she said firmly, "that *involvement* is too strong a word."

"Now, Elizabeth," he coaxed. "If we can't even agree on terms, how will we keep the lines of communication open?"

"That's one of my points," she offered hurriedly. "I doubt if we agree on much of anything. Outside of CCE, we've got nothing in common."

"I wouldn't say that," he reminded her smoothly.

"We don't think alike." She rephrased her argument. "You're conservative and pragmatic—"

"I'm an old softy."

"And I'm—"

"A hard-hearted woman."

"Would you let me finish a sentence?"

She pressed her palm to her forehead, feeling herself on the verge of yelling again.

Finally, dropping her hand to the table, she looked across at him sternly. "Will you please just let me be serious for a moment?"

"As serious as you want."

His words seemed sincere.

Heartened by them, she began to explain her position. "Getting involved with a member of my board goes against every ethical and professional standard I live by."

"Co-workers get personally involved every day."

"But you're technically one of my bosses. There's a big difference."

"I'll resign if it bothers you."

"Your resignation would bother me even more. CCE needs you."

"You need me."

"Certainly, as director of the coalition—"

"No. *You* need me, Elizabeth, in your life."

"Please, let's not go into that."

"But we can't get away from it, any more than I can escape the realization of what I've been missing."

"Oh, Mac—" she bowed her head "—this is getting too complicated."

"Life's complicated. And you're old enough and wise enough to understand it can't be tidied up conveniently."

"But I never intended..." Her voice trailed off.

His lips curved slightly. "Do you think I did? Do you really think I take off in pursuit of every attractive woman my mother dangles in front of me?"

His last words produced a surprised gasp.

"Although I see now," he continued thoughtfully, "that I was on my way the very first day when I admired your tush."

"Y-you wha...?" Elizabeth's voice failed her as a crimson blush flew up her face. She had a vivid memory of white cotton jockey briefs.

Mac paused to let his gaze linger appreciatively over her heightened color before saying softly, "And if you think I'm going to retire from the field, you're denying to yourself what happened that evening at Tracy's party."

He shook his head in a fatalistic manner. "No, I'm afraid it's too late to go back. Has been," he said with spurious resignation, "since our passionate clinch in the gazebo. That kiss of yours effectively sealed our fate."

Her head still bowed, Elizabeth sighed heavily. Still, she had to know more of what he was thinking. Through the veil of her lashes, she cast him a look.

His gaze held humor and desire and...

"Dammit, Elizabeth," he barely spoke above a whisper. "Every time our eyes meet, we make promises to each other. I haven't even touched you and yet—" He broke off and laughed ruefully. "Well, let's just say, I'd rather not get up from this table right now."

As if his own words compelled him, he took both her hands in his. "But it isn't just that I want you like hell. You appeal to me as a person. Do you really believe I need a woman who agrees with me on every issue?"

Since Elizabeth hadn't mastered words for several minutes now, she settled for a shake of her head in answer to his question.

"I don't want a docile woman—I want one who thinks."

"Who says I can't be docile?" Amazing how a sense of humor came to one's rescue. "I've restrained myself with you on numerous occasions."

"Yes, I know," he agreed solemnly. "With great effort, I might add. At other times, you haven't been entirely successful."

She laughed. Amazingly, incredibly, she'd begun to relax. Her hands lay slack on the table, absorbing his touch. His gaze seemed to wrap itself around her.

For just a moment, her look encompassed the room.

The restaurant hadn't been crowded that evening, and some of the other diners had already left. They might as well be alone in a world of their own in one corner of the dimly lit dining area.

As though they were in a place beyond time or space.

It felt right being with him, their senses telescoped on each other. Right and necessary and oh so inevitable. Her qualms and doubts were becoming difficult to cling to.

"What are you thinking?" His quiet words drew her look back to his.

She shook her head helplessly. "I'm not sure. My mind's a muddle. I don't see any solution to our problem. But I guess at this moment I'm feeling fatalistic."

His expression intensified. "Are you saying what I hope you are?"

There was a beat of silence before she confessed a little thickly, "Lord help me, I'm afraid I am."

CASSIE TAYLOR'S HOUSE was an old-fashioned bungalow set amongst the trees in a neatly mowed yard. As Elizabeth parked in front of it, she sensed that only one family had lived in and cared for the property.

On each side, homes had been remodeled and expanded as the west side neighborhood had grown fashionable. But this house must look much as it did the day of its completion, with a fresh coat of paint on the clapboard exterior and the windows gleaming in the morning sun. Elizabeth had a feeling the woman inside would have that same tidy air.

As soon as she rang the doorbell, the front door opened. A woman appeared who looked much as Elizabeth expected.

"Mrs. Taylor?" she asked.

"Yes. And you're...?"

"Elizabeth Waite. It's so good of you to see me on such short notice."

Cassie Taylor gave Elizabeth a polite survey before unlatching the screen for her to come in. "I enjoy talking to someone who's interested in local history. Why don't we go back to the sun room? It's a lovely day."

Elizabeth followed Cassie down the narrow hallway. She registered her appreciation as soon as they reached their destination.

"This is lovely," she said, glancing around the glassed-in porch. "I didn't realize your backyard was adjacent to the park."

"It's one of the reasons we built here. Jack, my late husband, added this room later." Cassie smiled in remembrance. "At my insistence."

"I can see why." Elizabeth waited until Cassie settled in one of the chintz-covered chairs and gestured for her to sit down. She chose a corner of the matching sofa, deciding she would let Cassie direct the conversation, as well.

"Are you a native Austinite?" Cassie asked her immediately.

"Yes. My father practiced medicine here."

"Oh, my heavens! Are you Dr. Waite's daughter?" For the first time Cassie's smile was spontaneous and open.

"Yes."

Cassie shook her head in wonder. "He was my physician for many years. What a lovely man he was. All his patients adored him."

"I've had many people tell me that."

"I was so sorry to hear he'd died."

"Yes. Although at the end, it was what he wanted. He had Alzheimer's disease."

Cassie tactfully changed the subject. "I bet you didn't know my grandmother was one of his patients."

"No, I didn't." Elizabeth's look sharpened.

"Toward the end, he treated all the ladies at the home. There were only a handful, not enough to justify maintaining the hospital."

"I had no idea. I knew very little about my father's practice."

"He was so good with old folks. Considering your line of work, you must take after him."

"I'd like to think I do," Elizabeth said, smiling.

Cassie leaned back in her chair with a reminiscing expression. "What a small world it is. Us meeting like this. My knowing your father."

Yes...and strange that lives should connect coincidentally, the patterns hidden to the casual eye.

"Jane told me," Elizabeth said, "that you knew several of the ladies."

"Oh, yes. I got to be kind of a pet around the place. They didn't get many youngsters coming by. You know how it is. Young people can't be bothered. They think the world started the day they were born. But even then I was interested in the old stories. And I was very close to my grandmother, being her namesake and all."

"Could you tell me some of those stories, and about the ladies?"

"I can do better than that. Mama Cassie kept scrapbooks. Let me get them. They'll jog my memory."

Cassie left the room and was gone for several moments.

While Elizabeth awaited her return, she sat in absolute stillness, trying to control the obscure excitement bubbling inside.

"...the one that covered her stay in the home." Cassie followed her voice back into the room, already opening the fragile scrapbook. This time she settled cosily next to Elizabeth and invited her perusal.

"The home was quite grand in its day," she said.

Elizabeth felt a faint tremor in her fingers as she turned a page. "I know. Jane showed me pictures."

"Here's one I wanted you to look at." Cassie pointed to a spot on the photograph. "That upstairs room was where Mama Cassie lived."

"Information and Referral for Older Adults is now located there."

Cassie laughed. "That would please my grandmother. She was the gossip of the home. Knew everybody's business. You know, the place was like a small community. None of the women went out much except to church. Most of them only had each other. They served tea every afternoon, and the north turret was used for a quilting circle. I still have two of the quilts they made."

Elizabeth couldn't muffle her intake of breath.

Cassie glanced at her curiously, and Elizabeth knew she'd have to explain the unlikely reaction. "It's just that...sometimes when I've been in the turret room, I've sensed...well, I've had this vision of the ladies in a circle—"

"Have you seen the ghost?" Cassie interrupted excitedly.

"Do you believe there is one?"

Cassie shook her head. "I don't know. There weren't any sightings while the home was in operation, or my grandmother would have told me. Oh, some of the ladies thought they saw things, but they were the ones who weren't quite with us."

"If..." Elizabeth paused, trying to figure out how to phrase the question. "If there were a lady so unhappy she couldn't rest, do you...well, do you have any idea who it might be?"

Cassie's expression turned reflective. "Many of them, had, you know, dealt with tragedy. They'd outlived husbands, children, friends, their good health."

"Yes." Elizabeth stared blindly down at the page.

"Grandmother saved the obituaries of each lady when she died." Cassie began to leaf through the scrapbook. "Sounds morbid, I know. But when you're older, you begin to understand the reasons. Sometimes these obits evoke images of the women's lives."

She stopped and gazed fondly at a picture Elizabeth recognized. "Dear Mrs. Hickman. You talk about someone who could tell tales about the good citizens of Austin. But she wasn't malicious. I don't believe Mrs. Hickman would need to come back from the grave."

She spied another write-up. "Now Annie Armstrong, she was a pistol. Had the home in an uproar half the time. Mama Cassie used to say Annie was going to live forever, because she was too mean to die. But as you can see, a heart condition caught up with her."

Cassie turned to Elizabeth, the scrapbook temporarily forgotten. "Grandmother was amazed at what killed her, since she didn't think Annie had a heart. I can't imagine Annie roaming that old place. But if she is, you'd better hire an exorcist."

Elizabeth chuckled and glanced down at a new page.

The laughter died. Her heart began to pound crazily.

"Wait." She stilled Cassie's fingers. "Could I read this one?" Her voice came out raspy, and she cleared her throat. "Sarah Elizabeth LeBow. Th-there was a piece on her in the material Jane gave me." It was the best reason Elizabeth could come up with for halting Cassie's progress.

"Certainly." Cassie looked at her strangely as she relinquished the book.

But Elizabeth couldn't begin.

Not for a moment.

She could only stare at the faded photograph that accompanied the funeral notice. It must have been taken many years before Sarah Elizabeth's death, because the woman staring unsmilingly at Elizabeth could hardly be older than herself.

The woman's face held beauty and character. But her expression was blank as she gazed into the camera.

Not at all like the beseeching look Elizabeth had encountered.

Still, she knew, was certain, that Sarah Elizabeth LeBow and her ghostly visitor were one and the same.

Finally, she read the words....

Our beloved friend Sarah Elizabeth Williams LeBow passed away April 11, 1959 at the age of ninety-seven. A longtime resident of the Confederate Widows' Home of Texas, she was a native of Bastrop...

After a few minutes, Elizabeth looked up at Cassie. "Did you know Mrs. LeBow?" she asked, trying to control a tremor.

"Yes." Cassie paused for a long moment. "Actually, I called her Aunt Sarah Elizabeth. She'd had a number of nieces and nephews and loved young people around her."

"I notice here that she taught English and American literature at Bastrop High School. Her husband and stepson predeceased her. But I see no mention of surviving kin. Didn't she have any children of her own?"

"No. By the time I met her, she had no family left at all, other than a great-niece in Dallas, who came by once a year. And a nephew living in San Jose, California."

Elizabeth read over a section of the write-up. "It says she was a longtime resident of the home."

"More than thirty years. She once told me she'd retired from teaching to take care of her mother. After her mother's death, she moved to Austin so as not to be a burden on her family. That seemed to be very important to her."

"Could you tell me more of what she was like?"

"Dignified and reserved." Cassie smiled at the memory. "What you'd expect from a teacher of that era. You notice she wanted to be called by her full name. She had an air of elegance the other ladies envied."

"They envied Sarah Elizabeth?"

"No. It wasn't like that. She was kind and understanding. One of the home's peacemakers. But she had an aloof quality." Cassie caught herself. "No, not aloof..."

Elizabeth spoke the words carefully. "Could it have been sadness?"

Cassie gazed into the distance. "Perhaps. But if she was unhappy, she contained her feelings. Until the end. That last year, she failed badly and seemed to inhabit a world all her own. She was often agitated and walked the hallways. I hated seeing her so confused."

Elizabeth looked down at the notice again. "How did she die?"

"In her sleep during an afternoon nap. It was a blessing."

No. Not a blessing. Or else Sarah Elizabeth would be resting with the sleep of peace.

"I wouldn't want to know if Sarah Elizabeth were haunting her old home." Cassie folded her hands and avoided Elizabeth's eyes.

"You cared about her, didn't you?"

"Almost as much as I did my grandmother." Cassie tsked faintly. "Rumors. That's all it ever was. Silly rumors and suggestive people. I admit the old place has a certain atmosphere—" she smiled anxiously at Elizabeth "—but you and I know ghosts don't really exist."

IT WAS AFTER SIX O'CLOCK when Elizabeth climbed to the second story, her footsteps echoing hollowly in the empty stairwell. She'd had to wait patiently for everyone to leave.

Patiently? It was hardly the word to describe her state of mind.

Distracted. Fearful. Dreading what might come. But knowing what she did was an inevitable consequence of what she'd learned.

She'd barely made it through the afternoon. The committee meeting. Mac.

No, she'd think of him later.

Now, she walked down the hall, hoping her legs would support her. Unlocked the door to the north turret. Stood for a moment in the middle of the room.

She felt alone and lonely.

After a moment, she went out on the porch.

The light was fading.

Yet the gloom was not as heavy as it had been that other evening.

She went to the same wicker rocker and lowered herself into it.

As she rocked, it made the same creaking noise as before. But this time her hands were shaking rather badly.

Still, Elizabeth knew... just as before... and looked up to see the woman's form come near.

Elizabeth's fingers clutched the wicker arms of the chair.

"Sarah Elizabeth...." she whispered.

The woman seemed to hesitate.

"Sarah Elizabeth...." The words came stronger. "You are Sarah Elizabeth LeBow, aren't you? I've seen your picture."

The woman nodded. Once. It was enough.

"Why?" Elizabeth asked. "Why have you chosen to appear to me? Is there a special reason? Because of my father? Is it... is it because we share a name?"

Sarah Elizabeth reached out a hand. Her agonized look tore at Elizabeth's heart.

Elizabeth felt the ineffable sadness wash over her.

"How can I help you?" she cried out. "You must tell me!"

But her cries were met with silence as the ghostly figure blended into the evening gloom.

CHAPTER SEVEN

June 23, 1895

I hardly know what words to write.

As I sit by Mr. LeBow's bedside watching the hours creep by, I know Johnny lies in the next room, as wakeful as I am.

He will leave tomorrow, not to return. I have asked that of him. And now I remain here weeping, feeling as if I had taken a Knife and carved out my Heart.

He should have married. Years ago, I told him he should marry. Then I would never have dreamed... never have hoped... none of this would have happened.

My mother was right. She understood far better than I the Dangerous Game we were playing.

And yet, today, when Johnny and I exchanged the words that had lain in our hearts for so many years, I was Exalted! No guilt I feel can sully that Sublime Moment.

But we can go no further.

Now that the words have been spoken, we hunger for an even greater closeness, and I must be strong. I look over at my Husband's face, so frail and wasted, the skin as thin and pale as parchment, and I understand where my Duty lies.

Johnny rages at our circumstances. He plans and schemes against it. But that is because he lives in a different world. And though I could join him in that world, I have lived too long in mine. It has bound and shaped

me into the person I am. And I could not bear a weight
of Guilt greater than that which I now shoulder.
  Oh God, please help me to remain Steadfast....

THE HAMMERING THAT ECHOED down the hallway made
it hard for Elizabeth to concentrate on her work. But the
sounds of the construction crew were music to her ears,
because they signaled the beginning of the restoration.

Once Mac had come up with money to pay off the
mortgage, he rammed through a proposal for the renovations.

And though Manley's plans still had to be approved
by the historical society, Mac's workmen were already
stripping away linoleum and tearing out the ceilings of
unoccupied offices, searching for the bones of the original structure.

Mac was somewhere in the building now. Elizabeth
would have known it even if he hadn't checked in with
Hope earlier.

Maybe she was developing extrasensory perception.
That speculation and its reminder of the ghost brought
her no comfort.

Her thoughts swung back to Mac. Some instinct always told her when he was near.

In the same room. Or close behind her. Or in her pe-
ripheral vision at the meetings they attended. Unless she
forced her concentration to the task at hand, he came
into her mind and possessed her thoughts.

Carol had taken to watching them oddly. Once, when
Mac had lingered over Elizabeth's shoulder while she sat
jotting notes on a report; another time, when his hand
had brushed hers. Elizabeth had looked at him for a
moment before she could control her expression. God
only knows what she'd revealed to Carol then.

Hope was even more difficult to handle. She'd taken to wearing a Cheshire cat's grin every time she was in Mac and Elizabeth's vicinity.

And Mary. Her frequent calls were ostensibly to find out how CCE was progressing. Yet she always managed to slip in a question about Mac.

Elizabeth felt exposed on every flank—with precious little reason.

Twice Mac and she had gone to dinner. Once they'd had tickets for the Austin Lyric Opera. Another time they'd seen a production at the Live Oak Theatre of a drama written by a local playwright.

Mac had been a charming escort. Their topics of conversation had ranged far and wide. As she'd predicted, they didn't agree on every issue, although Elizabeth often suspected he was less dogmatic than she. They'd certainly laughed together more than she'd expected.

And they'd exchanged exactly four frustrating good-night kisses.

Why on earth was Mac biding his time?

Staring blankly at the letter on workmen's compensation, Elizabeth finally laid it down and glanced at her watch. Four-thirty.

Soon, she'd leave to go home to shower and change. Later, Mac would pick her up for another dinner engagement.

Would he come by the office before he left? Should she search him out to say she was quitting early?

Was she reduced to this? Snatching every second she could with the man?

In a spasm of self-disgust, Elizabeth pushed away from the desk and stood. She'd just decided to call it quits for the day.

Her intercom beeped demandingly.

"Yes?"

"It's Mary on line one," Hope informed her.

Elizabeth punched in the blinking button.

"Hello, Mary. How are you today?"

"Looking forward to this evening."

"That's nice," Elizabeth said distractedly. "Now, how can I help you?"

"I thought we two women should decide on a restaurant for the evening. Men are no good at these kinds of decisions."

The implications of Mary's words sat Elizabeth back down in her chair. "Decide on the restaurant," she repeated faintly.

"Yes. Why don't we try the new place on Lavaca? The one that advertises continental cuisine. We'll see if it's a match for The Courtyard."

"Well, actually, I hadn't thought—I mean, I thought I'd let Mac..." Elizabeth knew she was dithering.

And she hadn't fooled Mary. "Mac did tell you we were going out together?"

Elizabeth remembered just in time that honesty was safest. "No, he hadn't. I expect he meant to surprise me." Stun the hell out of her, she meant. "And a delightful surprise it would have been, too," she finished lamely.

"Humph." The single syllable was eloquent. "Sometimes I wonder if my son has any sense. You can ask him that for me." Mary's voice changed perceptibly. "Not that you needed to be warned about tonight. We'll have a delightful time, just the four of us."

"Just the four of us?"

"Didn't I say? Herb rounds out the group."

"How wonderful. Since I'll have the three of you together, I'll pump you for advice. One of the reasons for

Mac's and my meeting was to discuss the renovations.'' She stressed the word *meeting* ever so slightly.

Mary laughed. ''That's not what Mac called it. No, Elizabeth, no business tonight—just the pleasure of good company.''

''In that case,'' Elizabeth said cheerfully, ''I'm sure we'll have a delightful time. And I'll bow to your experience and let you pick the restaurant.''

''You mean, you'll let me take the blame. That's okay. I can handle it. See you tonight.''

Elizabeth replaced the receiver more forcefully than was necessary. Slinging her purse over her shoulder, she marched into Hope's office.

''Have you seen Mac?''

''I think he's still in the office down the hall.'' Hope leaned back in her chair to examine Elizabeth closely. ''What did Mary say to upset you?''

''It's not Mary I'm upset with. I'm gone for the day.''

Without another word, she yanked open the door and stomped, no, trod purposefully, to the office in question.

When she entered, two members of the construction crew were chiseling up the flooring. Alongside them was Mac in faded denims and a dusty work shirt.

He looked damned sexy in the tight-fitting jeans. Somehow that seemed his greatest offense.

''Could I see you alone for a second?'' she asked, a fixed smile in place.

''Sure,'' he said, his brow lifting quizzically. Glancing down at his watch, he turned to his crew. ''You can quit for the day. I'll see you tomorrow.''

In another moment, Mac and Elizabeth were alone.

''What's the problem?'' he asked without preliminaries.

"So you noticed," she said coolly. "How perceptive of you."

He smiled faintly. "Well, you're having trouble unclenching your teeth."

"Don't grin at me that way."

"Are we about to have an argument? If so, I suggest we wait until we can do it justice."

"With your mother and Herb refereeing?" she asked getting to the heart of the matter.

"I see. You don't want to double-date with Herb and Mary."

"Double-date? I don't want Mary to know I'm seeing you at all."

"Mary wouldn't like that. She'd think I was shirking my duty."

"You know what I mean. Our seeing each other personally, after business hours."

"Impossible. Mary's spies are everywhere. I decided it was time for a coming out party."

"You decided? Without warning me? Mary said you were out of your mind."

"She did?" Mac looked skeptical.

"In so many words. Actually, she wasn't sure you had any mind to begin with. She called me a minute ago. That's how I found out. Mary was horrified you hadn't mentioned the evening to me." Elizabeth assumed a self-righteous air.

"In this instance, she's wrong. Which she rarely admits. An annoying habit of hers. I didn't tell you we were seeing Mary and Herb because I didn't want you obsessing about it."

"I do *not* obsess."

"You do constantly," he said firmly. "One of the hazards of an introspective mind."

"Better than barreling your way through life so sure of yourself you don't stop to think of another person's feelings."

Mac moved in close so they were inches apart. "Have I hurt your feelings?" he asked silkily.

Elizabeth felt his nearness like a wave of heat, but she wasn't ready to relinquish her indignation. It felt far too satisfying.

"Don't be ridiculous." She bit out the words. "You haven't hurt my feelings. You've insulted my intelligence. Not to speak of acting in a chauvinistic manner. I might have expected it."

"And what else were you expecting? This isn't a rhetorical question, by the way. Because I'm standing here thinking the matter through very carefully—just as you'd want me to," he reminded her gently. "I could kiss you to shut you up..."

She sucked in her breath.

"But since neither of us is in the mood for a single kiss, things could get out of hand, and you'd be a nervous wreck to face Mary. I've worked very hard to avoid that happening."

"I don't know what you mean."

"Don't you?" He smiled at her. "I want you to get used to having other people around."

"You mean around us?" She stared at him blankly.

"Yes. Before we go to bed together."

This time her gasp was sharp and disbelieving.

He cut it off by covering her mouth with two fingers. "And before you start wearing a hair shirt to work every morning."

Now he let his fingers fall from her lips and waited for her answer.

Despite her best efforts, the anger was gone. "You think you've figured me out, don't you?" she said finally.

"No. But I've spent a lot of time working at it lately. And I don't believe in doing a half-assed job."

Against Elizabeth's will, her lips twitched at the image. "It's such a nice one, too. Especially in those jeans."

For the first time since she'd known him, Mac was slow on the uptake. Then he grinned widely. "I'm encouraged to see you noticed," he drawled.

"How could I help it?"

With a daring she hadn't suspected she possessed, Elizabeth reached around and fondly patted his rear.

Displaying lightning reflexes, Mac captured her fingers and stuffed them into his back pocket, holding them there as he murmured, "Does this mean the fight's over?"

"I'm not sure." She looked away. "Mac, let go of me. If someone caught us like this . . ."

"Maybe we should reconsider that kiss."

"The fight's over," she said hurriedly, then couldn't resist adding, "although I'm not sure I've forgiven you. I had looked forward to our being alone this evening."

"Hold that thought." He smiled wickedly and molded her hand to the contour of his body.

"Mac . . . !" Blushing furiously, she jerked away and fled from the room.

ELIZABETH REMEMBERED that moment at several points during dinner. Each time she thanked heaven she didn't have further reason to blush.

Even so, it was disconcerting to parry Mac's attentions under the benignly curious gazes of the other couple. Elizabeth felt like wearing a sign proclaiming We're Just Good Friends.

Which was true in fact if not in spirit.

As it was, Mac's hand hovered near her elbow rather than around the curve of her waist. His look brushed her face with a tentative caress rather than with an expression that spoke of remembered embraces. His eyes held future intent rather than present passion.

And Elizabeth could face their companions with a direct look that masked no guilty secrets. Not many, at least. Mac was right, damn him. She could easily get used to being with him like this.

As for Mary and Herb, it was plain they shared a wealth of secrets and were by no stretch of the imagination just good friends.

They weren't indiscreet, just pleasantly relaxed in the company of friends. And content with only a fair amount of incidental touching. Yet, occasionally Elizabeth had to look away from what the lovers' eyes revealed.

Why was she still finding it difficult to accept their affair? She certainly harbored no moral qualms. As two consenting adults, their relationship harmed no one. Quite the contrary. Sometimes when they looked at each other they positively glowed.

She was jealous!

The realization struck Elizabeth and bowled her over. She felt envy pure and simple. Because Herb and Mary were so alive. Because they savored their feelings, delighting in each other. Because they exuded an exhilaration about what they shared. In a way, they were like a couple of kids.

Elizabeth suddenly felt like the oldest person at the table. It had been years since she'd experienced that giddiness. Perhaps she never had.

When she caught Mac looking at her intently, she smiled and tried to banish the feeling. But it lingered, dampening her enjoyment in the easy laughter, Mac's quips and Mary's attempts at dignity, which Herb took delight in skewering.

After they let Herb and Mary off at his house, Mac and Elizabeth rode awhile in silence.

Finally she came to enough to realize he wasn't taking her home. "Where are we going?"

"To my place."

"Oh?" She felt a wave of giddiness bubble up. "Are you planning to show me your etchings?"

"No." He glanced her way before turning his attention back to the road. "But I have a great view I'd like to share, if you approve."

"I approve." Amazing how level her voice sounded while she was on such a roller coaster ride of uncertainty.

What if he planned on offering her more of those frustrating kisses?

His intentions were probably above reproach, she thought with a wave of depression.

When they were met at the door by his son, Evan, she was sure of her assessment and had to conjure a smile as Mac made the introductions.

Without a doubt, Evan was Mac's child. He had his father's rangy frame without the years' accumulation of solid muscle. But Evan's face was finely drawn and had a touch of Mary in it.

"How do you do?" She held out her hand.

"Great. And you?"

"Stuffed at the moment. The restaurant was as good as Mary predicted. We found out after dinner that she knows the chef."

"Grannie knows everybody, I've decided. At least everybody who's anybody."

Elizabeth laughed. "Thanks, I'll take that as a compliment."

Evan grinned and she decided that his smile was pure Mac.

She was surprised when it vanished to be replaced by an earnest expression. "Dad tells me you're the new director of this coalition to provide services to the elderly. Did you specialize in gerontological studies when you were in school?"

"Whoa," Mac said, as they moved into the living room. "Before you two start talking shop, I'm taking orders for drinks. Elizabeth?"

"Mineral water, please."

"Nothing for me, Dad."

"I'll be back shortly," Mac said, and disappeared into the kitchen.

Elizabeth turned her attention back to Evan. "Actually," she said, since he seemed genuinely interested, "I first dealt with older clients when I was a member of VISTA."

"You belonged to VISTA?"

"More years ago than I like to remember."

"I thought seriously about joining the Peace Corps. But I know what I want to do and I'm anxious to get on with it."

"Mac said you were entering grad school this fall."

"I'll be working toward my doctorate. I want to specialize in the treatment of substance abuse and addiction."

"You couldn't have chosen an area of greater need."

"I know. But that isn't the only reason I'm going into the field. I think I bring a special perspective because of my own experience."

Elizabeth looked at him questioningly.

"Dad didn't tell you? I had to enter a drug treatment center when I was sixteen."

His honesty compelled her own. "I'm impressed with your decision. First because you conquered your own illness, and second because you want to help others conquer theirs."

"Then you don't think being a recovered drug abuser is the wrong motivation."

"Not at all. We get into the business of helping people for complex reasons. I know I'm concerned with problems of the elderly partly because of what I went through nursing my own parents. I have a sense of what they endured."

"Dad told me about your parents."

What else had Mac explained to him?

"Did I just hear my name taken in vain?" Mac came into the room carrying two glasses. He handed one to Elizabeth.

His entrance was apparently Evan's cue.

"I hate to leave good company," Evan said quickly, "but I'm studying for a midterm." He turned to Elizabeth. "Sometime, when it's convenient, I'd like to sit down and talk about your work."

"I'd be more than happy to. Come down to the center one day," she said on an impulse. "I'll show you around. You know, our fields interlap more than you might suspect. Alcoholism and overmedication are common problems for the elderly and their families."

"I'd like to discuss that," he said enthusiastically. His look cut to his father. "Another time. I need to ace this test tomorrow."

He waved at them both and exited the room.

Elizabeth turned suspiciously to face his father.

"Was there something I missed? Do you two have a system worked out between you?"

"Well, you know how it is. Two men baching it in the same house. We've learned to give each other space."

"For when lady friends come calling?"

He moved closer to where she stood. "Do you fit that description?"

"As I recall—" she took a sip of her drink "—I was lured here with the promise of a view."

"I like the view from here."

"Do you?" she whispered.

"Very much," he murmured, then abruptly changed the subject, disconcerting her immensely. "Did you enjoy the evening with Herb and Mary?"

"Yes," she confessed, trying to hide her disappointment. "I enjoyed meeting your son, as well. I admire his sense of direction."

"He's older than his years."

"I can see that."

She edged away from Mac slightly and took another sip to wet her dry mouth. "I also wanted to say that you were right. I was glad I could face your family and Herb with a clear conscience."

Mac sighed elaborately. "I wish you wouldn't think of our future lovemaking as a mortal sin."

"More on the lines of a grievous indiscretion."

Elizabeth moved away still more and turned away from him.

She was waiting for his response when he slipped the drink from her fingers. Seconds later she felt his hands glide over her back.

"When I think about our making love," he whispered against her ear, "I stop thinking and start reacting. And I feel as eager and anxious and cocky as a kid."

He took hold of her shoulders and turned her around. Without prior notification, he started to unbutton her jacket.

"What are you doing?" she asked faintly.

"This is an elegant suit," he said in explanation. "I noticed how well you fit into it earlier. But I've decided you're overdressed."

By now, he'd succeeded in divesting her of the offending jacket. The silky long-sleeved blouse he exposed seemed to melt beneath his touch.

"This is more like it," he muttered, and brushed his lips down her throat.

"Mac, I'm confused." She weakly pressed her hands against his chest.

"How's that, sweetheart?" As he asked the question, his fingers slid the top button on her blouse from the slit that secured it. He immediately nuzzled the collar aside.

"Wh-what are you d-doing now?" she gasped.

"Dammit, Elizabeth...." Suddenly the hunger in his voice was unmasked and aching. "I need a little skin. I can find it in one of two directions."

"Mac..." Her fingers clutched together tightly, then she slid them around his neck. "Mac..."

"Mmm?" The tip of his tongue grazed her collarbone.

She shivered in response and barely managed to repeat, "I—I'm very confused."

His lips discovered the line of her jaw and he nibbled its curve to the shell of her ear. "Care to be more explicit?"

"When you don't touch me, I'm frustrated—"

"And irritable."

"And—and I keep thinking about it. But when you do touch me, I'm terrified."

"You're obsessing again. Stop thinking and start feeling and turn loose of everything but me."

Before she could answer him, his mouth covered hers.

It was one of those kisses that started with the lips and ended with tongues and was wet and wild during the entire middle section.

By the time it was over, Elizabeth was plastered against Mac's body, clinging to him weakly, and she could feel his arousal through the fabric of her skirt. In case there was any doubt about his reaction to her nearness, Mac ran his hands over her hips and pressed them into his.

"Mac—Evan's in his room...."

"And he'd better stay there," Mac mumbled. "Damn, I want you."

"I...I noticed," she breathed softly, echoing other conversations.

He chuckled. "That's one of the things I most admire about you, Elizabeth—your keen powers of observation. That and..." He plucked at her blouse where it had strayed from her skirt band, running his fingers up beneath the silk until they encountered her puckered nipples. "That and your responsiveness."

"Ah..." She sighed, feeling boneless with desire. Conjuring what little sanity she had left, she croaked, "Mac—we're not alone. You've practically undressed me."

Mac growled somewhere deep in his throat. "If I were undressing you, you'd know it." He kneaded one of her breasts. "Under the circumstances, I'm showing admirable restraint."

"I'm not." Elizabeth clutched at him urgently. Heat swept through her, blazing away inhibitions. Her mouth found his again, and the mingling of their tongues stoked a conflagration.

Closer. She needed to get closer.

She rubbed her body against his.

He groaned and held her at arm's length while he bowed his head and tried to control his breathing.

"I think," he began at last, still struggling for air, "I think we've probably had enough for the evening."

Mac heard his own words and laughed briefly.

"Never were falser words spoken," he said. "This wasn't nearly enough. Not for either of us."

With that bald statement, he looked at her squarely. "This was why I've been such a gentleman, Elizabeth. Petting in the parlor won't cut it for us. The next time I get my hands on you, I'm taking you to bed."

CHAPTER EIGHT

June 21, 1900

Mr. LeBow has been laid to rest. His travail is ended.

I pray God will grant Johnny and me mercy for being the instrument of his death.

It was our mutual weakness that drew Johnny home. Our impetuous kisses that brought on my husband's paroxysm. Now I must live knowing we sent him to his grave believing his son and wife betrayed him.

So we did in our hearts.

I have sent Johnny away once more. When he asked me to leave with him and be married, I refused his offer.

He protested, then asked for my forgiveness. Yet when I pleaded with him, he would not ask for God's!

He said... But what good is there in recounting all we said? Finally, he agreed he would contact me no more without my consent.

Circumstances lead us to separate lives. Johnny has accepted the post of editor in chief of the Galveston Express. *He will no longer live in Austin, barely twenty miles away. There is no reason left for him to journey to Bastrop.*

I do not believe I will see Johnny again.

Why do my senses fail me as I write those words?

I read them over and still I feel nothing. No tears have fallen since our fateful argument. I listen now to the morning rain that cleanses and nurtures the dusty land,

and I hope a rain of tears can cleanse and nurture my heart, allowing it to ache again.

WHEN ELIZABETH RETURNED from her conference at the Travis County welfare office, the afternoon was late. She'd gone to talk over a possible grant that would enable CCE to offer limited free care.

The county officials had been polite, the meeting cordial. But Elizabeth got the clear message that funds were stretched thin and the commissioners were more interested in investing in established agencies.

Too many constituencies vying for too few funds. An old, old story.

Elizabeth only wished she didn't feel as if she'd somehow failed in representing the needs of the coalition. Her depression lifted when she saw Joe Beasley out in the side yard tilling his garden plot. Somehow his acceptance of life and willing participation in it always soothed her nerves.

"How's it coming?" she asked, walking over to where he worked and sitting on the bench nearby.

"Slowly but surely," he said, stopping for a moment to mop his brow. "There's no shortcut to a good growing garden. You got to take care with the hoeing and the planting and the watering and the weeding. Can't get impatient. You have to nurture a garden before it'll nurture you."

Elizabeth thought back to her unsatisfying meeting, her depression, the frustration that sometimes enveloped her.

She smiled at the elderly man who'd gone back to methodically breaking up the earth. "Mr. Beasley, I think you just said something very profound. I'll remember it."

Joe Beasley leaned on his hoe. "You got a garden, Miss Elizabeth, you trying to grow?"

She looked around the building, the grounds, the play equipment, before she turned back to him. "In a way. Do you ever get lonely, doing what you do? Out here by yourself?" she added casually.

"I'm never lonely helping God with his creation. Besides—" he looked over to Elizabeth "—sometimes she comes out to visit and sits awhile." He grinned slyly. "I think, like you, she enjoys my company."

Elizabeth thought of Mrs. Moreland, who'd taken a proprietary interest in all the building's activities. "Mrs. Moreland enjoys everyone's company. She's a dear, isn't she?"

"Yes'm." Joe stared down at the ground and attacked a lump of dirt.

"You're right, Joe." Elizabeth said quietly, referring to his previous statement. "I do enjoy your company. My world's a saner place after one of these visits. You seem so at peace." She laughed lightly. "It must come from being God's helper all these years."

"Yes'm." He stopped his work and looked at her directly. "I believe you're doing God's work, too, Miss Elizabeth."

She fought errant tears at his gentle pronouncement.

"I wish," he went on softly, "there was something I could do to ease your way." He stared up at the building. "Yours and hers, too."

Ease the way of Mrs. Moreland?

"Yoo—hoo, Elizabeth!"

Elizabeth's thoughts scattered as she turned to find Carol hailing her.

Carol hurried up to where Elizabeth sat. "Can we talk before Mac and Herb get here?"

The four of them were meeting after five to discuss the gala. It was close to five now.

"Sure. Joe, perhaps you've met Carol Summers, our board president, at the open house. Carol, do you remember Mr. Beasley and his hanging baskets? This garden is his project. He's promised us carrots, cucumbers and tomatoes by summer."

"Certainly I remember him," Carol said, smiling and shaking his hand. "And the projected harvest sounds wonderful. Today must be perfect gardening weather."

Despite her cheerful tone, Elizabeth could tell she was abstracted.

"Joe—" Elizabeth made a farewell gesture "—I'll visit with you later. Carol—why don't we go inside?"

"...HAVEN'T LIVED UP to Mary's expectations. I'm not doing a good enough job as president of the board."

Carol's anxious voice drifting out from Elizabeth's office caught Mac in the doorway to the hall. He stood silently, arrested by its tone.

"Of course you are, Carol." Elizabeth's response was immediate. "Listen, we all work under the shadow of Mary's accomplishments. But you're articulate, energetic, and you have goals and commitment. Believe me, Mary would be the first person to agree."

"Maybe. But this board's not working like it did when she was president. I can't seem to motivate people."

"Herb and Mac have put in service above and beyond the call of duty. Remember, Mac found the money we needed to clear the mortgage."

"Oh, the board couldn't get along without Mac and Herb," Carol said mournfully. "They're more valuable than I am. Don't you see? I should have found the money. It's like I abdicated my responsibility."

"Listen, Carol. I had some of the same feelings you did when Mac came up with that two hundred thousand. Our problem is, you and I want to save CCE single-handedly. But it's going to take all of us."

"That's the truth," Carol said with a sigh.

"A good board president," Elizabeth continued in her bracing manner, "utilizes the resources she has at hand. Mac's a resource and a damned good one. He's part of the good ol' boy network, and he can call in favors. Be thankful Mary handed him to us on a silver platter."

Mac grimaced, feeling a little like a suckling pig.

"Besides," Elizabeth added for good measure, "Mac could never function as board president. He's too impatient. Too used to doing things his own way."

Now he smiled faintly at her accurate perception.

"Have you noticed," Carol asked, "how at meetings he gets a blank look on his face every time we get into one of those convoluted discussions Mrs. Milton thrives on?"

"Yes, I have. He also walked away from her after a meeting one day when she'd cornered him and was spouting one of her crazy theories. Mac's no diplomat, Carol. Only someone like you can handle all the personalities on the board."

"You're right," Carol agreed, but she still wasn't happy. "It's just—we scale one mountain only to be faced with another."

For a moment, Mac could hear a hint of tears in her voice.

"Even without the mortgage payment," she went on forlornly, "we have problems with expenses. Now some of the agencies are squabbling about paying their share. They don't understand why we've gone forward with the renovations."

"We have to expect territorial skirmishes. It's inevitable when a group of organizations tries to act as one. Next week at our agency directors' meeting, I'll go over the budget so everyone understands our constraints. I'll also bring Mac in to explain the reasons for the remodeling."

Forget the suckling pig. Elizabeth meant to offer him as a sacrificial lamb.

Carol's mind was on another matter. "We won't have so many restraints if the gala's a success. Oh, Elizabeth, I know I'm dumping on you. But that's really what I'm worried about. If this fund-raiser's a failure, it'll be my fault. CCE could go down the drain."

"You and I won't let that happen."

"How will we stop it? Look at me now. I'm a spineless wreck."

"You're discouraged. We all feel that way sometimes. Which is why we're meeting tonight—to map out strategies and get moving." There was a slight pause before Elizabeth warned gently, "Mac and Herb should be here any minute."

"Listen," Carol said hurriedly. "You won't tell them I came apart and you had to put me back together."

"Of course not. We all need a shoulder to cry on."

"Whose shoulder do you cry on? You're always so confident."

Mac decided Carol's question was his entrance cue. He knocked on the open door to Hope's office. "Anybody here?" he called out.

"Come on in," Elizabeth responded.

When he entered the office, her expression was cheerful. But he could see the hint of concern around the eyes. Mac realized he was probably the only one who could detect it.

Carol had recovered enough to present a collected facade. "We were just going over some of the problems. I don't mind admitting, I'm discouraged right now."

"That's because," he said calmly, "you're not comfortable cracking a whip like Mother. But I have every confidence in your leadership abilities—yours and Elizabeth's. You're both a class act." He winked at Elizabeth, offering moral support.

She flushed. Her hands fumbled with the papers on her desk. For a moment, she was dangerously close to losing her composure.

Damn, Mac thought. And if he wasn't careful he'd just do more damage.

He'd watched her soothe disgruntled agency heads and teary-eyed board members. She protected herself from Mary like a pro. Yet one look from him and she blushed girlishly.

Only he could bring out her vulnerability. Only he had glimpsed her fragile side. That knowledge brought with it a sense of responsibility.

But it also brought on an intoxicating feeling that made him want to shout to the heavens. This competent, cool and collected woman could shiver at his touch. He and he alone ignited the fires of passion within her. Fires that were hidden to the undiscerning eye.

"Mac? Are you listening?"

He realized with a start that Carol had been speaking.

"I'm sorry. What were you saying?" This time, he carefully avoided Elizabeth's eye.

Carol started to repeat her words, when Herb bustled through the door.

"I'm not late, am I?" he asked.

"No. We were just getting started," Elizabeth said. "Let's go down the hall. This office is too small. We'll stop by the drink machine if anyone's thirsty."

Minutes later, the foursome had bought their soft drinks and settled comfortably in the downstairs conference room.

Elizabeth had regained her poise and was ready to deal with the major issue. "I think the gala's on everyone's mind."

"But Elizabeth," Herb said, ever gallant, "planning this event is the board's responsibility."

"I asked her to sit in," Carol spoke up. "I felt we needed her input. The committee's bogged down, and the rest of the board's not helping."

"We just have to involve them," Elizabeth said. "They need direction and specific tasks. For instance, I think we should give Jerry Tansy the responsibility for soliciting donations for the auction."

"The Silent Auction," Herb amended. When he saw Mac's questioning look, he clarified further. "Where we display donated items at the gala itself and take blind bids on them."

"Are you sure Jerry Tansy's the person for that important a job?" Carol was clearly hesitant.

"He's willing," Mac murmured.

"Eager," Herb added.

"With guidance," Elizabeth stated, "I think he'll do fine. After all, he was the one who came up with our computers. I bet he can beg two more for a worthy cause."

"We'll also send him to every business that has dealings with the elderly," Herb suggested, getting into the spirit of the discussion. "That's only about half the stores in town. When Jerry tells them they'll be named on the program as auction benefactors, most will be happy to donate a service or item.''

"And—" Carol's expression was animated "—my husband will chip in several software programs like the ones he gave to the office." She slapped her hand on the table. "Mrs. Milton..."

Mac muttered something under his breath.

"I know—" Carol turned to him "—she can be tedious. But she's on the Arts Commission and has all kinds of contacts. We'll tell her how much Jerry needs her. She should be able to come up with theater ticket donations. Probably even get us some original art."

As Carol talked, Elizabeth settled into the background. Mac wondered if anyone else had appreciated her strategy. It was all he could do not to wink at her again.

Damn, he loved watching her in action.

Damn, he loved her.

Mac took in a load of air, feeling momentarily winded.

Loved her?

Well, of course, he did. He'd been falling in love from that very first day when he'd listened to her impassioned speech on the needs of the elderly.

He not only longed for her body in his bed, he wanted her clothes cluttering his closet, her toothbrush hanging in his bathroom, his ring snug on her finger. He wanted to claim this special lady.

Marriage. That's what it was all about.

Mac leaned back in his chair, feeling remarkably calm considering the nature of his discovery. Calm and rather smug.

Assuming a thoughtful expression, he used it to hide a leisurely inspection of the special lady in question. She and Carol were engrossed in a discussion of mailing lists.

Elizabeth had never been married. The thought slipped into his mind, destroying his complacency. Oh, he knew the reasons why. But still, she'd been independent a very long time.

Did she, like Mary, guard that independence? Had her experiences with her parents served to make her leery of any relationship that might tie her down? Would she even consider marriage as a choice at this point in her life?

More important, would she consider marriage with him? He'd failed at it once.

Ah, but he was older and wiser this time. He had an idea about what was essential in a relationship.

He certainly knew what he wanted.

Expressive brown eyes. Wavy chestnut hair pulled back at the nape of a sloping neck. He itched to loosen those waves from their constricting barrette so they tumbled freely around her face.

A nice face, quietly attractive. With clean lines of the nose and brow. A strong jaw and a vulnerable mouth. With her classic bone structure, Elizabeth's looks were ageless.

And she'd been given a slim, graceful body, which spoke murmuring messages only to him.

Grinning at the thought, Mac's look settled on those vulnerable lips, remembering how they'd come alive under his.

She glanced over from Carol, caught his expression and choked on her cola.

He jumped up solicitously and went to pat her on the back, this time deriving perverse pleasure in her general unravelment. After all, she'd caused him many an uncomfortable night.

"I'm fine," she gasped in a second or two. He went on patting, only it was more of a stroke. "Really—I'm fine." She glowered up at him with those expressive eyes.

"Just making sure," he came back pleasantly.

Turning elaborately to Herb, she asked, "Do you think we should ask board members to sell a certain number of gala tickets?"

"Absolutely. They also should be responsible for one auction item."

Her demeanor regal, Elizabeth deigned to include Mac. "Do you have friends in the printing business who'd be willing to donate the invitations?"

"I think I can come up with somebody," he said.

She smiled at everyone. "Then we're on our way."

"I can also supply an able helper." He addressed this to Carol. "You know Tracy helped put on that shindig for the American Heart Association."

"Yes . . . ?" Carol began hopefully.

"Well, she's offered her services. And if I do say so myself, her experience with caterers, banquet rooms, possible entertainment—those kinds of things—could prove invaluable."

"We accept." Elizabeth and Carol spoke in unison.

"Good. Elizabeth, she asked for you to call her. She mentioned something about lunch and a concert."

"Oh. Yes. I'll phone her tomorrow."

After another few minutes of sorting out details, the meeting adjourned.

Carol took hold of Elizabeth's arm as they left the room, the men trailing behind them. "I feel a hundred percent better," she confided. "I guess I was just temporarily overwhelmed."

Now that the meeting was over, Elizabeth nodded distractedly. She'd set herself one more task this evening, one that made cheering Carol up look like a piece of cake.

"You want to grab a bite of dinner?" Carol asked. "Lane's out of town."

"I'd love to, but I have some things to finish here. I want to write up the meeting I had with the county."

Carol made a face. "Call and tell me all about it tomorrow. I don't think I want to deal with it tonight."

The two women waved their goodbyes. As Carol turned a corner and left their view, Herb gave Elizabeth a hug. "You did good tonight."

She looked at him, puzzled.

"I've been worried about Carol. Her husband, Lane, is a certified genius. And here she's having to follow in Mary's footsteps. I think you've helped her find a new confidence."

Elizabeth smiled at him gratefully. "Thanks, Herb, for your kind words. I'm sure Carol will hit her stride with this fund-raiser."

Herb said goodbye, leaving Mac and her alone. Silently, they walked down the hallway toward the main entrance.

For the first time, Mac found himself strangely at a loss for words. Having decided his pursuit of Elizabeth was of a permanent nature, he wasn't sure exactly how to proceed.

Finally, he settled on the obvious. "Let's go eat."

"No, Mac, I can't. Not tonight." Elizabeth's face had an oddly stubborn cast to it.

"This isn't a brush-off, is it?" he asked lightly.

"No. Of course not. I really do have some work to finish. I was out of the office the entire afternoon. But thanks for asking."

"You don't want to stay in this building alone."

It was exactly what she did want. "I'll be just fine."

Mac felt an immediate spurt of anxiety and frustration. He tried to control it. "Elizabeth," he said quietly, "I don't like you being here alone at night."

"Mac. I'm a big girl and more than capable of taking care of myself."

Fine. He'd finally found a woman he wanted to protect and defend, and she was trying to make a feminist issue of it. His jaw worked briefly. "There are a hundred ways to break into this place. The neighborhood crime rate is awful."

Leaning against a wall as though he meant to stay, he announced briefly, "I'll wait for you to finish. I've got all night."

Her eyes flashed a warning. "Don't do it, Mac. Don't treat me as if I were helpless. Our relationship doesn't entitle you to that."

With the premonition that this argument was different from others they'd had, Mac was smart enough to know when he should beat a retreat. Elizabeth wore a determined expression all out of proportion to the issue in question.

"Will you at least call me when you get home?" He raised his hands disarmingly. "For my peace of mind. Indulge me a little. You're so good at helping people with their problems. Will you humor me in this?"

"Yes." Elizabeth started to say something else and then thought better of it.

She wanted to do more than humor him. She'd like to walk into his arms and let him lead her out the door. But she had to be strong. Her task was important and had been carefully thought out.

"Yes. I'll call you," she repeated, and surprised him with a kiss before she pushed him out the door.

Once alone, Elizabeth walked back to her office through the dimly lit corridor. Inside she found the number she wanted and punched it in on her phone.

"Hello," said the feminine voice on the other end of the line.

"Mrs. Taylor. This is Elizabeth Waite. I hope I haven't caught you at an inconvenient time."

"Oh, no, you haven't bothered me." Cassie Taylor sounded sincere, but Elizabeth sensed her hesitation.

She hesitated herself before deciding how to begin. Finally she said, "I've thought a lot about what you told me the other day. I hope you won't mind my asking a few more questions."

"I don't mind."

"I'd like to know more about Sarah Elizabeth. I guess because she knew my father."

"There's another reason, isn't there?"

Elizabeth struggled with words.

Cassie said quickly, "No. Don't tell me. I don't want to know. Just—ask what you need to."

"Where was Sarah Elizabeth's room?" The question came out baldly.

There was a moment of silence before Cassie stated just as baldly, "Downstairs. The room facing east just before the south turret."

"Were there other places she particularly enjoyed?"

"The turret rooms upstairs and the second floor veranda."

"When she died, was there anything she might have left . . . in the building?"

A very long moment. "Yes." Cassie sighed and seemed to gather herself. "Her diaries. When I packed her belongings to send to her great-niece in Dallas, I couldn't find them. Mama Cassie and I knew she'd been keeping them for years."

A certain urgency crept into her voice. "Miss Waite—I've been meaning to call you. The other day—when you expressed interest in Sarah Elizabeth? I have a few of her mementos. I should have shown them to you."

"What are they?"

"Only a few books and a brass letter opener she willed me. She wanted Jack and me to have the opener as a wedding present, but she couldn't bear to part with it while she was alive."

"And the books?"

"The niece gave them to me. All of the front leaves are inscribed From Johnny."

"Her husband?"

"I assume so. Although I've never read through them, she made comments in the margins. I thought some of the things she wrote might reveal her character to you. Anyway, they're here if you want to come by."

"Thank you, Mrs. Taylor. I do want to. I'll phone you back to set a time. You've been a great help."

Their strained conversation ended with conventional goodbyes.

Afterward, Elizabeth sat for a moment, steeling herself for whatever might come.

It wasn't fear or dread that held her in her chair momentarily. It was the memory of that great enveloping sadness.

Loss. She knew something of the agony of it.

And Sarah Elizabeth's unknown loss seemed to invade her soul.

Finally, Elizabeth stood, carefully locked her door and made her way upstairs to the porch.

Her movements had a familiar quality to them, except that instead of sitting down on the rocking chair, she remained standing by the railing, looking out into the night. A newly risen moon cast her shadow against the building.

After a moment she turned.

Sarah Elizabeth waited.

"I'm here to help you," Elizabeth said. "I would have come sooner, but I was trying to gather my thoughts. Since you can't actually say to me the things I need to know, I've tried to reach out to you in my mind."

A whisper of a breeze ruffled the oak trees.

"Is there something in the building keeping you here?"

The figure wavered. Her pleading expression grew sharper.

"Is it near the veranda and the turret rooms?"

Sarah Elizabeth bowed her head and turned away.

"No? Is it hidden in the room where you lived all those years?"

Sarah Elizabeth's head came up; her eyes seemed to glow intensely in the moonlight.

"I've talked to Cassie Taylor. She told me your diaries weren't with your other belongings. Is that what you need for me to find?"

When Sarah Elizabeth's form wavered closer, Elizabeth could almost have touched it.

A hand reached out in its familiar gesture, telling Elizabeth all she needed to know.

"I'll find your diaries," she vowed softly. "Somehow I'll find them."

She felt another stirring of air like a caress around her as the figure drifted into the shadows of the night.

WHEN ELIZABETH FELT herself alone, she took a few deep breaths for the sake of sanity, then ran back downstairs, an urgency driving her.

She opened the door to the empty office where she and Mac had talked briefly that other day. Where Sarah Elizabeth had lived out her years.

The recklessness of Elizabeth's promise hit her abruptly.

This was just a room. A bare room, blankly guarding its secrets.

Where could Sarah Elizabeth have hidden her diaries?

The ceiling? Elizabeth stared up into exposed rafters and climbed the ladder Mac's workmen had left. After searching with her fingers, she moved the ladder into each of the room's four corners, thinking she might find a cubbyhole.

Instead, she found nothing.

The walls? All of the Sheetrock wallboard had been torn away, revealing the original plaster. She carefully made her way around the tiny room, feeling for inconsistencies in the texture. The plaster was smooth and mute to her touch.

Depression settled over her.

She stared down at the flooring. All the linoleum had been stripped away. The planks underneath were scarred and neglected.

Several of them had been loosened.

And suddenly Elizabeth knew.

Taking quick, shallow breaths, she surveyed the room hurriedly for a tool to help her pry at the planks. Finding one, she knelt. Under the fourth board she jimmied, Elizabeth discovered the bundled shawl.

For a moment, her fingers trembled so, she couldn't retrieve it.

Then, carefully, she lifted Sarah Elizabeth's treasures from their hiding place and unwrapped them on the floor.

It was much more than Elizabeth had expected. Four diaries. Letters—one left unopened. Newspaper clippings.

When she got home she'd decide what to read first. Without analyzing her sense of certainty, she knew she couldn't rush through the material. Sarah Elizabeth's plight cried out for patient understanding.

Still, Elizabeth couldn't keep from running her fingers over the diaries, anticipating their revelations. She opened one and then another.

Volume II, Volume IV...

Volume I.

Turning the page, she found Sarah Elizabeth's childishly rounded script.

April 11, 1880

This afternoon I am to be Married....

CHAPTER NINE

IT WAS A FINE March day. The birds were singing, the trees were leafing. A brief spring shower had polished the world.

Ignoring the piles of paperwork, Elizabeth propped her elbows on her desk, put her hands over her face and released a totally private moan.

So what if Tracy was having trouble finding a banquet room for the gala on the May night they had chosen? So what if every caterer she'd called was demanding an arm and a leg?

So what if Mac had been out of town for a week? So what if their relationship seemed to have stalled in neutral?

So what if today was her fortieth birthday?

Forty.

And what did she have to show for it?

A late-model car. A barn of a house. Three greedy cats. A job that seemed lately to drain her dry.

And no source of replenishment on the horizon.

Elizabeth felt as ancient as Sarah Elizabeth had felt the day she turned thirty.

Each night when she went home and journeyed page by page through Sarah Elizabeth's life, imagining this naive, breathless girl transformed into a weary, stoic woman, she realized that although time and custom separated them, the kinship was there.

More and more, she understood why Sarah Elizabeth, seeking understanding, had come to her.

Elizabeth had completed the second journal. When she read the last entry recording Mr. LeBow's death, she'd put all the diaries and papers away, unable to read further, feeling the other woman's remorse and fatalism as though it were her own.

She still sought the courage to open the third volume.

Courage. Was that what she wished for on her fortieth birthday? She wondered if there were a discount catalogue she could order some from. Courage generally was a very dear purchase.

Her intercom beeped.

"Yes?"

Hope's voice announced, "There's been an emergency in the day care cafeteria."

"An emergency?" Elizabeth's adrenaline started pumping. "An accident? Fire?"

"Neither. Although I do think it has something to do with an oven breaking down."

"Can't they find the maintenance man?"

"Billy's down there already. He wants you to come take a look."

"I don't know anything about stoves," Elizabeth protested, giving in to ill humor when she realized it wasn't a life-or-death matter. "Besides, I'm trying to wade through these damned insurance policies."

Hope calmly ignored the outburst. "Perhaps they want you to authorize a repairman."

"I thought that's what Billy was."

A patient silence emanated from the other office.

"Okay, okay." Elizabeth gave in gracelessly. "I'll go see what I can do."

Before visiting the disaster scene, however, she took a moment to get herself in hand.

It was one thing to use Hope as a safety valve. Hope encouraged it, and Elizabeth knew she couldn't find a more sympathetic ally. She also knew her occasional bursts of temper rolled off Hope's back like droplets of water.

No one else except Mac had seen her peevish side.

Thoughts of him only made her more peevish.

So stop thinking about him, Grumpy, and go be a director. And pick up Tinkerbell's wand on the way to pass over the ailing stove, so CCE won't be faced with ordering a six-hundred-dollar replacement.

After marching over to the new section of the building, Elizabeth stopped to peer through the double doors of the cafeteria. It looked deserted. All the parties involved must be in the kitchen viewing the patient.

She swung open the doors.

"Surprise! Surprise!"

The air filled with cheers as a multitude of people, blowing on noisemakers and wearing ridiculous hats, poured out from the kitchen.

"Happy fortieth birthday!" yelled various well-wishers with accompanying catcalls.

Elizabeth sighed very softly.

Another tide of voices turned her around as an additional horde crowded into the doorway. They swept her inside with hugs and kisses.

The entire building must have turned out for the party. Staff. The Adult Day Care Center. Herb, Carol and various other board members. Mary. Tracy.

Elizabeth was surrounded. And moved by the sentiment that had prompted the gathering, despite her instinctive recoil.

Laughing helplessly, she decided there was nothing to do but make the best of it. "Okay." She pivoted slowly to include everyone. "Who's the traitor? And how did he or she find out about the day of infamy?"

Her look stopped at Hope's beatific expression. She'd been a part of the second wave. She'd also copied Elizabeth's driver's license to attach to her employment form.

"Need I look further?" she questioned Hope menacingly. "Do you know," she asked the group, "how Hope tricked me into coming down here? She told me one of the ovens was broken. I had visions of a catastrophe. Do that to me again," she warned Hope, "and I won't make it to forty-one."

Everyone laughed and Suzanne called out, "Speech, speech! But make it short! We're all hungry for ice cream and cake."

With Suzanne's cue the group quieted down. Elizabeth looked around at all of them once more. Hardworking, dedicated, each of them facing his or her own disappointments. Finding their rewards in a hundred little ways. If she didn't speak soon, she might break down.

"I can't honestly say I was looking forward to my birthday," she admitted. "But I can't imagine another group of people I'd rather spend it with. Thank you all very much."

Her words were greeted with a combination of cheers and clapping.

"End of speech," she announced. "Let's eat cake."

"Presents first," Herb reminded her.

Tracy and Suzanne led Elizabeth to a table, which had miraculously appeared, laden with sandwiches, a cake, punch bowl and paper cups, and a small array of packages.

Most of the gifts were simple. Some of the agencies had only managed humorous cards relating to her advancing years. Elizabeth accepted them all with good humor and dutifully read each message aloud for the general amusement.

The Adult Day Care Center, however, in the person of Joe Beasley, presented her with a basket lavish with bougainvillea blossoms. Suzanne gave her a wall calendar celebrating the accomplishments of older Americans.

The board had chipped in and bought a leather briefcase. To complement her new red power tie, Elizabeth explained.

And Mary had found a book entitled *Gifts of Age,* which contained portraits and essays of remarkable women.

Elizabeth opened Tracy's present last. It was a small but delicately inlaid music box, which when opened played an unfamiliar but haunting tune. A reminder, Elizabeth knew, of their cosy visit of several days ago.

Elizabeth had discovered something alarming that day at Tracy's. Mac presented a triple threat.

He was not only charming, intelligent and sexy as hell. He also had two bright, down-to-earth, appealing children, who, as if they'd been scripted, were going out of their way to make friends with her.

Evan, true to his word, had dropped by the office asking knowledgeable questions as they toured the agencies. By the end of the visit, she'd almost forgotten he was Mac's son. Instead, she'd come to view him as a bright young man who possessed more than his share of compassion and insight.

And Tracy was one of the hardest working volunteers she'd ever been blessed with. *Blessed with* being the operative phrase, since Tracy had essentially stepped in as Carol's assistant, relieving Elizabeth of her job as presidential therapist.

Did she sense Mac's fine hand in Tracy's new role?

Late in the party, Tracy hugged her from behind and whispered, "Dad said to tell you he's sorry he couldn't be here. He'll call you tonight."

Elizabeth reddened and mumbled, "He doesn't need to do that."

"Oh, I don't know." An arch tone entered Tracy's voice. "He was awfully grouchy when he phoned me last night. I think he's missing you."

Elizabeth's blush deepened.

"He grilled me at length on how the gala was coming. I promised I was doing my part to lighten your load."

Elizabeth tried to change the subject. "Well, Carol certainly couldn't manage without you."

"That was my intent." Tracy grinned impishly.

Something about the smile reminded Elizabeth strongly of Mac. Perhaps that's why she lapsed into candor. "Is all the Reynolds family devious?"

Tracy's grin widened. "We only sink to subterfuge for the noblest of causes."

"I see." Elizabeth's mouth quirked. "I guess I should be flattered to fall into that category."

"Oh, no," Tracy contradicted her quickly. "You're not a cause. Evan and I consider you an important project."

"A project?" Elizabeth's brows lifted in mock alarm. "Is Evan in on this, too?"

"Sort of. He's a bit squeamish about meddling, though."

"Unlike other family members I could name."

"But he agrees with me you'd be great for Dad."

Tracy's breezy statement took Elizabeth's breath away. Any response could get her into trouble. It was just as well to realize that, since not a single quip popped into her head.

Tracy seemed to recognize Elizabeth's problem, for she continued confidingly, "I just wanted you to know, Evan and I approve." Her youth showed when she added, "We both think Dad needs companionship."

"I'm sure your father's touched by his children's solicitude."

Elizabeth's irony met with Tracy's delight. "A witty companion, too. We couldn't have picked better. I never liked Belin—" For the first time Tracy blushed and faltered.

Suzanne saved them both from acute embarrassment by sailing up just then and insisting that Elizabeth don one of the party hats.

But as the festivities wound down, Elizabeth kept remembering Tracy's stammer. Of course, she'd been about to mention another woman.

Well, what did Elizabeth expect? Just because she'd lived a cloistered existence didn't mean Mac had conducted himself like a monk. He was a virile man with sexual appetites. She'd have been astonished if there hadn't been women in his life.

So why did she feel depression envelop her when she went back to her office?

She answered her own question as she sat at her desk. Because she was forty years old and had never known an ardent lover. Just as Sarah Elizabeth, married for twenty years, had been bereft of her lover's embrace.

"Elizabeth . . . ?"

Startled, Elizabeth glanced up from the papers she was staring at blindly.

Mary stood in the doorway.

Elizabeth hurriedly rose. "I didn't know you were still in the building. Thanks again for the book. I hope it'll inspire me. Come in. Have a seat. What can I do for you?"

"I suspect I should ask what I can do for you. You didn't look happy just now. Do you need inspiration? Is the job getting to you?"

"No. Yes. Sometimes." Laughing lightly, Elizabeth sat back down to cover her confusion and gestured toward the papers in front of her. "I was just going to glance through these casualty and property policies. We really should fill the next board vacancy with an insurance agent. Our premiums are exorbitant."

Mary took her time responding as she also settled in a chair. "Are you sure it wasn't the party?" she asked.

"The party was lovely." Elizabeth was firm. "I can't thank everyone enough for giving it."

Mary surveyed her expression. "When Hope came up with the idea, we both decided the building could use a festive occasion. I hope you don't mind that your birthday served as an excuse."

"Mind? I was touched."

"I thought I detected a look of dismay."

Elizabeth fiddled with the policies, carefully arranging them into a neat stack.

"Well, you know how it is." She shrugged, avoiding Mary's eyes. "Birthdays come and birthdays go..."

"But this was a hard one."

Elizabeth sighed. "Yes." And then, because Mary's sympathetic voice invited confession, she blurted out, "I'm sure I'm overreacting, but I feel so old."

She immediately felt chagrined by her outburst, especially in light of their respective ages. But she should have known Mary would ignore her gaffe to get to the heart of the matter.

"Well, of course you feel old, Elizabeth," she said. "You *are* old."

Mary's blunt pronouncement got Elizabeth's attention. She stared openly.

"I'm younger than you are," Mary continued, "and I can give you thirty-five years. Age is a state of mind, Elizabeth. And youthfulness is nothing more than an openness to life experiences."

She snorted disparagingly. "Some of my friends are 103. First they won't go out at night, then they won't go out alone, then they're afraid to drive a car or take a trip or spend money. Before you know it, they're virtual prisoners.

"They've closed themselves off. No wonder they have so many aches and pains. There's nothing else for them to worry about. What good is a long life if you don't mean to live it?"

Elizabeth gazed down at her hands and clasped them together. "You don't think I'm living life to the fullest?"

"Do you?"

"No." Elizabeth's voice sounded thick to her ears. It took a moment for her to continue. "I'm not sure I was taught that particular lesson."

"You were busy learning others just as valuable. But you're free now to expand your horizons. Explore life, discover its possibilities. You're free and healthy."

Elizabeth's look met Mary's.

Mary leaned toward her, laid a hand on her wrist and said intently, "The trick is, Elizabeth, you can't be afraid. Fear is a tyrant. You mustn't let it rule you."

Courage....

Elizabeth covered Mary's hand with one of her own. "Will you promise me that if I follow your prescription, I'll grow as young as you are?"

Mary smiled and covered Elizabeth's other hand with hers, completing the bond. "You follow my directions and satisfaction's guaranteed."

AROUND EIGHT-THIRTY that night Elizabeth's telephone rang. With effort she restrained herself from snatching the receiver off its hook.

After three long rings, she answered, "Hello?"

"Elizabeth?"

"Mac."

Neither spoke for a moment.

Then Mac chuckled. "This is what you've reduced me to. Incoherency at eighty-five cents a minute."

"How's California?" she rushed in, her voice a little rusty.

"Lonely. I miss you."

"That's what Tracy said—" She halted.

"What else," he asked, "did my daughter say?"

Elizabeth's lips curved in remembrance. "That when you spoke to her you were an awful grouch."

"Sexual frustration affects some people that way."

"Tracy was more concerned with your need for companionship."

"I see. Sounds like you two had an interesting conversation."

"Oh, we did. She wanted me to know she and Evan approved. You warned me about Mary, but you didn't tell me your children were inveterate matchmakers."

"They've decided it was time I remarried," he explained.

"Have they?" she asked somewhat faintly, attempting a laugh. "Children. Only the very young think they know all the answers."

"I suspect in this case they're probably right."

"Do you?" Elizabeth's pulse thundered in her ear.

"Yes. Elizabeth?"

"Wh-what?"

"Do you know why I called tonight?"

"I'm not sure."

"To wish you a happy birthday. How are you coping with the dreaded event?"

"I'm ambivalent."

"I'm relieved."

"You're what?"

"That you've turned forty. I'm not interested in a younger woman."

Elizabeth could think of any number of younger women who would be interested in him.

"Mary thinks I'm too old for you," she said.

"Has she been offering advice again?"

"In a way. She thinks I should live life to the fullest."

"Did my mother say how you were to accomplish that feat?"

"She was vague on the details."

"Why don't we supply the details?"

Elizabeth took a long breath and let it out slowly. "Sounds good..." She was still breathless. "Sounds good to me."

She heard an indistinct growl, and his next words held urgency. "I'm a starving man, Elizabeth. How much have you missed me?"

"I've missed you. Very much."

"Have you been an awful grouch?"

"I snapped Hope's head off today."

"It's because you don't have me to fight with."

"It's because I don't have you...."

"Do you want me?"

A heartbeat. Two.

"Yes," she whispered.

"What are we going to do about that?"

"I'm not sure. I've been thinking."

"I told you not to think."

"You told me not to obsess. You also said seducing me would be a disservice to both of us. That is, I gather, what these last weeks have been about. You're waiting for me to make a decision."

"Ah, Elizabeth. You are a perceptive woman." He paused before asking with the faintest edge of uncertainty, "And have you come to a decision?"

"Yes," she said elusively, "I've decided your behavior's not terribly gallant."

He pounced on her words. "I see. You'd rather I swept you off your feet and carried you to my bed. So after our wild, passionate lovemaking you can deny responsibility."

"Do you guarantee wild passion?"

"Shall I draw up a contract?"

"No," she murmured. "A verbal agreement will do."

"Is that what we've just entered into?" he pressed.

"When are you coming home?" she evaded.

"Tomorrow."

"Shall I see you?"

"For what purpose?"

"Dammit! Do I have to come right out and say it?"

"Yes. Be brave."

"I want . . . I want for us to make love."

His soft sigh whispered in her ear. When he spoke, his voice held a peculiar intensity. "I'm warning you, Elizabeth, I'll ask for a lot more than that. I'm in this deeply, very deeply. Do you understand?"

"Y-yes."

"Do you still want to make love with me?"

She took courage. "Yes."

Once again no one spoke for a long moment.

Then Mac asked evenly, "Shall I come by for you at seven tomorrow evening?"

"You—you can't drop by the agency?"

"No."

She felt hurt by his curtness until he said, "I don't think I'm enough in control for a public greeting."

She laughed helplessly. "You make me sound like a seductress, when in reality I'm a staid social worker of forty."

He chuckled, too. His laughter had a sensual quality. "How little you know yourself. But that's okay. You have me to teach you."

"Are you a patient instructor?" she asked, already feeling a twinge of anxiety. "I may be a slow learner."

"Elizabeth," he said her name gently.

"What?"

"Don't worry about it."

"I'll try not to."

"Will you do something for me?"

"It depends."

"Don't think about tomorrow night. It'll just get you in trouble."

She laughed helplessly again. "Okay. I'll make every effort to follow your instructions."

"Very good. Now take care of yourself until I get home."

AFTER THEIR GOODBYES, Elizabeth wandered the house restlessly, trying to follow Mac's advice. When she took a bath, however, she couldn't resist the compulsion to assess herself in the mirror.

Her breasts were firm. Her butt didn't sag. Her tummy was flat and her waist...

She was thin. Her collarbones protruded. Her hips were sharp. She needed flesh to round out the curves.

Don't think about tomorrow night....

That was easy enough for him to say! He had current knowledge about the agreement they'd contracted. She had only a hazy recollection of the procedure involved.

Elizabeth crossed her eyes at the scowling reflection, jerked on her gown and went to bed.

Tom, Cleo and Jess took their customary places on the comforter, while she picked up a book recounting the latest research on custodial care. She settled herself under the covers with her scintillating reading.

Five minutes later she threw them off again.

Courage....

Climbing out of bed, she went to her closet, reached to the highest shelf and carefully drew down a carved wooden box she'd found on a trip to Mexico.

She took it back with her to bed, and after plumping her pillows, settled under the covers again.

Resolutely she removed the lid.

When she found the third volume of Sarah Elizabeth's journal, she flipped the pages to its first entry. The date startled her.

She checked back over the previous diary. Sure enough, five years had lapsed between the second and third books.

Questions buzzed in her head, but there were no answers. Somewhat bewildered, Elizabeth began to read.

September 25, 1905

My pupils and I have settled into a new year. We are preparing to face the rigors of Julius Caesar. *My consolation as always is that William Shakespeare has survived more barbarous attacks than those we will inflict upon him.*

Brother Caleb's youngest son may prove to be difficult. He mistakenly believes that as my nephew he is eligible for certain classroom privileges. I have taken pains to disabuse him of this foolish notion.

This year my class in American literature will test one of my newfound resolves. I am determined to teach the novels of Mark Twain, America's greatest living author. Several members of the community have objected strenuously to his works on moral and religious grounds. Rumors fly to the effect that the gentleman professes free love and atheism.

Unfortunately, Mama is one of those who holds to these beliefs and is a leader of the group of Concerned Citizens. I foresee pitched battles before the war is won, but I am determined to help lead Bastrop into the Twentieth Century.

As a teacher, I have the responsibility to broaden our eager young minds, even if on occasion they are less than disposed to the endeavor. Time will tell whether I can be effective in this pursuit.

Caleb has taken over the farm. Papa's heart is failing. I do not believe he can last out the year. I shall miss him sorely. When he is gone I will never again be anyone's "precious little girl."

What a vain, foolish fancy! Perhaps I should not have taken up my pen again in this fashion. Yet I have missed the process of sifting through my thoughts.

We shall see if I can turn away from futile remembrance.

I do not know what Mama shall do without Papa. He is the only one on earth who brings out her tenderness....

CHAPTER TEN

"HOPE," ELIZABETH CALLED as she searched a file cabinet located in the cubbyhole euphemistically known as CCE's file room. "Have you seen the folder with the grant request to the Lindell Community Foundation? They refused us last year, and I wanted to read why."

She listened for an answer, but none was forthcoming. Hope must have stepped out of the office for a minute.

Elizabeth had set herself the task of reviewing CCE's previous activities and that meant a search through the records. Since Hope was in the process of reorganizing their filing system, Elizabeth found herself lost without Hope's help.

Hope had, however, seemed singularly uncommunicative when she'd been asked a question several minutes ago.

Elizabeth wasn't up to ferreting out the reason for her unlikely behavior. Right at this moment she didn't feel competent to handle any human interaction. All she was trying to do was get through the afternoon.

The evening ahead loomed more and more ominously.

By eight this morning, after a sleepless night, she'd decided that lovemaking by appointment was not her idea of how to begin an affair.

She'd leave at five and run by the mall to pick up some lacy underwear. But what did lacy underwear consist of these days? A garter belt? Teddy?

Damn, damn, damn. She'd been wearing serviceable bras and panties too long.

And what did she intend to wear over her seductive apparel? Certainly not the shirtwaist dress she currently wore.

Muttering to herself, Elizabeth knelt to rummage through the bottom drawer, then crawled to the next cabinet seeking the folder in question. When her skirt got caught under a knee, she almost fell on her face. Next her hem snagged on a heel. She pulled off her pumps disgustedly.

"Need any help?"

Elizabeth whipped her head around and rocked back on her haunches. "Mac! What are you doing here? It's two o'clock. You said..."

He stepped inside and closed the door behind him. "I took an early flight," he explained, reaching down to haul her off the floor.

"But you said..."

He found the light switch and turned it off. Immediately, they were surrounded by total darkness. "I decided to surprise you," he murmured as he backed her against the one bare wall.

"But you said..."

He plastered himself against her just as she spoke. The impact of his body scattered her thoughts like confetti.

"Hmm?" His question was indistinct because his lips had reacquainted themselves with the slope of her neck.

"You said..." Her arms went around his waist of their own volition. "You said you weren't up to a public greeting."

"Is this public?" he asked as he discovered her ear with his mouth.

"Mac," she breathed. He seemed to be everywhere in the darkness. The scent of him. The heat of him. The hard contours of his body. His lips trailing moist, hot kisses over her skin.

His knowing hands. Roving down her back, over the slope of her waist, cupping her rear, pressing her against him. His fingers gathering her skirt until they found its hem and her thigh encased in nylon.

"Mac!" she gasped with what presence of mind she had left. "Someone could walk in on us."

"I locked the door. And Hope's standing guard. She's been instructed to say you've left the office for the day. Welcome me home, Elizabeth."

"I—" She moaned low in her throat as he stroked beneath her dress. She reached for his head and pulled it down to her face, her fingers tangling in his springy hair. Her lips sought his and opened beneath them.

The kiss they shared was seeking, demanding. He took her tongue into his mouth before delving urgently into hers.

Elizabeth's senses blurred with desire. She couldn't get close enough. Her breasts ached and she rubbed them hard against his chest.

His hand located the waistband of her hose and panties. He slipped inside and discovered soft bare skin. He began to peel away the layers.

"Mac...! Wha—"

"Sh," he murmured against her lips, nibbling at them, catching her bottom lip between his teeth, running his tongue along its sensitive interior.

His free hand slid up her dress front. His fingers skimmed a puckered nipple.

Elizabeth trembled with want. They could have been in his bed or on the moon. The only thing she knew was Mac and the velvety darkness.

When he pulled away slightly, she might have sagged to her knees, if her groping fingers hadn't connected with the top of a cabinet.

In a deft motion, he stripped off her hose and briefs. She was naked from the waist down beneath the demure linen dress.

From somewhere, somehow, her voice emerged rasping, "Mac... I don't think..."

"Don't think," he whispered thickly, "just want me."

"I do..."

His hands slid up her legs, taking material with them.

"Want..."

They circled her bare buttocks.

"You...."

Her murmur turned into a whimper of longing as his fingers skimmed the sensitive skin of her inner thighs, seeking her hot, pulsing center.

Seeking... finding....

Stroking her need....

Aching... throbbing....

Throbbing. She gasped wildly and dug her nails into his hair.

"Mac! I'm... I c-can't st-stop...."

"I know," he muttered intently. "Don't stop, love."

With sobbing breaths, she climaxed against his palm and fingers. For a long moment, Mac held her there, secure, dusting her face with murmuring kisses.

He tasted tears. She bowed her head against his chest, still breathing shallowly. Smoothing down her skirt, he took her into his arms.

"Thank you," he said softly, "for a lovely welcome."

"Do you realize—" she was still short of breath "—what I—what you—what we...?" She shook her head in disbelief, trying to decide whether her tears came from rage, relief or euphoria. "For heaven's sake—" her voice rose "—we've been making out in a closet!"

"Sh." He covered her mouth with his, muffling the sound of her voice.

"Oh my God," she whispered, pushing against his chest. "You don't think Hope heard anything?"

"No, love. The walls are thick. One of the benefits of old buildings. Besides—" his voice held repressed laughter "—you weren't very noisy."

She recoiled instinctively and would have slipped from his grasp if he'd let her. "Elizabeth, sweetheart, you can't go out just yet. You are definitely disheveled. Wait, I'll turn on the light."

"No!" She grabbed for him. "Not—not yet." She wasn't ready for him to see her. "How long have we been in here? What will Hope think? How can I face her?"

"Well," he said thoughtfully, "I can't answer the first question without looking at my watch. As to the second one, I assume Hope thinks I've used some of my patented charm to persuade you to leave with me. And we'd better damn well face her soon. I'm ready to move to more comfortable quarters. I have, though you might not have noticed, been practicing considerable restraint."

She'd noticed.

"Okay," she said, turning away and bumping into one of the cabinets. "You can turn on the light."

The single illuminated bulb hurt her eyes for a moment. Avoiding looking in Mac's direction, which was a feat considering the enclosed space, she cast around for her hose and panties. After finding them, she had to separate the two and struggle into them awkwardly. She slipped on her shoes and smoothed back her hair.

At last she felt capable of meeting Mac's eyes. The look she found in them made her insides melt into a puddle.

"Mac," she murmured, reaching out her hand. "Your hair's mussed. Let me smooth it."

"I don't think you'd better," he warned, raking his fingers through the unruly waves. "I've just found out that watching a woman dress is almost as exciting as undressing her. Can we leave now?" he asked, his voice even.

"Yes." Elizabeth glanced down and then up again quickly. She couldn't help the grin that appeared on her face. "You'd better button your coat. And walk with your hands in front of you."

"Don't tease me, woman. I can't take much more."

"You're the one who couldn't wait until this evening."

She brushed by him and opened the door, suddenly bursting with confidence.

"Hope—"

"I know." Hope barely glanced up from her typing. "You're gone for the day. Now hurry before someone finds out you're still here and corners you."

Elizabeth rushed into her office to collect her things. When she came out, Mac took her arm and opened the door.

"Have fun," Hope called after them softly.

Neither Mac nor Elizabeth thought it wise to reply.

A minor argument ensued when she headed for her car.

"No," Mac announced, steering them to his BMW. "I'm not letting you out of my sight for a minute."

"But Mac, someone will notice. Everybody knows my Honda. I'll have to come back for it eventually."

"Give me your keys and leave everything to me."

"Don't you think you're being arbitrary?"

"Yes. And if you don't get in the car, I'll arbitrarily kiss you."

Since they stood at the curb in plain sight of the building, Elizabeth slid onto the leather seat as he directed.

Silence reigned between them for several blocks.

Finally Elizabeth asked, a silky texture to her voice, "Are you used to winning fights with dire threats and blackmail?"

"Did I threaten you?" he asked, matching her tone with his. "I certainly don't recall any blackmail."

"Don't you?"

She leaned toward him and brushed his cheek with her lips, trailing her tongue against his skin for the fleetest moment.

"What a vile, arrogant man you are."

She rested her hand on his thigh and felt it flex beneath her touch. "Attacking me that way at the office. And me with a certain position to maintain."

Her hand inched upward.

Mac's lips twitched. The muscle in his thigh tightened. "Do you really want me to touch that line?"

"Why not? You touched everything else." Her fingers strayed over the bulge in his slacks.

The car swerved.

As he brought the steering back under control, he muttered various profane phrases.

"You are a dangerous woman." He took hold of her wrist. For just an instant, he pressed her palm against his length, then with a rueful sigh, he repositioned it in her lap.

The imprint of his maleness seemed to scorch her hand.

"I must be dangerous," she said dreamily, curling her fingers together.

Closing her eyes, she settled back in the seat. "Yet I've always considered myself rather prudish, you know. Just imagine, before I met you, I'd never even considered letting a man feel me up in a file room. It amazes me, how stuffy I was."

Elizabeth heard Mac chuckle as the car turned and slowed to a halt.

She opened her eyes. They were in the garage to his house. Mac switched off the ignition.

"We're home." He turned to her, his hand sliding over the back of the bucket seat.

"Yes."

They sat staring at each other. Elizabeth felt desire heating inside her.

The desire must have shown, for with an inarticulate murmur, Mac unlatched the door, got out and came around to open hers. As she stepped out, he offered his hand. When she accepted the offer, he took hold of hers tightly.

They were both silent as Mac fumbled for the key to the house. Once inside, he led her through the kitchen and down the carpeted hall. The first room he entered was the master suite.

"Where's Evan?" she asked, suddenly anxious.

"In classes right now, at a friend's apartment later—" he paused significantly "—for the duration of the evening."

"How can you be sure?" Elizabeth hadn't gotten used to Mac's cluttered life.

"I called him to discuss schedules after I talked to you last night."

The implications of his words caused her face to redden. "I'm not sure I like your children knowing the particulars of our love life."

"Welcome to the joys of parenthood. Don't worry, Evan's taken with you. If he thought I planned to bring another woman here, he'd have read me a lecture."

Her look slipped from his. "I'm taken with Evan, too."

Mac dropped her hand and cupped one of her shoulders. "How do you feel about his father?" He brushed her flaming cheek with the tips of his fingers.

"In light of recent evidence, I'd say I was putty in his hands."

"No." He moved closer until they barely touched. His look drew hers with its intense gleam. "You come alive in my hands. You shimmer and dazzle me."

She reached up and stroked his jaw lightly. "I've never dazzled anyone before. It's an intoxicating feeling."

"I want to dazzle you," he murmured, and began unbuttoning her dress.

Her very unsexy utilitarian dress.

"If you'd waited until this evening," she couldn't help mentioning, "I'd planned to wear something a little more slinky. A shirtwaist and cotton underwear aren't exactly seductive."

"Elizabeth," he said, "you could seduce me wearing nothing but a potato sack."

He unbuckled her belt and slipped it from around her waist. "On second thought, let me amend that statement. You could seduce me wearing anything, but I'd prefer nothing."

His thumbs hooked themselves under the tailored lapels and slid the material off her shoulders until the offending garment bloused silently to the floor.

"Why am I the only one getting undressed?" she asked breathlessly.

"I wondered that myself," he replied with a glint in his eye.

Obediently, she fumbled with his suit coat and slipped it down his arms. Her fingers trembling slightly, she began to unfasten his shirt, freeing it first from the confines of his slacks.

When she had loosed the last button, she spread the soft fabric aside, letting her palms linger on the contours of his broad, muscular chest. His nipples were nubs set in dark whorls of fuzz. A line of hair strayed down his flat stomach and disappeared beneath the fly of his trousers.

Suddenly she wasn't sure what else to do with her hands.

It was easy enough to play the wanton in the relative safety of a moving car. Now, however, when they were actually in Mac's bedroom with nothing hindering the logical progression of this mutual stripping, she felt a moment of panic.

What was she supposed to divest him of next?

She longed for that earlier blanketing darkness to hide her confusion. Sunlight sifted through outdoor greenery, but it met no resistance as it streamed in a wall of windows.

"I don't suppose you could pull the drapes," she said.

Mac stroked her throat with his palm, lifting her chin so that she was forced to look at him. He could feel her pulse hammering erratically against his thumb.

"Why? Are you nervous?"

"A little," she confessed.

"Elizabeth," he said softly, "I can't keep sneaking up on you in file rooms so you don't get anxious. It's hell on my nerves."

"I know," she said mournfully, and took a deep breath. "Mac, I've been to bed with three men in my entire life. I haven't entered a bedroom for—for this kind of purpose in over ten years. I know, sometimes with you, I act abandoned. I'm amazed by what gets into me."

Mac slid his hands around her waist and drew her tightly against him. "Sounds promising," he whispered. "How about me?"

He matched his actions to his words and covered her mouth with his, urgently seeking an entrance. As always when he touched her, she turned to flame.

Her nervousness flashed and burned. Her hesitation vanished. She pressed her hips to his in mindless invitation.

Before she could think or doubt, he peeled off her bra, then her shoes, hose and panties. Finally, he laid her on the bed.

"That's better," he murmured, allowing his look to roam freely over her bare skin. Where it lingered, she felt brushed with the delicate stroke of a painter.

Odd—the thought skittered through her brain. She didn't feel at all anxious or embarrassed. Instead, a delicious lassitude had taken control of her body.

Her eyelashes fluttered shut and then opened slowly.

When Mac saw her expression, he took a sharp breath, shrugged out of his shirt, kicked off his shoes and fumbled for a moment with the zipper to his slacks before he succeeded in discarding them.

Finally he dragged off his socks and straightened, wearing a look of desire, and low-riding white jockey briefs, his readiness for lovemaking evident against the soft knit of fabric.

He tugged at the elastic.

"Wait," Elizabeth commanded. She rose to her knees with a small smile on her lips. "Let me."

Mac's brow rose expressively. His hands fell away and hung at his sides. "Be my guest," he said huskily.

"That first day at the board meeting," she reminisced as her hands molded his tight buttocks, "I imagined you wearing these and nothing else."

"Elizabeth, I'm shocked." His voice, however, didn't reflect that censure. It was low, sexy and tinged with laughter. As he spoke, his hands moved to free her hair from its confining barrette.

"I thought I saw something in your eyes when I caught you staring," he recalled as he tangled his fingers through the shoulder-length waves.

"Of course," she went on, rubbing her head like a cat against his caressing palms, her own fingers inching around to the front of his shorts, "I hadn't pictured them fitting you in quite this way."

"Oh, no? If you'd kept looking at me the way you were, they might…" His voice died to a strangled groan when she ran her hand sleekly up his hard male length.

"Will you stop toying with me, woman?" he begged her hoarsely. "Remember, I've been in this condition for close to an hour."

"I guess," she said, stripping away the briefs, "we'd better do something about that problem."

"It's not exactly a problem," he growled. "But it does need attention."

He pushed Elizabeth flat on her back and stretched out beside her, immediately pulling her into his arms.

When they were skin to skin he let out his breath with a sigh. "Damn, you feel good."

He freed one hand and found the mound of her breast. His thumb flicked urgently across the swollen nipple.

When he heard the low sounds that came from the back of her throat, his leg urged open her thighs.

Without conscious volition, Elizabeth began to rock against him, her own throbbing heat unleashing a driving hunger.

"This one's going to be fast," he muttered against her lips, his tongue beginning to mimic the anticipated union.

"Yes."

He ran his fingers down her stomach, through the soft tuft of hair, finding the cleft where his thigh had exerted its erotic pressure. Her hips rose to meet his touch, and he delved into the moist heat.

"You're hot and ready for me, sweetheart."

"Yes," she breathed hurriedly. "I want you inside me."

She stirred restlessly under his knowing touch. Her eyelids drifted shut, freeing her other senses.

A moment later, she felt him cup her hips, spread them and plunge deeply into her silken sheath.

With a surprised gasp, she pulsed helplessly.

His motion quickened, became thrusts of need.

She cried out with exquisite pleasure as she clutched at his shoulders.

"I can't wait...." he groaned.

"Don't wait...Mac...I want..."

His tongue plunged into her mouth.

The pulsing throbs seized her body once more.

He drove once, twice, cried out...

And collapsed over her with a shuddering completion.

ELIZABETH SEEMED TO DRIFT in a haze of sated exhaustion. Only when she felt a sudden chill of air did she realize Mac had moved off her. She opened her eyes to find him close by, his head propped on his palm.

He was staring down at her with a tender concentration. As soon as her gaze met his, he rested his hand in the hollow of her stomach and leaned over to brush her lips ever so gently with his.

"We promised each other passion," he reminded her, "but not even I knew how much we had to give."

"I didn't know, either," Elizabeth whispered. "Mac..." She turned away from him slightly. "At the office and just now...well, I was never like that before."

"You mean—" he stroked the damp hair from the hollow of her neck and nuzzled into it "—the way you go up in smoke for me."

"You have a rare way with words, Mr. Reynolds," she drawled, fighting an absurd sense of shame. "Yes, that's what I mean. You don't suppose it's because I'm a sex-starved female."

"I think—" he lifted his head and said judiciously "—it's because you're wildly attracted to me and you're falling in love.

"Now—" he turned her body so that they were facing each other "—ask me why a grown male of forty-six flew home from California like a madman, conspired with a certain lady director's secretary, then waylaid that director for a torrid quickie in a closet when he had a perfectly good bed at home."

Her eyes widened. "I don't know. Why did he?"

"Because he's wildly attracted to said lady and he's fallen in love."

"Already fallen?" she asked, searching his face.

"Irretrievably."

He recognized her look of stunned disbelief.

"I don't know about you," he said lightly, "but I suggest we take an afternoon nap for the sake of our evening. You didn't get much sleep last night, did you?"

"No," she whispered, still wide-eyed.

"Neither did I."

Moments later, they'd settled under the covers. He gathered her to him so that her face rested on his shoulder.

In love with her? Mac?

Was she in love with him?

Her thoughts whirled around like leaves in a windstorm. She was so sleepy after the anxious night, the intense passion.

Elizabeth rooted against Mac's chest as though she were nesting in a pillow. His arm tightened over her back reassuringly.

She'd somehow avoided dealing with issues of commitment, never quite believing their relationship would come to that, despite what Mac had said on the phone last night.

Now she didn't feel capable of grappling with the notion.

All she knew, as she lay draped over Mac's powerful, protective body, was that sharing his bed was a damned sight more pleasurable than napping with Cleo, Tom and Jess.

February 9, 1918

Mama is doing poorly. She roams the house at night, muttering and confused. Ever since I have taken over the care of her, she has seemed fretful and disoriented. Of course, she's never been the same since Papa's passing years ago.

We all knew the move off the farm would be hard for Mama to endure. Yet it was necessary she come to live with me. When my nephew Bobby died in the Second Battle of Ypres, my sister-in-law could no longer cope with her demands.

So many young men sacrificed to war. I anxiously survey the lists of dead and wounded in the paper. Many of my former pupils are fighting on the blood-soaked fields of Europe. I pray Mr. Wilson can someday forge a lasting peace.

At least poor Mama isn't aware of the death of her favorite grandchild. Her mind seems riveted to years ago when she was a little girl on her father's Georgia plantation. We rattle around this house, two aging, lonely widows, each trapped by her own memories.

Since I gave up my teaching, my solitude has troubled me, but Mama requires my constant care. So I read and piece quilts and tend to Mama's needs. We go out to our porch chairs during clement weather.

It is just as well I resigned my position. Bastrop's citizens always saw me as an unsettling influence on their youth. Yet my students had come to think of me as a relic of the past.

I sometimes think it the work of capricious fate that I never settled comfortably in my time and place....

CHAPTER ELEVEN

WHEN ELIZABETH AWAKENED it was late afternoon. Slanted rays drifted through the numerous windows, and the landscape of Mac's room was patterned with shadow and light.

She lay alone in the king-size bed. Her clothes were no longer scattered around the floor, but a robe had been draped invitingly over a nearby chair. The bathroom door stood open, as did the one to the hallway and the rest of the house. She heard no sounds coming from either direction.

Feeling dazed and a little disoriented, Elizabeth threw off the covers and padded over the plush carpeting to the waiting robe. When she shrugged it on, the sleeves hung off her fingers. The material was a fine silk burgundy, and it clung to her curves like the caress of water.

She walked through the entrance to the bath and stood staring for a moment at a room as spacious as the average kitchen. The floor was patterned with Mediterranean tile. The ceiling consisted of a series of skylights. The tub was enormous. And a shower stall had been installed for hurried morning ablutions. She peered into a walk-in closet the size of three of her wardrobes.

Mac certainly wasn't one to stint on creature comforts. The rest of the house had already shown her that. The square footage was ample, the decor informal but tasteful. He obviously enjoyed a quality of life commensurate with the fortune he'd made.

Right now she had more important things to worry about than his life-style. Like where was he? And should she seek him out?

For a moment Elizabeth looked longingly at the sunken tub. Then shaking off her fantasies, she slipped out of Mac's robe and into his shower.

Ten minutes later she stepped out refreshed and flushed from the needle spray of hot water. She reached for a towel on the vanity where she'd placed it and touched Mac's hard male torso, instead.

"Oh!" She jerked her hand away and wiped the moisture from her eyes, finally peering at him through wet lashes. He was buck naked, aroused and leaning against the lavatory, surveying her nudity with a lazy grin.

"Finished already? I was planning to join you."

"I can see that," she said, flustered and trying to hide evidence of it. "But you've taken a shower. Your hair's still damp."

"Yes. But it wasn't much fun without you."

"Oh?" She searched again for the towel. Mac deftly took it from her grasp.

"Do you need toys to play with at bath time?" she asked, still unable to meet the gleam in his eyes.

He wrapped the towel around her and began to dry away the moisture. Only instead of rubbing vigorously, he lingered over every inch of skin.

He also took his time about answering her question. When he did, the words were light but the tone wasn't. "I'm not into rubber duckies, if that's what you mean. But I'd sure as hell like to find you in my tub every night."

Since one of her fantasies concerned the tub, Elizabeth found herself momentarily breathless.

By now she'd been adequately dried and thoroughly fondled. Somewhere along the way, the fluffy towel had been replaced by his caressing hands.

She leaned against him weakly, her sensitive breasts pressed against the solid expanse of his chest. He framed her face and molded her lips with languorous kisses.

"Instead of a shower," he whispered, "why don't we go back to bed?"

"Aren't you getting hungry?"

"Yes," he murmured. "But not for food."

Without waiting for permission, Mac picked Elizabeth up, went back into the bedroom and laid her on the bed. Staring down at her, he remained standing for a moment. It was hard to lie still under his hooded gaze.

"Why don't you come here?" she asked, suddenly itching to explore the contours and texture of his body.

"Because I don't think we've been properly introduced."

"Oh? Not even after this afternoon?" She stretched languidly, aware his eyes followed her every movement. "And what would you call a proper introduction?"

He sat down, crowding her hip. "This..." Without warning, he leaned over and slowly licked a nipple.

It puckered immediately and she shuddered with need.

"And this..." Now he covered the same breast with his mouth and began to suck and fondle it until the flesh was wet and exquisitely tender.

Moaning softly, she arched to meet his tongue. His hand molded the other breast, plucking and kneading the nipple.

Deep inside, Elizabeth started to ache. She could feel herself begin to weep with wanting.

"And this..." His other hand brushed over her body with long, lingering strokes. Her arms, her ribs, her belly. Up over her knees and her raised thighs, which were already spread for him.

Each teasing, knowing foray approached, retreated then circled nearer.

"And this." He trailed kisses by her navel, halting to explore it with his tongue, before his lips moved downward, nibbling, tasting, over her triangular mound of hair.

She gasped, realizing his intention. "I—I'd call this a highly improper introduction. Mac...!" Her tone held shock, but her hips writhed with anticipation.

"We're past introductions," she heard him say. "I am now establishing intimate regard."

"Oh...."

His mouth and tongue found what they searched for, and Elizabeth was entirely bereft of speech. All she could do was moan helplessly, riding a crest of dizzying passion.

She felt his body move between her legs. He pulled her thighs over his and slid slowly into her.

It was good. So very, very good. He filled her completely. She sighed and drifted with mindless delight.

When her eyes fluttered open, she found Mac watching her with a look of fierce tenderness, as though he took his delight in the pleasure he gave.

She reached up and ran her palms over his chest. He leaned down and kissed her deeply on the mouth. Then he nuzzled between her breasts and once more suckled a swollen nipple.

She felt the draw in the ache between her thighs. The ache that he stroked again and again—with a rhythmic control that undid her completely.

His hands were everywhere, pleasuring, urging.

"Mac! Ah...!"

She pulsed all around him, her ripples of ecstasy washing over them again... and again.

She was faint and gasping when his control shattered.

He took her hips high and drove into the depths of her, crying out with his own fulfillment.

Afterward, he fell forward and rested his cheek against her breast.

IT WAS SEVERAL MINUTES before either of them spoke, only their shallow breathing rustling the air.

At last, Mac rolled onto his back and pulled her up over him. He took her face between his hands, gave her a peck on the lips and smiled lazily, his expression satisfied and, yes, a little smug.

"It's Doris's day off," he said in a low, sexy voice. "How do grilled hamburgers sound for supper?"

"Hamburgers?" she said stupidly. A giggle popped out. "You're suggesting hamburgers?"

He raised a brow and his lips quirked enchantingly. "Too plebeian for you, huh? The sirloin steak will take longer to thaw."

"I—I see," she said. Another giggle escaped. "You're offering me a choice of entrées."

"Man cannot live by sex alone."

She clapped her hand over her mouth. The giggles kept coming. Finally, she fell back on the bed, laughing uncontrollably.

Mac propped himself on an elbow and watched her, his expression enigmatic.

"I left work in the middle of the afternoon," she gasped, "to have a roll in the hay with one of my board members—"

"You could have chosen the shower," he reminded her.

She laughed harder. Tears were beginning to stream from her eyes. "I've acted irrationally and impulsively—"

"We've known each other almost two months."

"Thrown l-logic and judgment to the winds—"

"You accepted the inevitable."

"I'm h-having fantasies about orgies in the bathtub—"

"Now that sounds interesting."

"I've had the most un—" her breaths came in spasms "—unb-believable afternoon of my life. And we're discussing what to thaw for dinner."

He wiped away a tear as it trickled toward her ear. "What would you like to talk about?" he asked quietly.

For some reason his tone effectively muffled her laughter. She stared at him, still gulping for air.

"I don't know," she said at last, huskily.

"Shall I tell you how beautiful you are?"

Elizabeth turned away, muttering, "Don't be silly."

"No." He caught her chin and made her face him. "Haven't you been listening all this time? You *are* beautiful—in every way."

"You're biased."

"It's a lover's prerogative."

"You don't think I'm too thin?" As soon as she asked, Elizabeth grimaced horribly. "You—you don't have to answer that question. I don't need reassurance."

"I think you must," he said softly.

"No...no." She shook her head.

"Elizabeth, don't deny me my rights and privileges." His tone was stern and she stared at him blankly.

"A man wants to tell the woman he loves how she looks in his eyes."

Her gaze widened.

"I see," she whispered. "And how do I look to you?"

"Utterly enchanting. You take my breath away."

His fingers brushed a cheek and settled over her throat, where he caressed her slowly.

"I never want to stop touching you, Elizabeth. Your skin's like satin. Your body's sleek and incredibly giving... and exciting."

"How do you feel about small breasts?" she asked.

Mac grinned. "All I want is a mouthful."

"I guess I asked for that." She laughed, chagrined.

"No," he said, proving just how well he knew her. "What you're asking is if I really love you. I do, very much. And I'm ready to show you and tell you in every way I know how."

"Oh, Mac." This time her laughter held joy and, yes, even triumph. "I love you, too."

She launched herself at him, pinning his shoulders against the mattress. When he didn't resist, she grabbed fistfuls of hair and rained small, moist kisses over his eyes and nose and mouth and jaw.

"I am desperately, passionately in love with you," she said. "I've never felt so crazy or wonderful in my life. I don't have room for doubts or questions. All I have to do is look at you and I turn to mush."

She bowed her forehead to his and shook with mirth. "And I'm starved for a hamburger! With cheese, pickles, lettuce, tomatoes, mustard and onions. So if you think you've got what it takes to join me in the tub later, you have to promise to eat onions, too."

"Lady," he said menacingly as he grabbed her around the waist, "it's dangerous to question a male's sexual prowess."

"Oh, really?" she asked, her lips pouting.

In answer, Mac flipped Elizabeth over and straddled her ribs, proving to them both that his sexual powers were more than adequate to meet her needs.

This time their lovemaking was uninhibited and brazen, a tangle of limbs and sheets accompanied by sensual laughter, torrid whispers and breathless exploration. At the last, their bodies joined together in a union of celebration, culminating in a driving, elemental release.

When it was over, Elizabeth wasn't sure she'd ever move again. She was sore and tender in a number of places. When he nudged her lazily, she grunted and rolled over.

"Go away," she mumbled, and felt him get out of bed.

In a moment, a whisper of silk tumbled over the small of her back. She reached to identify the sensation and realized he'd dumped the robe on her.

A second later, he lightly slapped her behind.

She let out a yelp and sat up to glare at him.

He shrugged and grinned. "Supper's waiting and it won't fix itself. Remember, you're starving."

Her lashes fluttered shut. "Not anymore."

Mac laughed. "Well, I need to maintain my strength. A certain lusty lady keeps demanding my attentions."

Grumbling, she climbed out of bed and belted the robe around her waist. When she'd finished rolling up the sleeves, Elizabeth glanced up to see that Mac had tugged on a pair of jeans and slipped into a shirt without bothering to button it.

He turned and eyed her appreciatively. "You look a hell of a lot better in my robe than I do."

"That's because you have this thing for dishevelment." She pushed away a lock of hair that had fallen over one eye.

He chuckled and threw an arm around her shoulders, leading her out of the bedroom for the first time that afternoon.

The next hour was easy and companionable between them. She sliced the lettuce, pickles, tomatoes and onions and explored the refrigerator for mustard, mayonnaise and olives. He grilled the meat they found in the freezer.

Both of them ate as if they hadn't seen food for a week.

"Open up," Mac said, selecting the last olive. She obeyed and he plopped it into her mouth.

Elizabeth chewed on it thoughtfully.

"Marry me," he said.

She choked and grabbed hastily for her drink.

"Why do you always do that to me?" she complained after a moment.

"Do what?"

"Come out of left field."

"Are you really surprised?" He took her hand, kissed it and laid it against his cheek.

"No." She faced him and answered honestly.

He surveyed her features with a strange intensity. "You're not a woman a man could bed and not want to marry."

His tone had a kind of detachment that caused her to say in a rush, "You don't have to feel obligated—"

"No. You misunderstand me. I said it poorly." He sent her a rueful glance. "I'm rusty at this."

"So am I," she said faintly.

"You are a person of rare generosity. I could never love you casually or carelessly. This afternoon was unique for me, too."

"Why didn't you ask me to marry you earlier," she asked, "when you said you loved me?"

"Because what I feel goes far beyond passion. And I didn't want you to feel that desire alone prompted my proposal."

"No." She laid her hand over his. "I wouldn't think that."

He took a deep breath. "I need you, Elizabeth. And every time I'm with you I need you more and in different ways. Now that I've made love to you, I don't want to sleep in that bed alone. I don't want to wake up to the day without you by my side. I want everything for us that marriage means to two people."

Her look fell from his. "What if I told you I'm not sure I know how to be married."

"I thought you might be worried by that."

"I am, Mac. And we can't avoid the issue. I've lived many years essentially alone."

"But you know what it means to care for someone. You know how to love. That's what's important."

"But it's not enough in a marital partnership. Maybe I've gone my own way too long to learn the give-and-take a relationship demands."

"I honestly don't think that will happen, Elizabeth."

"But don't you see? I can't be sure."

"None of us is ever sure. You know that."

"But at least you've been in a marriage. You know how it's supposed to work."

"And I've felt like a failure. Anyone who's ever gone through a divorce, especially if there are children involved, wonders what could have been done to preserve the marriage. I've had to ask myself if I'm such a bargain."

"Is that why you haven't married these last ten years?"

"Yes. And no. There've been women since Karen. I'm no Don Juan, but . . ." He shrugged.

"Of course," she said, forcing sympathy into her voice. "I understand."

"Oh, no, you don't." He had the nerve to grin. The grin faded and he said quietly, "I haven't slept with another woman since I met you."

"You didn't need to tell me that."

"Oh, yes, I did. To help you understand. It wasn't a conscious decision on my part—at least not at first. But I think I sensed from the start that what we could have would be very special. Because unlike you, I have been around the block a few times. Do you see what I'm saying?"

"Yes." She stared down at the counter and the remains of supper. "Are Tracy and Evan part of the reason you stayed single?"

"Yes," he admitted bluntly. "There were some tough years when Karen wasn't around, and I didn't think bringing another person into the equation would solve any problems. But you can't use Tracy and Evan against me, you know, because they're two of your greatest fans."

"I would want them to accept me. I would want to do what was best for them. Sometimes children are threatened by such a major change."

"They're generous like you. My happiness is important to them. In any case, I don't intend to live my life for my grown children. What's really bothering you?"

He assessed her closely. "Come on, sweetheart, let's
have a little honesty."

She traced an imaginary doodle on the counter with
one of her fingernails. "What if this thing between us
burns itself out like a Roman candle? All sparkle and
flame, in one brilliant display?"

"Is that what you believe?"

"No. I don't know. Oh, Mac, don't you see? It's be-
cause I've never acted this way that I'm not sure what
I'm doing. You—you go through life confident and sure.
You never second-guess yourself."

"Are you saying," he drawled, "that I make snap
decisions?"

"No, not exactly. But we don't think alike. I have to
reason things through very carefully. Consider the consequences. Proceed with caution."

"By all means, you should proceed cautiously, Elizabeth."

She heard the irony in his voice and gave him a look
tinged with exasperation. "I just don't want you to get
into something you'll later regret."

"I'm in it already," he reminded her bluntly. "And
you are, too."

A look of distress crossed her features.

His look softened. "Don't worry. I do understand. I
love you because of who you are, and I wouldn't want
to change you. I knew when I proposed you'd have to
get used to the notion. That's why I brought it up, to
begin negotiations."

"Oh, Mac." She rubbed her hand along the hard line
of his jaw. Her tone was pleading and a little breathless.
"Please don't give up on me."

"Not a chance."

"I do want to marry you very much, it's just that—"

"I'll give you a month. That should be more than enough time for you to work yourself into a tizzy."

"You really do think you have me figured out."

He smiled lazily. "I'm getting there, lover. And you and I are lovers. Don't forget it for a minute. After today, the rules have changed."

"Are you saying you'll be applying your own method of persuasion?"

"Don't you want me to?" He leaned nearer.

"Oh, yes," she whispered as their lips met, "every chance you get."

THEY MADE LOVE once more late in the evening, and the quality of their lovemaking was again different. There was a slow, languorous tenderness to the physical joining.

For one thing, Mac was solicitous about the soreness she was feeling. But more than that, they seemed to want to savor each moment, as if they both were poignantly aware of how ephemeral happiness could be.

When Mac drove her home, midnight had come and gone. He'd wanted her to stay, but Tom, Jess and Cleo were waiting hungrily. To Elizabeth's surprise, he hadn't pressed his case.

She was also surprised to find the Honda parked in her driveway. She'd forgotten all about it. Mac had evidently taken care of the matter while she was asleep. As he walked her to the door, he handed over the keys.

Their farewell kiss was simple. Mac promised to call her in the morning, then left her to face a lonely bed in a haze of exhaustion.

Maybe that's why Elizabeth could face it at all. By the time she climbed gingerly between the sheets, her thoughts were already wandering. Sleep was very near.

Mac. Marriage.

Her eyes popped open. She stared up at the darkened ceiling.

Marriage meant children.

A child. Her child. Their child.

The child she'd longed for desperately.

The child she thought she'd never have.

Elizabeth's hands slipped over the concave of her stomach. Perhaps she was already pregnant. They hadn't used a condom.

Maybe Mac thought she'd taken care of it.

Maybe she hadn't mentioned birth control on purpose.

A simple mistake would make everything so simple.

She smiled, giddy joy bubbling through her. She could almost feel the new life growing inside her.

Mac had decreed a month. She didn't think it would take her that long to decide.

THE NEXT MORNING, Elizabeth awakened still giddy. When she opened her windows, the morning air was like wine. She breathed it deeply, her head swimming with spring.

When she dressed for work, she chose one of her more elegant outfits, a navy sheath that hinted at her "sleek" curves.

As soon as Hope saw her, the older woman smiled broadly. Elizabeth didn't care. She grinned right back.

The day progressed as usual. She waded through a frantic phone call from Carol, two agency emergencies and a grant rejection. This on top of the usual chaos. Yet when five o'clock came, she still felt fresh and renewed.

And she realized suddenly that the stresses of the day hadn't drained her. If anything she felt a rebirth of purpose.

She'd given her love to Mac, and this was his gift to her. Just as he'd spilled his seed into her womb, he'd filled her with strength.

It was all she could do not to jump up from her desk and dance down the hallway.

She was up to any task. Mac's love had inspired her.

He'd made her feel equal to the compelling dilemma she had yet to resolve.

Feeling a new commitment to another special someone who needed her, she waited once more for everyone to leave, then climbed the stairs to the second story. Her heart was in her throat; her hands were clammy. She felt an air of unreality about her mission.

But this was something she knew she wanted to do.

Again she sought the familiar rocker, and waited, rocking and gazing out into the yard.

She didn't need to look around to know when Sarah Elizabeth joined her in the chair close by.

"Why," Elizabeth asked, "haven't you written Johnny's name in the third volume of your journal? Tell me what's happened. It's been almost twenty years with not one word about him."

The rocker beside her creaked as if a breeze had nudged it.

"I know you loved him. How could you send him away when your husband died? Mr. LeBow's death was a release, just like my father's. You shouldn't have allowed your guilt to come between you and Johnny."

The creak grew louder as if the wind swirled in agitation around the wicker chair.

"You'd already sacrificed twenty years. Your youth, your dreams." Elizabeth's voice showed her frustration. "I've seen what you went through. I've felt your burden."

She closed her eyes for a moment, feeling a sharp, stabbing pain.

An icy cold crept over her. It was as though the same wind that swirled around them brought a winter's chill to banish the promise of spring.

She shivered and rubbed her arms, but she couldn't stop the questions. "How could you sacrifice two people's lives? How could you condemn yourself to loneliness? To never share your lover's kiss? To never lie with him?

"Sarah Elizabeth. I need to know so I can understand."

She turned. The air was still. The chair stood motionless.

And empty.

October 21, 1924

I will be leaving tomorrow to begin a new life in the autumn of my years, taking the few possessions of which I have need.

I am not sorry to go. This house has not been a happy one. Perhaps the new tenants will fill it with love and erase the sad memories that seem to linger in the rooms.

As long as Mama was alive there was a reason for me to abide here. But she is gone, her death peaceful. And I do not choose to be dependent on my relatives' charity. Somehow the charity of strangers seems much more palatable to me. With room and board provided, my small pension will be sufficient to my needs.

I have heard Austin is a congenial city, the Confederate Widows' Home a pleasant one, the other ladies friendly, their habits compatible. Certain of my fellow boarders have even formed an afternoon quilting circle. Communal living may come as a welcome change.

In any event, I will surely find those who need comfort and aid. The thought of living out my days alone has become intolerable to me, however long is the time I have left....

CHAPTER TWELVE

IT WAS THREE WEEKS LATER, a workday, and Elizabeth stood in Hope's office. The mail had just been delivered, bringing with it a moment of high drama. Now Elizabeth's hands shook as she tore open an embossed envelope. Hope, watching at her desk, sat inordinately silent. Both women recognized how much difference this letter could make to CCE. Neither of them dared voice their fears and prayers about its contents.

She carefully unfolded the single sheet of typing. Her eyes scanned the page.

When she gave out a whoop, Hope jumped from her chair.

"We did it!" Elizabeth cried as they hugged each other. "The foundation gave us a grant for sixty thousand dollars over a two-year period. For subsidized home and adult day care. As an adjunct they've provided funds for the Guardianship Program."

The women danced a manic jig over the tiled floor.

"Listen..." Elizabeth tried to catch her breath so she could quote aloud. "Listen to this. 'We make it our policy to fund innovative projects that effectively meet the needs of the elderly population. The programs and agencies that form Capital Coalition for the Elderly meet our high standards for goals and performance.'"

"This is our first major acceptance," Hope reminded her excitedly. "The first of many."

"I certainly hope so. We need that high-speed copier I asked for from the Longhorn Foundation. But it was harder to wax eloquent over copy machines."

Without questioning her instincts, Elizabeth walked into her office. "I have to call Mac."

"Don't you think—" Hope's voice trailed after her "—that Suzanne and Betsy might be interested? We're talking about their clients. And what about Carol?"

"I'll get to them in a minute."

Luckily Mac was at his office and available for calls.

"Mac," she said as soon as he came on the line, "do you remember that day Suzanne came to my office and I promised to help her?"

"You're as bad as Mother," he complained. "How about a 'hello, how are you, I love you,' for starters?"

"You know how I'm doing." She lowered her voice even though the door was closed. "And I told you I loved you this morning in bed."

"So you did," he remembered. "But that was a long time ago. Have lunch with me and refresh my memory."

"I can't. I'm meeting Tracy at noon."

"I don't trust you two alone," he grumbled. "Is there a chance I could wangle an invitation?"

"No, you can't. So don't try to get around me." Tracy had made it clear she wanted a cozy tête-à-tête.

"Then tell me over the phone to help me get through the day."

"Mac...." It was one thing to whisper love words in the throes of passion. She found it harder to make bald statements over the telephone lines.

"Elizabeth. You wouldn't deny a starving man," he wheedled, "would you?"

Since he was anything but starving, considering the frequency of their lovemaking, she couldn't help uttering a disapproving harrumph.

But as there was precious little she knew how to deny him, she also gave in and whispered, "I love you."

"That wasn't so hard, was it?" he said. "Now what's your news about Suzanne?"

"Oh," she said breathlessly, "you almost made me forget. We got the money for subsidized care. Every bit we asked for. And the grant I wrote helped them decide in our favor. I knew it was a good one."

"That's important to you, isn't it?"

"Of course. This time I came through for the coalition. I made the difference."

"You make a difference every day. Don't you really know how good you are, Elizabeth?"

"Well, I—"

"I love watching you work with people. You respect their opinions. You care and it shows."

"Thank you, Mac." Her voice was husky.

"In fact, at the risk of having it go to your head, I'd say you were pretty hot stuff as an executive director."

"Just as a director?" she asked softly.

He chuckled. "I thought you didn't want to get personal over the phone."

"You wouldn't deny a starving woman?"

"You're pretty damn hot in bed, as well. If you have a minute, we can discuss particulars. This morning, for instance—"

"No! That's okay." She stopped him hurriedly. "Details aren't necessary. I have to hang up and deliver the news."

After their call ended, she headed out the door, explaining to Hope, "I'm off to tell Suzanne. And the day care center."

Thirty minutes later, she waved goodbye to an exultant Betsy and headed back to her office to telephone Carol. On the way, however, she lingered in the corridor, wanting to savor her triumph for a moment.

Everything seemed to be coming together. First the mortgage had been paid, thanks to Mac's grateful friend. The renovations were proceeding, also Mac's doing.

Now the grant.

And every day the membership agencies were linked together more securely. The Guardianship Program, for instance, had found a volunteer to be Mrs. Cooper's trustee, who in turn had located an adult foster home where she could live. And the Adoptive Grandparents Program was getting rave reviews. It had even been written up in the newspaper.

Every goal the coalition dreamed of was possible.

Bring on Travis County and the city! She'd have them crawling to her to fund CCE's projects.

Elizabeth launched another jig, realized where she was and looked around guiltily. To her relief the hallway was deserted. She was very much afraid this triumph had gone to her head.

But it wasn't just the grant she'd written so meticulously. The job itself rewarded her efforts. She came to work every morning ready to tackle the day. She no longer felt drained, overwhelmed and inadequate.

And why should she? After all, a reliable source had informed her, she was pretty hot stuff as an executive director.

Elizabeth grinned wickedly and hugged herself for just a second, imagining Mac's arms around her.

Having a lover was great for morale.

Mac, true to his word, hadn't pushed the subject of marriage. And Elizabeth had been so intoxicated with love she'd found it hard to look into the future.

Her menstrual period had come—a mild disappointment. But there was time, plenty of time. When she did accept Mac's proposal, she didn't think he'd want a long engagement.

As soon as they made definite plans, he'd have to resign from the board. Their personal involvement still troubled her for ethical reasons.

Not that Mac would mind stepping down, she admitted. He'd be the first to remind her he'd served Mary's purpose. The fate of the building was no longer in doubt.

Mac was, however, chafing under the rules she'd set down in the interests of discretion. Unfortunately, those rules had served very little purpose in disguising their affair.

After that day in the file room, Hope was certainly aware of the change in their relationship.

Herb and Mary must be suspicious. They'd gone out for dinner together for a second time, and Elizabeth's eyes had given her away.

Evan knew. She blushed at the thought. But how could he not? During these past few weeks, Mac had left her bed several times at dawn.

And if Evan and his sister hadn't conferred, something had put a gleam in Tracy's eyes and contributed to her proprietary air. She seemed ready to claim credit for an anticipated addition to the Reynolds family.

Elizabeth smiled. Like Evan, Tracy was mature for her years. Yet only the very young assume true love leads to a happy ending.

Thinking of Tracy, Elizabeth glanced at her watch and saw she had barely twenty minutes until they met for lunch.

When Elizabeth arrived at the restaurant they'd chosen, she could tell Tracy was wilting in the late spring heat.

Odd, when she was around Tracy these days, Elizabeth no longer felt a trace of envy. Instead, a certain protectiveness had taken its place. Despite Tracy's infectious enthusiasm, Elizabeth detected a fragile quality she hadn't seen before.

Tracy, however, began the conversation in her usual breezy manner. "Evan's joining us as soon as he gets out of class."

"Evan? Then I should have let your father come. He asked to join us."

"Daddy? Oh, we don't want him."

Elizabeth looked at her suspiciously and started to speak, but the waitress interrupted to take their orders.

When she left, Tracy changed the subject. "The invitations are out. We've got a great lineup for the Silent Auction. The program's been sent to the printers. I think we've just about got the big evening wrapped up."

"What about the catering?"

"I found a new service that's just starting out. Two women—and they really can cook. I sampled the menu. Anyway, they've given us a deal in return for publicity."

"What about the publicity?"

"Two different articles are due to run this week and next. And—the society editor's writing us up in her column. She was one of Carol's sorority sisters in college. I suggested Carol renew their friendship." She grinned smugly. "I'm giving your president a crash course in pushiness. After all, I learned at the feet of a master."

"I'm sure she's grateful for your counsel and advice."

"Well, I don't intimidate her like Grannie does. So she can accept my suggestions better."

Elizabeth laughed and shook her head. "Sometimes you frighten me a little, Tracy. I'm just glad you're on CCE's side."

"Oh, I didn't do all this work just for the coalition. You know why I got involved." Her look was arch.

Elizabeth decided to play dumb. "It *was* sweet of you to help your father."

"Daddy?" Tracy giggled, then said rather thoughtfully, "Well, you could say I was also coming to Daddy's rescue."

"I've been worried lately. You're doing too much."

"If I didn't have the gala, I'd be bored to tears. Besides, your committee was floundering without me."

Elizabeth decided to let that one pass, trying hard to stay noncommittal.

Tracy picked up on her reticence. "Oh, I know you can't gossip about board members. I'll stop trying to lead you astray." She sent Elizabeth a wicked glance. "And leave that to my father. Now, I wouldn't mind any tidbits of information you might be willing to share on how you two are progressing."

Just how much did Mac's daughter already know?

"That's not a loaded question, is it, Tracy?" Elizabeth smiled to soften any censure the other might feel. "Is pumping me the reason for our lunch today?"

"Do we need a reason?"

"No, of course not."

Yet from Tracy's expression, Elizabeth knew the question had troubled her.

"Elizabeth?" The note in Tracy's voice had changed. "You won't hurt him, will you?"

"Your father? No! I mean...I'll try not to." She paused before adding honestly, "In any relationship there's always the possibility of pain."

"I know. And I don't mean to sound protective."

"It's a daughter's privilege."

"You see, it's just that I love him so much. And he's always been there for me. I don't know how much you know about Karen, my mother."

"Very little."

"I love her, too. But she doesn't have a lot of stick-to-itiveness...if you know what I mean?"

"I think I do."

"Life's little problems always defeat her. In her own way, she was crazy about Daddy. But when she found out marriage wasn't all champagne and moonlight, she opted out. Husband number three has just been sent on his way." Tracy's voice tightened. "You might wonder how falling in love comes so easily for her."

"Tracy, are you sure you want to—"

"Yes. You should know about her. So you'll never consider her a rival."

"I hadn't thought—"

"Not yet. But you will if you meet her. We women can't help wondering."

Elizabeth stared at her clasped hands. "True," she admitted.

"Karen's kept herself looking very youthful," Tracy explained lightly, "with a lot of help from her cosmetic surgeon. She's had liposuction, a tummy tuck and a nose job. Her second face-lift has been arranged for the summer, conveniently scheduled in between men.''

When she noted the troubled look on Elizabeth's face, Tracy asked anxiously, ''Do I sound bitter?''

''More disillusioned.''

''Maybe that's the right word. When Evan had so much trouble a few years ago, Karen opted out of parenthood, too. Oh, we see her every month or so, in between cruises. Although the sightings haven't been so frequent lately. She's resentful because we keep piling up birthdays. They're reminders of how old she's getting. And I doubt Squirt would be forgiven if he called her Grandma.''

Any more than her children would be pardoned for calling her Mom, Elizabeth mused.

Tracy shrugged casually. ''Actually, Evan and I long ago accepted Karen as she is. She can be utterly delightful when she wants to. As long as you don't disturb the cadence of her life or be so selfish as to need her for something.''

''Sometimes—'' Elizabeth watched Tracy carefully ''—that's hard not to do.''

''Yes, it is.'' Tracy blinked once or twice, then made a dismissive gesture. ''Evan's the one who's really suffered from her desertion. He's the sensitive Reynolds. I'm tough like Mary. I guess I hoped...you and Evan have so much in common. I can tell he admires you.''

''I'm certainly available if he ever needs to talk, if that's what you mean. Although I wouldn't presume...'' Elizabeth stopped and began again differently. ''You know, Tracy, I've appreciated the way you and Evan have accepted me.''

''What's not to accept? You're everything Karen isn't. Loyal, dependable—''

"You make me sound like a guide dog."

"Funny."

"A stitch."

"Without a trace of vanity."

"Tracy," she pleaded, "please, leave me some small frailty. I'm not sure I can stand all this sanctification."

"Oh, I'll leave it to Daddy to keep you sinful."

Elizabeth laughed helplessly and decided a change of subject was in order. "What I want to know is, how are you holding up? You look like the heat's getting to you."

"Ugh. It is. The doctor says I have about a month to go. But I'm not sure Squirt agrees with his prognosis." Tracy patted her protruding stomach. "And Allen, the worrywart, is driving me crazy. I've decided those stereotypes of pregnant husbands are true."

"Men can sometimes be more trouble than they're worth," Elizabeth agreed.

"Oh, Allen means well." Tracy perversely came to his defense. "We go to Lamaze class every week. He's the picture of solicitude. But if I told him how I really feel, he'd panic."

"I promise not to panic. Why don't you tell me how you feel?"

"Like a big, fat, ugly cow." Tracy's look settled somewhere to the left of Elizabeth's ear. "And since we can't make love anymore..."

"That makes it more difficult."

"Yes. I feel like a big, fat, ugly, *sexless* cow. All udders and belly. I can't ever seem to get comfortable. I don't sleep at night."

"I thought you looked tired."

"You mean I look awful."

"No. You're just a lady who's very pregnant. Maybe this last month of misery is nature's way of helping us cope with labor."

"I don't know. Sometimes it's like I'm driving down a road, and all of a sudden I realize there aren't any detours. I mean, I can't even backtrack. I'm having this baby whether I'm ready or not."

"I don't think it's possible to prepare for giving birth."

"I try not to be scared."

"It's all right to be frightened."

"I mean, I say to myself, other women do it."

"And other women are anxious, especially with the first."

"That's just it. I don't know what to expect. Karen had cesareans with both of us. After six hours of labor with me, she decided a scar on her stomach wasn't so awful, and she insisted they put her to sleep."

"Everyone's labor is different, I gather."

"Come on, Elizabeth. Six hours is nothing. What if I can't stand the pain, just like my mother?"

"You know, Tracy—" Elizabeth took hold of her hand "—you don't have to prove your courage with this baby. It'll come, no matter what. And Allen will love you both very much. We all will."

"I just don't want to embarrass myself. I don't want people to think . . ." Tracy's voice trailed off.

Elizabeth patted her hand.

Tracy's clung for a moment.

Elizabeth's grip tightened. "Now you sound like me. Listen, we don't give a hoot how you behave. All we care about is that you and Squirt are healthy."

"What if he doesn't have all his fingers and toes?"

"He will. He'll be beautiful."

"Will—would you be there?"

"If you want me."

"J-just to spell Allen. Just in case."

"I'll be there every minute. I have a feeling I'll need to prop up your dad."

"He might be as much trouble as my husband."

"Don't worry. I can handle them both. And I promise, you won't be alone in the hospital, or between now and then. If you need to talk, I make a good listener."

A look of gratitude crossed Tracy's face. She started to speak, when Evan interrupted them.

"Well, I'm happy to see you waited, dear sister."

"Well, dear brother, I'm glad we didn't." Tracy pointedly studied the watch on her wrist. "You said you'd be here by twelve-thirty. Need I remind you, it's almost one?"

"You never miss a chance to nag, do you?"

"I do not nag!"

"Not much, you don't! I feel sorry for Squirt."

"Now listen here, buster..."

"You're bossy, too."

"I am not bossy!"

"You're as bad as Grannie. You even give Dad a hard time. Watch out, Elizabeth, or you'll be next on her list."

"Children, children," Elizabeth said pacifically.

Startled, they turned to her and began to laugh.

Evan's look held a glint she'd come to know.

"Gosh, Elizabeth," he said. "How come you're so lucky? All this and sibling rivalry, too."

"I'll try to bear up under my numerous blessings."

For some reason, her drollery sent Tracy into gales of mirth.

Evan looked concerned. "Has she been like this the whole time?"

"I think she sees irony in the situation."

"What situation?"

"Oh, come on, Evan," Tracy said, fighting for breath. "We all know we arranged this meal with Elizabeth to soften her up, so she'll take pity on Daddy and put him out of his misery. Instead, we're instructing her in the hazards of acquiring a stepfamily."

Evan stiffened. He turned to Elizabeth. "I hope you don't think—"

"Of course, I don't, Evan. You're the only one in the bunch with any tact at all."

"Just as I suspected," Tracy said. "She has a soft spot for you. Now she'll think you don't approve of the match."

"Of course, I approve." He reddened and mumbled, "That is to say...I approve if you do, Elizabeth. I mean, it's what you want that I want. If you know what I mean."

"Yes. And I'm touched by the sentiment—"

"You so eloquently expressed." Tracy accompanied her words with a comical grimace.

"Lay off, Tracy," Evan said abruptly.

Elizabeth thought it wise to create a diversion and embarked on a discussion of Evan's classes. The rest of their meal was spent in relative peace.

As Evan was paying the bill, Tracy asked quietly, "Did you mean what you said before Evan got here?"

"Yes, I did. Call me any time you want."

"Why don't you come by the house after work tomorrow? Invite Daddy, if he's free. It's hot enough to use the pool. And swimming's one of the few things I still do gracefully."

"I'd love to come. With or without Mac."

"It's a date." Tracy stretched to kiss Elizabeth on the cheek. The gesture was unexpected. But Elizabeth recovered in time to return the favor, adding a quick hug for good measure.

Tracy waved and went to her car.

Evan lingered. "Can I come by CCE and pick up that book you suggested on prescription drugs and the elderly?"

"Sure," Elizabeth said. "I'll meet you there."

A short time later, they arrived at the building and exchanged pleasantries with Hope before Elizabeth ushered him into her office.

"I think the book's in one of my desk drawers." She began to rummage.

"Do you have a minute?"

Elizabeth glanced up at Evan's tone to find that his face held a sober expression.

"Yes, of course," she said, ignoring the report that was due. "Have a seat."

After asking Hope to hold her calls, Elizabeth closed the door and settled in her chair as though she had all afternoon.

"I won't keep you long."

She smiled. "You're not keeping me."

"I just wanted to thank you."

"For what?" she asked, surprised.

"Making friends with Tracy."

"You don't have to thank me. She's been an enormous help."

"I know. But, well, just because you're involved with my dad doesn't mean you have to be concerned with his children."

"I don't mind, as you put it, being concerned with Mac's children. In fact, I'm enjoying getting to know you both."

Perhaps now was the time to deal with a matter that had been troubling her. "I just don't want you ever to feel I might come between you and your father. That's the last thing I would want to do."

"Aw, Elizabeth, don't worry. Dad and I are close. Besides, his loving you just works to our advantage. I mean, the more people someone loves, the more love they have to give. Isn't that the way it works?"

For a moment, she had trouble answering. Certainly, the truth of his simple statement touched her profoundly. But she was also discovering just how much she cared for this child of Mac's.

"Yes," she said finally when she saw he looked worried. "Yes, Evan. I'm sure that's how it works."

"I guess that's why I thought I could talk to you about Tracy."

"Tracy?"

"I mean, if you are involved," Evan said hurriedly, "you know, seriously with Dad."

This time his look was questioning.

"It's serious," she admitted.

His grin was broad before he corralled it and assumed an earnest expression. "I think Tracy could use you. She needs a woman to talk to. Our mother's absence has been difficult for her. I don't know how much you've heard about Karen."

"Tracy's talked to me a little."

"Then she's already come to you."

"Yes. And I told her I'm available whenever she needs me."

He was obviously pleased by how she'd handled the matter.

"You see, it's easier on me, being a male," he explained. "I have Dad as a role model. Although sometimes I wonder how I'll ever measure up to his successes."

"I don't think Mac would want that. He'd rather you choose your own path and use an individual yardstick to gauge your accomplishments. I do know he already respects and admires you."

"You think so?" Evan's voice held an eager quality.

"I know so. I also think he believes you're more mature than he was at the same age."

Evan laughed ruefully. "Sometimes I don't feel very mature."

"Sometimes, I don't, either."

"It's hard," he said, "not to have doubts about how good I'll be in my chosen profession. All the training in the world can't prepare us to meddle in people's lives."

"When you were helped, did you feel it was meddling?"

"He—heck, no. But that was different. Now we're talking about my abilities to help someone else."

"A certain amount of self-doubt keeps us honest and humble. Two admirable qualities in our line of work."

"Why?"

"Because then we won't think we know all the answers. We help each person find his or her own salvation."

"I'd never thought of it exactly in those terms."

"I didn't, either. Until I was much older. So see—you're further along than I was at your age."

Evan looked at her slyly. "Am I getting a pep talk?"

Elizabeth laughed, leaned back and folded her arms. "We all need them occasionally. Do you mind?"

"Hell, no. They could get to be a habit. I think I see why Dad's head over heels."

As her look fell away from his, she couldn't control a blush.

"When *are* you going to put him out of his misery?" he asked.

"And I said you were the only one in the family with tact."

"It's just that I'm beginning to believe we all need you."

Her vision blurred momentarily. "It's kind of you to say so."

"No, it isn't. What you see is enlightened self-interest. Besides, we men have to stick together." This time Evan's grin was deliberately provocative. "Putting the make on you was Dad's smartest move in years."

June 5, 1936

Alex, one of my former students, came to see me to-day. He was in the region visiting relatives and took the trouble to ascertain where I was staying. I was very touched by his kindness in coming. We had a lovely chat on the second floor veranda.

I must admit, when I taught Alex years ago, he didn't seem receptive to the lessons I offered. I worried for fear he would fritter away his talents, which I saw as exceptional. I was wrong, however, in my estimation. We teachers take comfort in our fallibility.

I found out today that after a wastrel period, Alex entered college and became a lawyer. Now he has a lovely wife and three blooming children. He told me he wished they had the privilege of being challenged by my tutelage, since teachers capable of inspiring that emotion are rare.

As a boy, he said, he had thought book learning was unimportant. Later, however, he realized how valuable were the lessons I had taught him, not only in grammar and literature, but about life and fortitude. His words were extravagant but moved me deeply, and I had to blink away hasty tears.

I have never asked nor sought gratitude from students. Teaching, I discovered early, is its own reward. I always saw the opportunity to nurture and mold young minds as a great privilege. To see those minds grow and blossom and to know that in some small way I influenced them, has made my life worthwhile.

People have sometimes asked me if I missed bearing children. What a stupid, thoughtless question! Every childless woman feels sorrow at some time in her life.

Yet every pupil I taught became one of my children. For a short while, each was put into my care to comfort and cherish. Isn't that in the end all any parent has?

Only one true sorrow has dominated my existence. Only one regret has gnawed at me constantly.

No, it is more than regret! I must admit to my feelings. I live with an agony compounded of remorse and longing.

I must write the words! They have festered inside me. I was never a wife to the man I loved.

CHAPTER THIRTEEN

AS ELIZABETH STRETCHED lazily on the recliner, water from Tracy's pool cooled on her skin, diluting the sun's afternoon rays. A glass of iced tea beckoned within reach, if only she had the energy to retrieve it.

When Tracy snored delicately from the next lounger, Elizabeth turned her head and took a peek at her companion. Tracy's swollen body was shaded from the heat. Her eyes were closed; her mouth hung slightly open. Her face in sleep evoked a childlike peace.

Satisfied with the scene, Elizabeth turned her face skyward once more and shut her eyes, content for them both to doze into the evening.

A sybaritic life held definite allure.

Elizabeth remembered Mac's swimming pool and decided it only added to his charms. There were all sorts of activities for which a pool could prove useful....

Stretching again languidly, her lips curved into a sensuous smile.

That smile was suddenly covered by a male mouth, cajoling and taking her breath away. She gave in to its gentle demands, beguiled by the onslaught.

Two callused palms slipped over her arms and pinned her wrists to the lounger's hand rests. A solid thigh nudged her hips to one side, and her chair creaked under the added weight. A broad bare chest brushed tantalizingly against her dampened bikini-clad breasts.

Elizabeth opened her eyes to find Mac's face hovering inches away. Her look ventured lower. His swim trunks were snug, and she could see for herself he was semiaroused.

"Behave yourself," she whispered vehemently.

"Sh, you'll wake Tracy up," he murmured, his lips exploring the side of her face. He discovered her ear and dipped his tongue inside it.

She shuddered and let out a drifting sigh. At least, she thought fatalistically, it was the ear away from his daughter.

But Elizabeth was fast losing what willpower she had in reserve.

"Mac, will you stop that?"

"Stop what?"

"You know what."

She tried to free her hands. He held them fast.

"Have I mentioned," he asked softly against the shell of her ear, "that you looked very sexy lying here wearing a satisfied smile and two scraps of cloth? Were you thinking of me?"

"Maybe."

"And what was on your mind?"

She closed her eyes and smiled again, content to bask in his attentions. "That I'm glad there's more than one pool in the family. I hadn't realized till now all their possibilities."

"Many more than a tub?"

"Mmm-hmm." The purring sound came from deep in her throat.

His lips wandered to her shoulder and sampled sun-warmed skin. Taking her strap in his teeth, he tugged on it gently.

She stiffened. "Don't you dare, Mac Reynolds. This is not the file room. Allen should be here any minute."

"Daddy," Tracy muttered as she stirred from sleep and struggled to sit up. "Will you stop nibbling on Elizabeth? I have a perfectly good dinner prepared and waiting."

A strained look appeared on his features.

"If that's the case, I'd better take a few laps to work up an appetite." He slipped from the chair and plunged into the pool.

With a grin, Tracy watched his precipitate actions. "Serves him right for canoodling in front of his grandchild. What will the baby think?"

She turned, asking Elizabeth innocently, "And what did you mean about the file room just now?"

Elizabeth stood hastily and shrugged on her toweling robe. "I'll go set the table."

"I'll come with you."

Tracy vainly tried to rise from the low-slung lounger. "Ugh. You're going to have to help me. I'm like a beached whale."

Elizabeth offered a hand for Tracy to pull herself up with and stayed close as she ponderously made it up the flights of stairs.

"Are you supposed to be climbing like this?" she asked at one point, steadying Tracy's elbow.

"No. But I'm sick and tired of always doing what I'm supposed to. And _ m tired of everybody getting on my case." Tracy's tone was truculent. She wore a mutinous expression.

Elizabeth wisely decided to let the matter lie.

But Tracy wasn't ready to. As they went inside the house, she asked, "Aren't you going to scold me for being a bad girl?"

"I'm not in the scolding business."

Easy tears began to slide down Tracy's cheeks, startling Elizabeth with their sudden appearance.

"See how terrible I am?" Tracy mumbled. "I bite Allen's head off. I snap at you."

"It's okay." As soon as Elizabeth appraised the situation, she took Tracy into her arms and patted her consolingly. "We all understand how hard the ninth month is. Don't worry about me. My hide is tough."

Tracy let out a chuckle in the midst of a sob. "I bet that's not what Daddy thinks."

Elizabeth pulled away slightly.

"Now listen here, young lady," she said with mock sternness.

Giggling again, Tracy nuzzled her face into Elizabeth's robe. "You're nice, d'you know that? Make Daddy tell you that at least once a day."

"I'll speak to him about it."

"No, I will."

"Tracy."

"Tracy what?" Allen asked as he strolled into the room. When he saw Elizabeth comforting Tracy, his expression grew alarmed.

Elizabeth shook her head quickly, her look an unspoken signal.

Allen seemed to read it correctly, because he went over and relieved Elizabeth of her armful, kissing Tracy's brow as he pulled her close.

"What's the matter?" he asked. "Is Squirt being obstreperous?"

"Squirt's mother is." She burrowed into his embrace.

Leaving the kitchen quietly, Elizabeth went to summon her frustrated lover, who'd emerged from the pool and was toweling himself dry.

He really was a magnificent specimen, she decided as she approached him. A big man in every sense of the word, with a large frame, muscular shoulders, solid thighs and well-defined calves.

Yet for all his size, he moved with an economy of motion and an air of male grace she found hard to resist. If he had an ounce of fat, she couldn't detect it, in spite of the fact he said he had to watch what he ate.

Since they'd started going to bed together, he'd come up with novel exercises to fight the battle of the bulge.

Interestingly enough, Elizabeth had gained weight. Being fed by Mac on a regular basis had something to do with it. But she decided the five pounds she'd put on were more probably the result of love.

"Now what are you grinning about?" he asked as soon as he got a good look at her expression.

She assessed him slowly. "I was just thinking I really caught a big one."

"You're not considering throwing him back?"

"Nope. Not a chance. This one's a keeper." Settling her hand on his furry chest, she gave him a circumspect peck on the chin.

He laid his hand over hers and asked insistently, "Does that mean what I think it does?"

"Maybe." Elizabeth let her lashes fall to her cheeks.

"Do you know," Mac said menacingly, "what punishment I reserve for coy females?"

"Pooh. You don't scare me."

"Just wait till I get you at home alone."

She wriggled her eyebrows. "As long as I get a moonlight swim as part of the punishment."

"Are you propositioning me and my pool?"

"Yes."

"I accept," he said promptly, and was about to put his hand to interesting use when he tensed and pulled away. "Damn, this place is too public."

Elizabeth turned to find that Tracy and Allen had appeared on the upper patio and were beckoning to them.

"We'll get back to your proposition later," he said, and gave her a brief but eloquent kiss.

"Is that a promise?" she asked breathlessly.

"Yes. And I mean to extract a few promises, as well."

THREE HOURS LATER, Elizabeth slipped into Mac's swimming pool and moved slowly to the man who waited in waist-deep water, his nude body a shimmering play of reflected light. The stars above were faint against the nighttime glow of the city, but a half-moon hung brightly over their heads. And the gently warmed water, just like Mac's gaze, felt like liquid velvet as it slipped over the sensitized contours of Elizabeth's skin.

"You're overdressed," Mac said when she came close.

He reached around her, deftly unhooked the upper half of her suit, then tossed it onto the pebbled deck. Making for deeper water, he pulled her with him so that the waves lapped at her upper body.

"I thought you might enjoy undressing me."

She clasped her arms around his glistening shoulders. The heat of his body against her wet skin sent a shudder of desire rippling through her.

She arched her breasts into the wall of his chest.

"You have a point," he murmured, reaching the side and bracing against it. He slipped his hands beneath her bikini bottom, pulled her high against him and found her aching nipples with his mouth.

She laughed then gasped with pleasure as he teased and suckled first one, then another, driving her wild with his tongue and teeth.

Instinctively she wrapped her legs around him, so that his jutting erection nudged the thin material between her thighs.

"You're still overdressed."

Pulling away for a moment, Mac worked her suit down until she was as nude as he.

"Mmm, that's better." He grunted his satisfaction, cupped her buttocks with his palms and once more urged her thighs around his waist. "Much . . . much better."

Slowly he eased into her, causing an anticipatory flutter deep inside her belly. The water eddying around their joining licked at her heated desire.

"Is this what you had in mind earlier?" he asked, settling her firmly until she was filled with his sex.

"Yes . . . ah . . . something . . . like this."

Holding on with one hand, she lay back buoyant, staring at the moon, dazzled by the sensations of liquid passion.

All the while, Mac roamed her torso. He nipped at her breasts with teasing fingers. He spanned her waist and rocked her against him. One hand delved into her triangle of hair and began to pleasure her swollen nub.

She felt herself tightening. An inchoate sound welled in her throat.

"Mac. . . ."

"Yes. Let it happen," he urged her intently.

His caresses beckoned her. Their watery bed rocked her. The bright white moon kissed her skin.

"Mac!"

The throbbing came fast and over and over until she lay limply cradled by Mac and the whispering waves.

When he pulled her to him, she clung to his neck.

His thrusts came into her harder and harder.

"God, it's hot inside you," he moaned through labored breaths. "So good. So tight. We fit…so well…."

"Yes, oh, yes…." She sighed against his hair.

Yet again, her body began the instinctive flexing. Her nails dug into his rippling back.

Then there were no words.

Only a wild communion that culminated in cries of ecstatic completion.

Their joined bodies sank to the bottom of the pool.

Seconds later, they broke the surface of the water, laughing and choking. Mac tried to stand and they both toppled over, again sinking below the waves. Finally, he righted himself, lifted her under the knees and back, secured her against his chest and plowed toward the steps leading out of the pool.

"Where are we going?" she sputtered, her arms tight around his neck.

"To dry land. I've just been reminded I'm not a fish. If we go on like this, we're liable to drown."

"Oh. Okay." She smoothed away a curl that trickled water down his forehead and brushed her lips along his temple. "It was fun, though, wasn't it? I'd like to add moonlight swims to our permanent repertoire."

"Permanent?" he asked, his look meeting hers.

"Insistent, aren't you?"

"On the contrary. I've been remarkably patient." By this time, he'd stepped out of the pool. Now, without stopping for them to towel off, he made his way into the house.

"Mac, we'll ruin your carpet."

"To hell with the carpet."

She realized he was taking her straight to his room.

"We'll get your sheets all wet."

"No, we won't," he assured her, ignoring the bed and heading directly for the bath.

Only when he put her down to turn on the spigots in the shower did she understand his purpose. As soon as the stream drifted out and over them, Elizabeth realized she was chilled as well as damp.

"You have the most marvelous ideas." Stepping inside the enclosure, she let the water sluice over her.

"You're hogging." He stepped in behind her and plastered his body along her length. She leaned against him, enjoying the prickles of heat tingling her skin.

They stood that way for several minutes.

Then insidiously Mac's hands began to mimic the liquid sheets that outlined her hills and plains and valleys. She could feel him grow hard and press against her backside.

"You're insatiable," she murmured as he turned her around.

"Yeah. Aren't you glad?"

"Yeah." She laughed.

He silenced her with his lips. The kiss they shared was wet and hot and steamy.

"Mac," she got out finally, "I don't know how to make love in a shower."

"Just watch," he whispered.

His hand slipped down her thigh, lifted it and rubbed the sensitive inner skin along his furry leg.

"Do I just get to watch?" she asked as she clutched him tightly.

"You can join in if you want."

Without another word, Mac lifted her slightly, pinned her against the tile and thrust himself between the juncture of her legs. Male flesh nuzzled female flesh with an erotic friction. Yet he stopped short of entering her, as if waiting for an answer.

"I...want..." she whispered, already dazed with need.

"What do you want?"

"You—inside me."

"Enough to marry me?"

Her eyes rounded and she stared into his. They held a sensual gleam. He smiled at her lazily. But she glimpsed more than her own passion reflected in his face.

"I thought..." She tried to settle herself down on him, but he wouldn't let her. "I thought you were against using lust as a tool of persuasion."

"A desperate man uses any tool he can find."

"And are you desperate?" she asked, and hitched one foot around him.

"You could say so," he muttered.

She insinuated herself closer.

"Elizabeth!"

"I'll marry you."

"When?"

"Whenever you like."

"Good," he said shortly.

His look intensified.

"This is what I'd like." He drove up into her.

Her eyes widened with the shock of pleasure.

"Watch me love you, Elizabeth." He held her gaze steadily.

As their love and need and want and hunger flashed in each other's eyes, they coupled hard and fast...and climaxed with a raw passion.

Minutes later, pleasantly exhausted, they lay dry and warm between his sheets. He pulled her to him so they were skin to skin.

With a lusty sigh, he hauled one of her thighs over his belly. "I'm going to have to go into training if we plan to keep up the water sports."

"They say, with athletes, the legs are the first to go."

Laughter rumbled in his chest. "Just as long as the major organs stay in working order."

"I'd say one of them works just fine. In fact, I really think we had better marry quickly. Since we haven't used birth control, I may already be pregnant."

His fingers stilled where they had delved into her hair.

"I'm sorry," he said after a moment. "I should have explained that first time we made love why I didn't use a condom. I've had a vasectomy."

She stiffened, trying to assimilate his words, and suddenly needed a large gulp of air. Rising to her knees, she stared at him blankly. "A vasectomy?"

"Yes." He smiled as if to reassure her.

"I—I didn't realize. I must be stupid."

"Just inexperienced. So, you see, you don't have to worry about a shotgun wedding." He reached for her hand. "However, I'm all in favor—"

"Worry? Worry!" She jerked away from his grasp, panting for breath. "When—when was it done?"

"After Evan was born. Karen didn't think—"

"Karen did this to you?"

Sitting up Indian fashion, Mac studied her face. "Karen didn't do anything to me. It was my choice, as well." One of his brows lifted ironically. "If you're concerned about performance . . . ?"

"I don't give a damn about performance!"

He smiled faintly. "That's not what you said a minute ago."

His look beckoned her to come back into his arms. Still on her knees, she skittered away from him.

"A minute ago? I don't care about then."

"Elizabeth—" he paused and watched her closely "—what's the matter?"

"You mean, why am I upset? I'll tell you why. I want to have a baby!"

She could see the shock of her confession washing over him in waves.

"A baby? My God! Why didn't you tell me?"

"I didn't think you'd have a problem with it."

"Elizabeth, I'm forty-six years old."

"Plenty of men become parents after they're forty. Women, too. I still have time."

"Time has nothing to do with it. I have two grown children."

"Well, I don't!"

Unfair! It was so unfair!

"Do you know how much I've longed for a baby?" Her voice as she tried to explain had a strange intensity. "For as long as I can remember. It's one of the reasons I got engaged."

"Getting married to have children isn't a very good basis—"

"Don't preach to me, Mac! Just shut up and listen."

She heard her note of hysteria and tried to calm down. "Everything changed when my parents became ill. My whole life was taken up with caring for them. But later, when I was alone—" she shrugged helplessly "—I even considered having a child artificially. In the end, I couldn't go through with it. Because I knew that wouldn't be fair to the baby. Not having a father."

"No child," he said roughly, "should be deprived of a parent."

"I know. I know." She flung out her hands. "But when I fell in love with you, I thought . . . it seemed so right. I . . . I was planning to get pregnant as soon as we married. Mac—I detour by the nursery every day at work. I was even jealous of Tracy when I first met her.''

"I'm sorry. I wish you'd shared this with me." He shook his head helplessly. "I didn't know."

"You do now." She wiped at the tears that had begun to fall. Her hand stilled on her cheek, and she stared at him again. This time her look held eager excitement.

"It's okay." She leaned forward. "We can have it reversed."

"Twenty years have gone by."

"But now the procedure is much more sophisticated. What with microsurgery to repair the damage, the success rate is climbing."

She covered his arm with beseeching fingers. "I realize results aren't guaranteed, but it's worth a try."

"Guaranteed? For Pete's sake, Elizabeth!" Mac's burst of laughter was brief and harsh. "The odds in my case would be less than fifty-fifty. How would you handle it if surgery's not successful? Would you feel I'd failed you?"

"Right now we don't have to worry about that. . . ." Her voice died out.

There was a tense moment of silence. A controlled look slipped over Mac's features.

"I don't think I want to attempt a reversal."

Even though she had an intimation of what was coming, his evenly spoken statement still hit her like a blow.

"Not—" she searched his face frantically "—not even for me?"

"Elizabeth, I can't make up for what you've lost in your past. All I can do is offer you a future."

"What good is a future between us," she blurted out, "if I can't have a child?"

As soon as she spoke the words, she covered her mouth with her hand. Still, she was glad, *glad* she'd said it! An unreasoning resentment simmered inside her.

She'd tried to make him understand, but he refused to listen. Couldn't he see how much this meant to her?

"Elizabeth...." His voice was calm, although his face was grim. "You're not being entirely rational right now."

Rational?

His use of that word was the final blow.

She scrambled from the bed and grabbed for her overnight bag, the one she'd packed this morning when hope was young.

"Please, wait. I shouldn't have said that." His voice tightened. "Don't run away from me."

"I'll dress first," she assured him, and rushed into the bathroom.

"We have to talk. We have to listen to each other."

She shut him off by slamming the door.

When she came out moments later, he'd shrugged into his clothes. She tried to brush by him, but he forcibly detained her.

"You're not leaving until we've sat down quietly and worked out an understanding of the problem."

"Oh, I understand perfectly. You're willing to have a discussion if I see your side. But what about *my* side?"

"I thought we shared a common purpose."

Pain welled in her throat and almost choked her. "I thought we did, too."

Breaking away, she rushed through the door.

"Elizabeth, dammit! Don't go like this."

He caught up to her and twirled her around, grasping her shoulders.

They faced each other, both breathing heavily.

"Let me get this clear," he said, struggling with anger and frustration. "You're saying my love's not good enough unless I service you with a child."

"And how much is your love for me worth? Answer me, Mac. How much do you really care about my happiness? You've already implied you see my needs as inconvenient and irrational."

"Needs?" He fairly shouted. "From here, these needs of yours look like an obsession."

"How dare you say that!"

"I'm sorry," he said instantly. "I went too far." He took a deep breath. "But Elizabeth—sweetheart—you're scaring me to death. Just for a moment, hear me out."

His voice grew pleading. "I love Tracy and Evan dearly. But I spent ten long, hard years as a single parent. I need to be free of that kind of responsibility. That part of my life is over and complete. Now I want you as my wife. I need a friend. A companion. A partner. A lover. There's so much for us to share. So much I want to give you. Please, don't do this to us. Don't make our happiness conditional."

As she stood rigid in his grasp, his entreaty beat against her rage.

"You talk about giving," she said at last, raggedly. "Yet you won't grant me the one thing to make me complete."

"What if I can't!"

"You're not willing to try!"

His hands fell away from her and dropped to his side. "Don't you see what you're saying? That the love we share isn't enough to complete you. Is bearing a child the only way for you to prove you're a woman?"

"No! I—I don't know. You're trying to confuse me."

"Dammit! I'm trying like hell to understand. What would you have done if I hadn't come along? Have you asked yourself that?"

"I'm not sure." She turned away, refusing to look at him. "Having no one to love was getting harder and harder...."

"But you have me to love now. And Tracy and Evan. They need you—"

"No! It's not the same. I want a child of my own."

"A person isn't like a possession, Elizabeth."

"Stop!" she cried and covered her ears with her hands. "You're twisting my words. Please, just let me leave. I need time alone."

"How much time?"

"I—can't say. I have to get use—I'd made so many plans. It meant so much..." She pushed him away. "Just let me *go!*"

He heaved a deep sigh and moved away from her slowly. "Okay. I can see we're not getting anywhere. But promise me we'll try to work through this when we're both calmer."

She shook her head. "I can't make promises."

"Elizabeth...this is crazy." He reached for her again.

"Don't touch me! I couldn't bear..." Her voice broke into pieces.

"For me to hold you." Mac completed her words with a bleak finality. "I understand."

He stepped aside in a curiously formal gesture.

She burst into sobs and rushed out of his house.

THE DRIVE HOME took much longer than usual. She had to keep stopping on the shoulder as, again and again, her tears overwhelmed her.

Pain. So much pain. She felt as if she'd been stripped and beaten. Even her flesh seemed raw and hurting.

She sought refuge in her bed like a wounded animal. But even her sheets carried the faint scent of Mac.

If only she had someone. To go to.

Who understood her emptiness.

Struggling upright, she reached for the final diary, where it lay on the bed stand.

The entries were becoming more difficult to read because the last few years they recorded held a dreary sameness. Sarah Elizabeth had noted the comings and goings of the home with a growing detachment.

Now...somehow...the other woman's painful endurance became a beacon to her own.

For so many years they'd both repressed their longings....

October 2, 1958

I saw Mama today outside my Room. I met her in the Hallway. She was Weeping. Is Papa sick? I asked her. But she wouldn't answer.

Perhaps she is Angry. Perhaps she's found out about Johnny. He sent me a Letter. I am Certain he did, for I know he is coming. He Promised me I had only to ask him. He said we would be Together. Why hasn't he Returned? It's so hard to Remember....

The widest land doom takes to part us....

There are Strangers all around me. They ask Questions I cannot answer.

Everyone is Dead.

Mama. Papa. Mr. LeBow.

I sent Johnny Away....

I sent him to Die....

CHAPTER FOURTEEN

OUTSIDE, THE EARLY MAY morning was gray and muggy. Later, the sun would scour away the clouds, but for now the air had a turgid quality. Elizabeth felt the weight of it as she sat alone at her desk.

Although it was early, Hope's office teemed with activity. Board members with ticket sales arrived and departed. Auction items were being sorted and labeled. And Carol was on her way over to put the programs together.

With CCE's gala only days away, anticipation had gripped the entire building.

Except for Elizabeth.

Behind closed doors, she was hiding out.

Hope had agreed to corral chatty board members as well as coordinate the fevered preparations. She'd also promised to take charge of Carol when she came.

Thank God for Hope. She'd taken to hovering unobtrusively, picking up the slack in a dozen little ways. Without her, Elizabeth didn't think she could make it through each day.

Only six hours to go.

She'd been counting off time like this for two long, dreadful weeks.

Since the night she'd driven home from Mac's house.

A night she'd relived over and over.

She wasn't sleeping. When she'd seen herself in the mirror, she'd looked gaunt and bruised around the eyes. Sometimes she wandered her house at night as though she were searching for something.

A small, mournful sound echoed through the room, and Elizabeth realized it came from deep in her throat.

She took a sip of coffee and discovered it was tepid.

How long had she sat staring at the skin of cream that had settled on the surface? She pushed away the cup and rose from her desk.

When she went to the window, she saw Mac's car.

Instinctively, she backed against the wall, clutched the top of a chair and sat down slowly, waiting for the spasm to subside in her gut.

Since that night she'd neither seen nor heard from him. He'd been by the building several times to check on his crew. But he never lingered. And the business side of the renovations had been conducted through Carol or Herb.

Did she have the courage to seek Mac out? Now? Today?

If they met face-to-face, what could she say to him?

That she regretted the hurtful words she'd hurled at him? That she'd been too shattered to stay and discuss things calmly? That she'd run away because she was as frightened as he? Frightened by the yawning chasm between them.

Yet part of her fear lay in facing herself. And how she'd led her life these past several years.

Wanting a child was instinctive and primal. It wasn't wrong, she told herself again and again. But somewhere along the way the wish had grown into a fantasy. A fantasy that consumed her. A way to escape the loneliness she felt inside. When Mac said she was obsessed, he wasn't far wrong.

And oh, dear God, it was hard to relinquish that fantasy, as long as a band of resentment and longing squeezed her heart dry.

Since that night she hadn't been able to shed a tear. Her chest felt tight with unresolved emotions. Sometimes she felt as if she could scarcely breathe.

Staring back out the window, she saw that Mac's car had vanished.

The office walls seemed to close in around her, making her feel trapped and claustrophobic. She rushed from the room.

"Hope, I'm going for a walk. Be back in a while."

Without further explanations, she headed out the door.

She'd just passed the conference room when she heard muffled crying.

Elizabeth stopped. Turned. The sounds came from behind the door, which was slightly ajar.

For a long moment, she closed her eyes and stood there, wondering if she was capable of rendering aid and comfort.

In the end, her question was a moot one. She could no more walk by than she could fly.

Shoving her own troubling thoughts to one side, she cracked the door and peeked inside. Mary stood facing a wall, her shoulders slumped forlornly.

Elizabeth stepped into the room and closed the door behind her. When it creaked noisily, Mary's back stiffened.

"It's just me," Elizabeth said, walking to her side. "What's wrong. Can I help?"

Mary frantically wiped at her eyes. "You mustn't let anyone see me like this. Mary Clark Reynolds does not break down in public."

"Mary Clark Reynolds has a right to cry the same as anyone else does. What happened?"

Mary hesitated. She seemed to be searching for a reserve of dignity. When the search proved futile, she admitted in a rush, "Herb's just driven off in the car. I don't think he's coming back."

"He left you?"

She nodded. "We came for the task force on community outreach. After everyone had gone, we started talking, and suddenly the talk became a fight."

"There's a lot of that going around," Elizabeth muttered. "Look—" she paused "—you want to get out of here? We could both use some air."

Mary's lack of answer signaled her consent.

Elizabeth returned to the door, opened it a crack and peered out into the hallway, feeling like a truant schoolgirl. Glancing back to Mary, she saw the other woman had regained a modicum of composure, although her face still bore witness to her recent tears.

Elizabeth signaled for her to follow, and they made their escape.

"There's a neighborhood park a couple of blocks down the road," Elizabeth said as they reached the sidewalk. "That's where I was headed. I'm not very good company right now, but you're welcome to come along."

"I might as well," Mary said wryly. "I seem to have lost my ride."

The two women walked to the park in silence. When they arrived, the playground equipment was deserted.

Their glances met and each registered the other's discouraged expression.

Something seemed to spark between them, and giggling like idiots, they beat a path to the swings. In a minute, two grown women in high heels and hose were swinging back and forth madly.

"Oh my goodness," Mary panted as she slowed herself at last. "I haven't done this in forty years. No, make that sixty."

"It may become part of my weekly schedule. Monday lunch. Stroll to park. Swing like a monkey and howl at the sky."

"Why howl? No. Don't answer. It was a stupid question. I know you and my son had a terrible fight."

Both women stared across the grassy expanse.

"You know," Mary said, "it's your fault Herb and I argued."

"My fault?"

"Yours and Mac's."

"Oh."

"Herb used your quarrel as an excuse for a confrontation. He said he was tired of waiting for me to make up my mind. He pointed out that the strategy hadn't worked for Mac."

"And that's when you began to fight?"

"No. That's when he launched into this speech he'd prepared. He said I might be comfortable with the status quo, but he couldn't continue. I quote, 'I'm an old-fashioned man, with old-fashioned values. I want to marry the woman I love. If that's not on your agenda, I want to know now so we can go our separate ways before we get hurt any further.' In other words, he issued an ultimatum."

"And how did you respond?"

Mary looked over at her. "Are you sure you're up to a blow-by-blow account?"

Elizabeth knew she'd already committed herself when she'd walked into the conference room. "I'll be glad to listen, if it'll help you think things through."

"It might." Mary sighed. "You asked me how I answered. I said the first thing that came into my mind. That I didn't like being dictated to."

"I see."

"And then he—he made rather a point of explaining that that was the trouble. I wanted to be the one who dictated the terms."

"That was a pretty harsh statement for him to make."

"But accurate." She looked Elizabeth straight in the eye. "Let's face it, I'm nothing but a bossy, selfish old woman who wants to have her cake and eat it, too."

"That's not true," Elizabeth protested. "You're a generous person who's spent the last twenty years helping other people."

"On my terms—as Herb would say. Face it, Elizabeth, I'm the one who decides the degree of my involvement. And when I want to disengage, I take off on a trek to the Himalayas."

"Is it so bad to find a way to be useful?"

"Herb would say I've made it my life. That wasn't how it all began, you know. When Greg died and my children were grown, I was looking for some way to channel my grief. I wanted badly to stand on my own. I was so concerned about becoming a dependent, whiny old lady."

"I don't think there's any danger of that happening."

"No. Herb says it's my whole problem. I have to be in control because I'm so afraid I'll lose my precious independence. He says I won't let myself care for people to the point of needing them.''

"You care fiercely.''

"In the abstract. In the interest of one of my causes.''

"Oh, come on, Mary. That's absurd. You love your children, your grandchildren.''

Mary looked at her. "I've grown very fond of you.''

"It's mutual,'' Elizabeth said, touched by her words.

"So shall we consider ourselves best friends? Because right now I could use one. I feel so alone.''

Elizabeth knew what she meant.

"We're bosom buddies,'' she countered lightly. "And as your buddy, I'm asking . . . how do you feel about all Herb said?''

"I can't deny any of it. I haven't let myself lean on anyone since Greg died. I insulate myself with appointments and speeches. My calendar's filled for weeks ahead. I always have something more to be doing. Or a trip to plan. Although, lately, I've found myself more and more detached. I feel like I'm burning out.''

"Maybe projects and trips aren't enough anymore.''

"Perhaps. The awful part is, Herb's wrong about one thing. I'm in love with that dirty old man. I can't bear the thought of living my life without him. But I'm scared to say yes. When he told me I had to make a choice, I panicked and lashed out at him. Now that I've made a mess of things, what am I going to do?''

The irony of Mary's question struck Elizabeth forcibly. "I'm not sure I'm the person to offer advice.''

"Perhaps you are. I've felt a kinship with you from the first time we met.''

"Well, I could repeat a lecture a good friend once gave me.''

"Did it do any good?''

"For a while." Elizabeth sighed and gazed down at her shoes. "Before Mac and I realized we wanted different things from each other."

"Just like Herb and me. Do you know Herb's the first man I've gone to bed with since Greg?"

Despite their buddy status, Elizabeth squirmed uncomfortably with the new topic of discussion.

"For heaven's sake, Elizabeth, don't blush," Mary said. "If I can't admit it to you, who can I admit it to? Do you think I don't know we're in the same boat?"

Elizabeth had to laugh. "Yeah, and the boat's sprung a leak."

Mary laughed, too. Her expression lightened. "I'll tell you a secret, but if you ever repeat it..."

"Mary!" Elizabeth was indignant. She spoiled the effect with a cheeky grin. "Your secret's safe with me. Cross my heart and hope to die."

"After Greg," Mary said confidingly, "I didn't think another man could stir me. Oh, I swoon over Kevin Costner. What female doesn't? But never anyone I'd actually met."

Her tone grew smug. "That's not to say I haven't had a few offers. But Herb was different. He knocked my hose off. It was such a novelty, I said, why not? I thought having an affair would be like a cruise down the Amazon. Just another adventure. How was I to know we'd fall in love?"

"But it seems to me, falling in love would be the greatest adventure of all. You told me to be open to life experiences."

"An Amazon cruise takes less than a month."

"I see. And falling in love—"

"Is the risk of a lifetime."

"Mary—you just admitted you can't bear the thought of living without Herb. You told me to risk. You have to risk, too."

"Most people don't know Herb has angina."

"Are you afraid he'll die on you? We all face death. You could keel over tomorrow."

Mary's look had a sheepish quality. "Herb said it would be his luck to outlive me. He had such a difficult time when his first wife died."

"Well, then, Herb's not chicken. He's willing to make himself vulnerable."

"Are you?" Mary asked.

"We're not talking about me."

"Perhaps we should be. You and Mac are so good for each other."

"Please, I don't think I can talk about it."

"I thought you were doing so well," Mary pressed.

"We were," she admitted. "But it seems our lives don't match as well as we thought."

"I know you've been through a lot. Just as Mac has."

The way Mary said the last caused Elizabeth to look up sharply.

"I never will forget," Mary said, "the day he had to commit Evan to the treatment center. Evan was strung out and denying he even had a drug problem. When he found out what Mac planned to do, he went into a rage. Told Mac he hated him. Said he never wanted to see him again. Can you imagine how that must have made Mac feel?"

"I don't think I can," Elizabeth said huskily.

"But Mac held on to his resolve and signed Evan in. He went back the next day and the next until Evan would see him. They reconciled and went into family therapy, but even then the road back was rough. Unlike Karen,

Mac's never avoided his problems. And the problems of single parenthood are almost impossible to imagine. He's due some freedom and happiness. That's why I'd hoped . . . Surely whatever's happened—''

Mary's words shook Elizabeth badly.

"You don't understand. . . ." Her voice broke, and she had to take a deep breath. "We might have set ourselves up to fail each other."

"Is it the children? The place they hold in his life?"

Mary's question was close enough to the truth to make Elizabeth flinch.

Seeing her reaction, Mary asked anxiously, "Surely you can appreciate how he feels about them? He's been their only real parent—''

"Of course I understand. . . . I would never begrudge—''

"Tracy's very upset. She thinks she put too much pressure on you."

"No, no, she's a lovely child. The problem isn't Tracy or Evan. I—I'm very fond of them."

"They're fond of you, too. In fact, I'd hoped— Both of them could use some maternal affection." Mary sighed faintly. "A grandmother's not the same. Especially not a globe-trotting grannie."

"I know." And Elizabeth had encouraged them to come to her. To trust her. To depend on her.

What an awful mess she'd made of her love.

Mary leaned toward her. "Surely whatever's happened—'' She stopped in midsentence. The color left her face and she turned away blindly.

When Elizabeth glanced around to find the cause of Mary's reaction, she noticed a familiar car parked at the curb.

Herb climbed out of it and headed toward them.

"Go on," Elizabeth urged softly, her own problems momentarily forgotten. "Don't be afraid to meet him halfway."

Mary stood. She began the walk haltingly before her stride gained confidence.

As Elizabeth watched, the figures approached each other, stood for a moment, then dissolved into one.

She didn't need to hear the words being spoken. The lovers' reunited bodies told the whole tale.

After a long moment, she rose from the swing and began to skirt around them, not wanting to intrude on the tender scene.

"Elizabeth," Mary called. "Let us drive you back to the center."

"No." She made a gesture of dismissal. "Go away, both of you. You need to be alone."

"Are you sure?" Herb asked with Mary penned in his embrace.

"I'm sure."

"Okay," Mary yelled, then sent off a parting shot. "But remember what we talked about. You might find it useful."

Elizabeth shook her head helplessly. "You just remember to take some of your own advice."

HALFWAY BACK to the center, the sun came out, blistering the pavement. Yet when Elizabeth arrived, she was reluctant to go inside.

The talk with Mary had affected her strongly. Dealing with someone else's troubles had brought her out of her self-absorption. But the echoing themes of the two arguments left her feeling exposed.

And the final scene she'd witnessed had moved her deeply. She knew she held her emotions barely in check.

When she saw Joe weeding his garden, she approached him, grateful for the respite he offered.

He looked up and bestowed a smile upon her.

"It's hot out here," she said. "Are you sure you should be working?"

"Weeds love the heat. They'll take over if I let 'em."

"Can I at least get you something cool to drink?"

"No'm, I just refreshed myself." He pointed to a half-gallon container and a package of paper cups. "These days my granddaughter makes me a thermos of tea to bring out here."

"Your granddaughter takes good care of you."

"She sure does. And I told her to brew enough to take care of my visitors. Well, most of them, anyway. You look like you could use a little refreshing."

"Thank you, I could." She took the container and a cup, poured some of the cold, lemony liquid and drank thirstily. "Mmm. She makes it just the way I like it."

Taking a break, Joe stretched his back and glanced over her way.

"I was wondering when you were coming out to sit with me again. Haven't seen much of you lately."

"I've been busy. The office has gotten very hectic."

"It always is, Miss Elizabeth. But you shouldn't get so busy you don't take time to replenish your soul."

"Are you scolding me, Joe?"

Although his grin twinkled, his answer was serious. "No. Just looking out for you. Don't seem to be as happy as you were."

"I've had things on my mind."

"Have you and Miss Mary's son had a falling-out?"

Good Lord, did everyone in the building know?

"Joe," she said slowly, "I wish things were that simple."

"Things generally are. We humans are the ones who complicate 'em up."

"Isn't that the truth." Elizabeth stared at the ground.

"She's not happy, either," Joe said without preamble. "Else why would she be here? She comes and visits most every day now."

Who was Joe talking about? Mrs. Moreland?

Then something about Joe's words and the way he spoke them made Elizabeth meet his look with a startled expression. He gazed at her expectantly, yet his look was serene.

"You see her, too," she whispered. "Just as I do."

"Yes'm. Most every day." He smiled and surprised her by saying, "I thought sure you'd met her."

"Then you see more clearly than I. I didn't know she'd appeared to anyone else. I thought at one point I was losing my mind."

"You're not crazy, Miss Elizabeth. Lots of wonders in this world and the next we don't understand. We just have to accept them."

"Like you accepted her coming."

"I figured she had her reasons."

"Yes. She led me to her diaries, which she'd hidden in the floor of her room. Her name is Sarah Elizabeth, and I know why she visits you. She was raised on a farm. I think she feels a kinship for the earth and the people who tend it."

"I figured something like that. She just sits where you are now, watching me work."

"You must bring her peace."

"Yes'm."

"Like you do me."

"She reminds me of you. I knew she wasn't here for any bad purpose."

"She's never asked anything of you?"

"Just my company." He smiled. "And the smell of the dirt as I turn it."

"She wants more from me."

"What?"

"I'm not sure. To undo a tragedy. She and the man she loved spent their lives apart. But I don't know how to change what happened. How can I help her when I can't help myself?"

Elizabeth's look flew to Joe's after her revealing words had been spoken.

But instead of questioning her, he said quietly, "Maybe when you find your way, you'll be able to take care of her."

"Is that why I've failed her?"

"You haven't let her down. You're just struggling with life. Like she did. You don't have to tell me all she went through. I can read her troubles in her face." He paused and sent Elizabeth a penetrating look. "Have you ever thought maybe she came to you for more than one reason?"

"What do you mean?"

"Maybe she doesn't just want something from you. Maybe she feels a bond. Maybe she wants to give something, too."

"Our lives have parallels," Elizabeth said distractedly. "I've felt that bond. Especially these past couple of weeks."

"Just like I figured." He nodded sagely. "I want you to think about it, Miss Elizabeth. Maybe she's come so you don't make the same mistakes."

FOR THE REST of the day, Joe's supposition haunted her. As soon as everyone had left that evening, she hurried upstairs. With the approach of summer, the sun was still high on the horizon.

The slanted rays of light seemed to filter through Sarah Elizabeth's form.

"I didn't know you and Joe had met," Elizabeth said as soon as she felt her. She settled into the chair and sensed more than saw Sarah Elizabeth settle, too.

"I visit him often. He's very restful, isn't he? I have a feeling he's been more comfort than I. I'm sorry I got impatient before."

She said the next words more slowly. "Joe said you've come to help me. Was he right? Is that true?"

The air around her seemed to still expectantly.

"It is true. I feel it." She gazed out into the trees.

"I—I have to ask you something," she began after a long moment. "Remember when your student Alex came to the home? The entry you wrote about having children?

"You said then, 'People have sometimes asked me if I missed bearing children.... Every childless woman feels sorrow at some time in her life.'

"I dreamed of having a baby. I longed to bear one. Even when the dream was out of reach, I only yearned for it more....'" She choked back a sob.

Every pupil I taught became one of my children. For a short while, each was put into my care to comfort and cherish.

"Yes, I know. Mac's children need me. Mac needs me. But I'm afraid I've driven him away as you did Johnny. Because I demanded he give me a child. I let my dream come between me and the man who loves me."

Only one regret has gnawed at me constantly.

"And if I've lost him, I'll always regret it."

No, it's more than regret!

"Mac's no fantasy to cling to as a retreat from loneliness."

I must admit to my feelings.... They have festered inside me.

"He's real, and he's offered me a lifetime together. If I lose him, how will I bear to live each day?"

I live with an agony compounded of remorse and longing.

"I'll hate myself for what I've destroyed. We bring each other joy and passion and fulfillment. I love him. He is the only man I shall ever..."

I was never a wife to the man I loved.

Elizabeth's tears began to fall silently.

Mourning tears for the child she would never bear.

Healing tears washing away anger and resentment.

A rain of tears to cleanse a heart, allowing it to ache again....

When Elizabeth stopped crying, she found Sarah Elizabeth had gone.

THAT NIGHT, Elizabeth spread Sarah Elizabeth's possessions on her table. The diaries, the newspaper clippings, the packet of letters. The books and letter opener Cassie Taylor had given her.

After completing the diaries, she'd examined the clippings. Most of them were written under Johnny's byline.

Sarah Elizabeth was right; he'd been an insightful reporter. She began to know him better through the events he covered, as well as through the letters he'd sent to Sarah Elizabeth, their tone changing subtly as the years had gone by.

But there wasn't a scrap of his correspondence or writing after the death of Mr. LeBow.

What words had Sarah Elizabeth spoken to send him away? Why had a man of self-confidence and decision accepted those words as final?

And what about the unopened, returned letter from Sarah Elizabeth to Johnny, dated two months after Mr. LeBow's funeral?

What were its contents? Why had Johnny sent it back?

Several times, Elizabeth had been tempted to open the envelope. But if Sarah Elizabeth could never bear to unseal it, how could she?

She turned to the books Cassie had given her. Elizabeth knew from Sarah Elizabeth's entries they were gifts from Johnny.

The Twain novels. Dickens's *Great Expectations*. Elizabeth noted the thoughtful comments Sarah Elizabeth had made in the margins.

She browsed through the book on the Eiffel Tower, remembering Sarah Elizabeth's excitement at Johnny's Paris adventure.

Finally she turned to the small poetry volume.

Sonnets from the Portuguese by Elizabeth Barrett Browning. Love poems from a wife to her husband.

Elizabeth's mother had always loved Browning. Elizabeth suspected that was the reason for her name. Her mother and Sarah Elizabeth must have had similar tastes. The book was well-worn.

There was Johnny's inscription. A tear had smudged it. Elizabeth gently brushed over the stain.

As she began to scan the sonnets, she was captured by their beauty. She turned a leaf.

A newspaper clipping had been pressed inside, along with a page of Sarah Elizabeth's script. She'd copied the poem that appeared on that page.

Elizabeth started to scan the lines when she noticed the phrase, ''The widest land doom takes to part us....''

It had been a cryptic inclusion in one of Sarah Elizabeth's last confused entries.

Elizabeth stopped reading silently and began to recite aloud, listening to the words as they spoke to her heart.

''Go from me. Yet I feel that I shall stand
Henceforward in thy shadow. Nevermore
Alone upon the threshold of my door
Of individual life, I shall command
The uses of my soul, nor lift my hand
Serenely in the sunshine as before,
Without the sense of that which I forbore—
Thy touch upon the palm. The widest land
Doom takes to part us, leaves thy heart in mine
With pulses that beat double. What I do
And what I dream include thee, as the wine
Must taste of its own grapes. And when I sue
God for myself, He hears that name of thine,
And sees within my eyes the tears of two.''

CHAPTER FIFTEEN

"I'VE RESIGNED from the board of the coalition."

They were almost the first words Mac had spoken to Elizabeth since he'd escorted her, gowned, groomed and jittery, out to his car.

"I see," she said with admirable control.

"I doubt it," he murmured.

Her control slipped a notch, and she snatched at it. Her eye shadow and liner mustn't run. She'd spent too much time applying them. Not that she considered the results a howling success.

Howling. That's just what she felt like doing. Now she knew why Mac had called and asked if she would be his date for the gala evening.

He'd wanted a moment alone so he could deliver his bombshell. What else had she expected? Or hoped?

"Of course, I'll remain in charge of the renovations," he went on smoothly.

"Yes. Well, I'm sure the rest of the board appreciates your dedication."

"Was that a sarcastic note I just heard?"

The worst part of it was, Elizabeth could detect an undertone of humor in his question.

"Yes," she snapped, and sat stiffly staring through the windshield.

"Are you upset that I didn't come to you before I talked to Carol?"

"Certainly not. The president of the board was the appropriate person to go to. You don't answer to me."

Somehow the last hadn't come out exactly as she'd intended. The lights that whizzed by them were beginning to blur.

"I thought, under the circumstances, it might be better if I discharged my obligations—"

"Of course," she said, holding on to her voice tightly.

"So I could get on with my life."

"Look," she said, frantically trying to halt their conversation, "I don't know all the reasons you've escorted me tonight—"

"We need to talk."

"But if you make me cry, I'll never forgive you."

"Forgiveness might be a good place to start."

"In approximately ten minutes, I have to walk into a crowded room wearing a gracious smile. With my makeup in order. A hundred pair of eyes—"

"At last count, four hundred."

"What do you mean, forgiveness?"

"It can wait. I don't want to smear your makeup."

"How," she wailed, "do you always manage to rattle me?"

Mac pulled into the crescent-shaped driveway in front of the hotel's main lobby, turned to her and said, "Good. You have color in your cheeks. I was beginning to worry."

He took a thumb and delicately wiped away a glistening drop. "And the hint of tears makes your eyes sparkle. You look lovely in that dress. Is it new?"

The doorman opened her door, and she stepped out of the car.

As a matter of fact, the expensive gown was hot off the rack and bought in a moment of insanity. It was teal blue, slinky, with very little back.

Mac came around and took her arm through his.

"You don't think I went too far?" she asked uncertainly.

"Too far where?"

"With the dress. It's not my usual style."

"You've regressed, Elizabeth."

"I beg your pardon?"

"Never mind." His look intensified, and his voice deepened. "If you bought it for me, I entirely approve."

"Mac—" she laid her other hand on his tuxedo-clad arm "—why...why did you bring me tonight?"

He turned and waved at a familiar looking couple. "Because," he said, "if I hadn't, it would have looked damned odd. There were already rumors flying."

"Oh." She braced her shoulders and strode ahead of him.

His voice drifted after her. "And I missed you like hell."

"You did...?" She stopped in her tracks, her heart suddenly pounding.

"And I want us to clear the air," he finished enigmatically.

"So do I," she agreed in a rush.

He'd caught up with her by now. "But not now. Paste on that smile, sweetheart, the performance is about to begin."

With a curiously light heart, Elizabeth obeyed his instructions. As soon as they walked into the ballroom, however, she smothered a gasp.

Mac hadn't exaggerated when he'd estimated the gate.
Close to four hundred people milled about, surveying
the auction items on display, deciding on bids, sampling the hors d'oeuvres, sipping champagne, seeing and
being seen.

She recognized two city councilmen and a county
commissioner candidate pressing the flesh. Nearby, the
district's congresswoman held court.

Austin's mayor bore down on Mac and Elizabeth.
After Mac performed the introductions, Elizabeth
smoothly answered the mayor's questions. Only Mac
knew she held on to his sleeve for dear life.

When had all this happened? she asked herself as Mac
and the mayor chatted. She knew they'd gotten a good
initial response on the invitation mailing. But she'd been
oblivious lately to the tide of acceptances.

Smiling brilliantly, she focused her attention once
more on the two men as they talked.

"Ms. Waite," the mayor said, "I think Capital Coalition for the Elderly is an idea whose time has come.
Someday soon, I'd like to sit down and talk to you in
depth about your various programs."

"I'd like that, too," she assured him.

"Good. Make arrangements with my office. Mac, I'll
see you later."

The mayor walked off, and Elizabeth and Mac continued to float around the room.

Carol, standing by her husband, waved, and Mac
herded Elizabeth toward them.

"Everything's running smoothly," Carol confided as
soon as they got close. "I think we're a smash."

"Darling, you and CCE are the talk of the town."
Lane shook hands with Mac before circling Carol's waist
in a possessive gesture.

Elizabeth could almost see her bask in the glow of his admiration.

"We should make several thousand off the Silent Auction alone. And just wait until we bring on the entertainment." Carol was beside herself with excitement. "Elizabeth, we did it. We really pulled it off."

"You did. You and the board. Lane, I just wanted to tell you how much your wife has meant to me these last few months. I couldn't have made it without her support. I know CCE's taken a lot of her time."

"Time obviously well spent," Lane said, putting his seal of approval on the venture.

"Well, I just wanted to let you know, Carol stepped into Mary's shoes and took off running. I hope as her fame spreads, some other board doesn't grab her."

"Never," Carol vowed. "My heart belongs to the coalition. Which reminds me, have you seen Tracy?"

"Not yet." Elizabeth's pleasure dimmed. She wasn't sure of her reception with Mac's daughter.

"When we do," Mac said, starting to move away, "we'll tell her you want to see her."

"To celebrate," Carol said. "She was a noble assistant. Mac, I intend to nominate Tracy for the board, since you're determined to abdicate. We need at least one Reynolds. Are you sure you won't reconsider?"

"Not a chance."

"Well, under the circumstances, I understand." Carol smiled knowingly at the couple. "Glad to see you're together tonight."

"I rest my case," Mac said after they made their break.

But Elizabeth felt as if she were sinking in quicksand. Tonight could give everyone the wrong idea.

Although her tears of grief and acceptance had blessed her with a sense of peace, nothing had been resolved between them.

Without realizing it, she slowly deflated.

Mac turned, saw her expression and leaned over to ask, "What's wrong?"

"I feel like a fraud."

"Why? Are you here under false pretenses?"

"We are. Together...."

"Elizabeth!" Mary hailed them. "Come sit with us. The show's about to begin."

Mary and Herb stood by one of the large round tables, where Tracy, Allen and Evan were already seated.

Tracy watched the couple's approach in wide-eyed apprehension. Until Mac, with a deceptive ease, looped his arm around Elizabeth's bare back to fit her to his chest.

He couldn't have timed his maneuver better.

Tracy smiled tentatively. For once, Elizabeth was grateful to Mac for taking unilateral action. She leaned into his shoulder and smiled back gamely. She could stick to their impersonation for the evening, at least.

When the lights went down and the audience hushed, Elizabeth and Tracy shared a small, anxious look. The latter had been instrumental in arranging the evening's ensemble entertainment. Elizabeth crossed her fingers that all would go well.

Ten minutes later she relaxed and enjoyed.

Several well-known Austin artists had donated their talents, and the air was filled with a medley of Cole Porter tunes.

In between acts, Herb went to the microphone to announce the winners of the auction. The amount of the bids as he named them brought the requisite oohs and aahs.

Carol was right—CCE would make a killing. Elizabeth couldn't help turning to Mac in glee. She stared when he smiled crookedly, took her hand and brushed it with his lips.

For Tracy. He was putting on a performance for Tracy and Evan.

Yet Elizabeth couldn't bring herself to disengage her fingers. Instead, she allowed herself to luxuriate in the warmth of his touch.

After the auction was concluded, Herb made various introductions. There were even more local bigwigs attending than Elizabeth had counted. She dutifully rose when he called out her name and title.

"I have one more person I'd like to introduce," Herb said finally, beaming out into the audience. "The founder of Capital Coalition for the Elderly. Mary Clark Reynolds. Soon," he said before the clapping could begin, "to be Mary Clark Reynolds Briscoe. Ladies and gentlemen, I'd like to present my future wife."

Herb's announcement brought forth cheers and whistles, then a standing ovation as Mary went to stand beside him.

To everyone's delight, he kissed her soundly.

When Mac's clasp tightened around Elizabeth's fingers, she returned the pressure and glanced over to see how Mary's grandchildren were reacting.

Surprised, she saw immediately that Tracy wasn't happy. Instead, she seemed to be in deep distress.

No, that wasn't distress convulsing her features.

Elizabeth leaned over worriedly. "Tracy...?"

"Will you come with me to the rest room?" she whispered.

Elizabeth nodded, murmured something to the men and followed in the wake of Tracy's faltering gait.

As soon as they made it through the lounge door, Tracy collapsed into one of the chairs. She moaned softly and rubbed at her side.

"I've had these low back pains all afternoon. They seem to be worse."

"Are they coming at regular intervals?" Elizabeth's mouth was dry.

"No, but they're more frequent and harder, and they've come around to the front. Elizabeth, do you think...?"

"I thought you weren't due for a couple of weeks."

"I told you Squirt was impatient. Have I... am I really going into labor?"

Hell, Elizabeth didn't know! She'd never been pregnant, much less been around someone about to give birth. At this moment, she felt woefully inadequate. But as she glimpsed the white line around Tracy's mouth, Elizabeth knew panic wasn't an option.

"We're going to assume you have," she said calmly. "Neither one of us has a watch to time your contractions, and we're not about to sit here dithering for the next twenty minutes."

"What *are* we going to do?" Tracy's voice was uncertain.

"You'll stay here for as long as it takes me to round up Allen and Mac. I'll have Allen call your doctor, then we'll drive to the hospital."

"You don't think we're rushing things?"

Elizabeth smiled faintly. "That's Squirt's prerogative. And since I don't think you want to deliver this baby in the middle of a formal function, I suggest we get you to the hospital, where you can get down to business."

"I guess you're right." Tracy gasped and clutched at her stomach.

"Elizabeth," she panted after a moment, "you and Dad will stay at the hospital in case Allen needs support?"

"Every minute," she assured her. Before leaving, she stroked Tracy's hair back from her dewy brow.

"And don't let anybody else know." Tracy clutched Elizabeth's hand for a moment. "I don't want to disrupt the evening. I worked too hard to make it come off."

"The evening's a smash. And you're about to go on to a greater triumph. Just hold on. I'll be right back."

Hurriedly, she returned to the ballroom to get reinforcements.

Something about her expression must have given her away, because as soon as Allen saw her without Tracy, he stood up wild-eyed.

Mac glanced her way concernedly. Evan looked puzzled. Herb and Mary, who'd returned to their seats, shared an anxious expression.

And as Elizabeth motioned them to follow, the entire table exited en masse.

So much for discretion. Elizabeth would have to get a waiter to deliver a note to Carol explaining their conspicuous departure.

As soon as everyone was out in the lobby, they crowded around.

"Tracy's in the lounge," she announced briefly. "I think she's in labor. Allen, call the doctor while I bring her to the entrance. Mary, come with me. Mac, write Carol a note saying why we left. Evan, have the door-

man bring your father's car around. We'll drive Allen
and Tracy and pick their car up later. Herb, you take
Evan and Mary. We'll form a caravan.''

''Very well-done,'' Mary said as they went to retrieve
Tracy.

''Working at CCE has honed my delegating skills.''

When they hurried into the lounge, Tracy was having
another contraction. The trio had to wait for it to re-
cede so she could get her breath.

The menfolk were pacing outside the lobby doors as
the three women emerged moments later.

Allen bundled Tracy into Mac's back seat. Mac and
Elizabeth scrambled into the front, and Mac pulled out
of the driveway with a roar.

Ten minutes and three traffic violations later, they
pulled into the hospital's emergency entrance. All the
while Tracy and Allen had been whispering comfort to
each other.

At one point, when Tracy had gasped out loud, Elizabeth had glanced Mac's way and noted his grim expression. She'd reached over and patted him consolingly
on the thigh.

The life of a grandpa-to-be wasn't always easy.

Everyone felt relief when the expectant mother was
transferred into professional hands. Then everyone realized there was nothing to do but wait.

And feel helpless. And watch the minutes tick by.

After the doctor arrived and examined Tracy, he came
out to the waiting area where Allen and the rest of the
group were congregated.

''It's going to be a long labor,'' he announced mat-
ter-of-factly, introducing himself as Dr. Cable.

He took in the gowns and tuxedos. ''Well, I've heard
of making this a formal celebration, but I suggest you go

home and get changed for now. There'll be no popping the champagne cork for several hours."

Dr. Cable's quip broke the tension. Elizabeth, however, read a hint of concern into his expression.

"How many hours?" she asked after the humor subsided.

"Hard to say. Tracy's small, and this baby's good-sized. If she gets too tired, we'll do a C-section."

"Tracy doesn't want that," Allen protested.

The doctor nodded his understanding but said noncommittally, "We'll see how it goes. She's ready for you to go in, Allen. Remember," he said to the congregation at large, "if things get hectic, we'll have to cut out the visitors. But for now she can see you one at a time—if she feels up to it."

Allen left the room and came back somewhat later, grinning broadly. "She's doing great. Her contractions have eased off, and she wants to say hello to everybody. While you all keep her busy, Herb can take me to my car so I can run home, get her suitcase and change."

His news didn't encourage Elizabeth as much as it might have. Being a doctor's daughter had lent her some understanding of Tracy's medical situation. And if Tracy was determined to be brave through a difficult labor, it could turn into an ordeal for them all.

Mary, Evan and then Mac went in for their audience.

As soon as Tracy saw her father, she raised her arms, and he bundled her into his.

"You don't look so good, Daddy," she teased against his coat.

"Humph," he grumbled, and pulled up a chair beside her bed. "The question is, how are you feeling?"

"Don't worry about me," she said airily. "Having this baby is going to be a piece of cake. Some women are just cut out to be mothers."

"Oh, really?" He grinned down into his daughter's face while inside he felt aching tenderness. "And how did you decide that you were one of those females?"

"Heaven only knows. I certainly didn't have any obvious role models. I mean, Grannie's wonderful, but she's hardly maternal."

"No." He chuckled.

"And Karen . . ." Her voice trailed off.

He took her hand. "You want me to phone her?"

She looked at him, horrified. "Good Lord, no. She'd drive us all crazy."

Especially Tracy. Mac settled back in his chair.

"So," he said to divert her, "how did you decide you were the maternal type?"

"I've always wanted to have a baby. Ever since I could remember."

Her words, so evocative of Elizabeth's, caught Mac up short.

"Why?" he asked baldly.

"Oh, come on, Daddy." This time the look she sent him was condescending. "The usual reasons. To love, to care for, to cherish. Your trouble is, you've never been around a nurturing woman. Until Elizabeth."

"Yes," he said musingly. "That's a good way to describe her."

"You won't let her out of your clutches, will you? I've been worried I was going to have to step in and take charge." Her tone was light, but he detected a note of anxiety underlying it.

He smiled faintly. "You just take charge and have this baby and leave Elizabeth to me. I'm not going to let her get away."

Tracy grinned back at him. Then her face convulsed with a prolonged contraction.

Alarmed, Mac leaned over her. "Are you all right? Should I call for a nurse?"

"I'm just following your instructions," she panted. Her expression grew abstracted. "I bet Elizabeth wishes she'd had children. Me—I plan on Squirt being the first of several. I haven't decided yet just how many."

"Do you think," he asked grimly, "we could take care of this one first?"

"Daddy—" she smiled tenderly at him "—don't worry, I'll be okay. Don't you see? I don't mind the pain, if it's for a good cause. I'm just impatient to hold Squirt in my arms for the first time."

"Yes." He stared down into her delicate features. "I can see that you mean it. I love you, little one."

"I know. And it's hard for you to watch me hurting. So be a good father and go fetch Elizabeth. I want to see her."

Although she smiled gamely as she said this, Mac knew the last pain had been a sharp one.

His own expression was abstracted as he went to do as she bid.

Elizabeth noted his expression and was surprised to find Tracy waiting for her, a cheerful smile in place.

"You look better," Elizabeth commented as she went to the bedside, "than when I saw you two hours ago."

"I was just scared," Tracy explained as she offered her cheek for a kiss, "because I wasn't sure what was happening. But now I'm in for the long haul. Dr. Cable says it'll be at least tomorrow before Squirt makes an appearance.''

A spasm of discomfort crossed her face.

Elizabeth cautioned gently, ''Relax when you get the chance. Try to sleep if you can.''

''And miss all the fun?'' Tracy asked brightly.

''Just don't expect too much of yourself. Remember that conversation we had.''

''I'll be fine. It was just the waiting.''

''Probably so.'' Elizabeth took Tracy's hand. ''But don't think you have anything to prove. Get help when you need it. Promise me that?''

''I promise.'' Tracy looked at Elizabeth from under her lashes. ''You know, you make a good mom. Anyone would think you're applying for the job.''

Elizabeth laughed and started to place Tracy's hand on the coverlet. The younger woman wouldn't let her.

''Promise me you'll work things out with Daddy?'' she whispered. ''Fair's fair. You extracted a promise from me.''

''Now I know you're feeling better. Emotional blackmail from your labor bed. I'm ashamed of you, Tracy.'' Elizabeth said the last with a teasing grin.

Tracy didn't return it. ''Promise me you'll try, at least,'' she pleaded, rising to her elbow.

''Of course, we'll try,'' Elizabeth said soothingly.

Tracy fell back, sighing with satisfaction, her expression a little too innocent for Elizabeth's peace of mind.

''Just what kind of promise,'' she asked suspiciously, ''did you get from Mac using these tactics?''

''Oh, Daddy already knows what he wants.'' She smiled at Elizabeth serenely. ''You can go now. Everything's going to be all right.''

But by the next evening, they all knew everything wasn't going well.

Tracy was exhausted after twenty-four hours of intermittent labor. And the occupants of the waiting room looked as if they'd been carted in from a graveyard.

No one wore party finery any longer. Evan had taken Elizabeth home early that morning so she could bathe and change. All four men wore a day's growth of beard. And each of them had an owlish stare that came from too much coffee and not enough sleep.

Allen stayed by Tracy's side almost constantly. But each time he was spelled, he seemed less and less in command. Mac's expression had grown grimmer and grimmer. Evan wore a bewildered look as if he couldn't take in what was happening. And for the first time since Elizabeth had known her, Mary wore an air of fragility that accentuated her age. Herb hovered nearby, looking endearingly hapless.

Elizabeth stood when she saw Dr. Cable and Allen come out of the double doors, conferring. Allen made a helpless gesture, and the doctor shook his head.

She and Mac met them in the corridor.

"Mac...Elizabeth," Allen said, turning to her instinctively. "Dr. Cable says we need to do a Cesarean. But Tracy won't agree to it. She keeps insisting she wants to wait longer."

"And I told Allen we don't have any longer. He must make the decision. Tracy's too tired to be rational. When her water broke five hours ago, I put her on a Pitocin hormone drip to induce hard labor. But she's still not dilated sufficiently. If she starts hemorrhaging, her life could be in danger. And the fetal monitor is picking up signs of distress."

Dr. Cable looked at Allen hard. "We don't want to lose this baby or its mother."

Mac made an inarticulate sound, and his jaw worked spasmodically.

Elizabeth took a deep breath. "Let me go talk to her."

Allen grabbed at her suggestion as if it were a lifeline. "Would you, please?"

He looked back to the doctor. "Dammit, I'll sign the papers. But I want Tracy to agree. If she can."

Elizabeth marched down the hall and into the labor room. Tracy lay motionless, her face as white as the bed sheet. Lines of pain were etched around her mouth and eyes.

When Elizabeth bent over and whispered, "Tracy... ?" her lids fluttered open.

"Elizabeth—" her voice was barely audible "—I know I can do it."

"Listen to me, young lady," Elizabeth came back in her starchiest tone. "Remember that job you want me to apply for? Well, these are my terms, take 'em or leave 'em. You'll do exactly as I say and you'll do it now. Your husband wants to please you so much he's let you put your life and your baby in danger. Your father's working himself into a bleeding ulcer. And Mary looks like she might not make it through the night.

"You've earned your medal of bravery. Now it's time to stop putting yourself and everyone else through hell. Do you understand what I'm saying?"

Tracy wore a stunned expression, but she managed a "Yes."

"Squirt's got a lot of love waiting for him—"

"Or her."

"Or her. And right now your stubbornness is getting in the way. Have I made myself clear?"

"Yes." Tracy's lips quivered slightly.

"Good. Now I'm going out to get Allen and Dr. Cable, and when they come in, you'll consent to surgery. Are we agreed?"

Tracy nodded mutely.

Elizabeth leaned to kiss her before leaving.

"Elizabeth...." Tracy weakly lifted her arms, and Elizabeth gathered her up.

"It's going to be all right, honey," she whispered, stroking Tracy's back. "Just let go and stop trying to do it all yourself."

She could feel the tension ease out of Tracy's muscles as she let Elizabeth support her.

"That's a good girl. Just let go," she repeated, cradling Tracy's body. "You've been very brave. But it's time to get you some help."

Tracy let out a sobbing sigh and lay limply against her.

She rocked Tracy gently. "Everything," she vowed, "is going to be okay."

IT WAS CLOSE TO MIDNIGHT, and for the first time since morning, Elizabeth found herself alone in the waiting room.

Allen was in delivery watching his baby come into the world. Thank God, Elizabeth thought, for medicine's humane advances.

Herb and Mac, concerned with Mary's pallor, had insisted Herb take her home to rest until Tracy went into recovery, at which point they were to be notified of the blessed event.

Mac and Evan, prowling the halls like caged tigers, had been sent across the street to an all-night café. Elizabeth expected them back momentarily.

But for now, the corridors were practically deserted. The rest of the hospital had quieted for the night. And she had only her thoughts for company. Not that they frightened her. Dr. Cable knew what he was doing. She fully expected Tracy and the baby to come through fine.

As if her pronouncement were an omen, she saw the doctor exit the delivery room doors.

She hurried out to meet him.

"Tracy's fine. And so is the baby."

"And the father?"

"I think he'll pull through. They are now the proud parents of a seven-pound, twelve-ounce baby girl. The pediatrician's examining her, but she looks just great. She'll be taking up residence in the nursery soon."

"Thank you, Doctor."

He waved. "I'll see everyone tomorrow."

After he left, Elizabeth walked back into the waiting room, dazed and trembling with happiness, her forty hours of sleeplessness magnifying the moment.

As she sat down to wait for the men to return, her mind and emotions began to meander. To wander down unexpected paths.

Tracy's life. The life she'd given birth to.

Life. Death. Love. Separation.

The eternal verities of existence, which in times like these sweep away the daily fictions.

A child is born.

Tracy's child. Mac's grandchild.

The child she would never bear.

Love. Mac's love. Would he still offer it to her?

Separation. Must she face the rest of her life alone, as Sarah Elizabeth had been left alone because of the ultimate estrangement?

Death. Elizabeth had already mourned the death of her dream.

Now grief washed over her again. For the passing long ago of a man she'd never met yet knew through the eyes of the woman who loved him.

She knew now how and when Johnny had died. The news clipping she'd found with the poem had shown her. She'd read it over many times, reconciling herself to the tragic finality. The words were etched in her memory.

The Democratic Statesman
September 4, 1900
Thousands Feared Dead In Killer Storm

Galveston, Texas—A hurricane of monstrous proportions has swept over Galveston Island bringing with it the rampaging sea and leaving unbelievable destruction and death in its wake. This reporter finds it difficult to describe the scenes of devastation. Where days ago a prosperous seaport stood, now lie piles of rubble with bodies scattered like mannequins amidst the debris.

Among those missing and feared dead is our own beloved Johnny LeBow, late of this newspaper, who had recently taken up a position as editor in chief of the *Galveston Express*. Confirmation has come that he ventured out during the height of the storm to report its fury. If he must be gone, this is the way he would have wanted it. We mourn his passing and the many more who went with him.

The death toll is already estimated to be in excess of five thousand, and the grim task of identifying the bodies has begun. This newspaper will print casualty lists as they are provided. Authorities ask relatives to notify them of missing loved ones. They also urge relatives and curiosity seekers to stay away from the island.

A cholera epidemic is feared . . .

CHAPTER SIXTEEN

AT FIRST ONLY his anxious words whispered by her. "Elizabeth, wake up. Has there been any news?"

Then she felt the sweep of Mac's strong arms.

"She's been crying." Evan's voice, when he spoke, seemed to come from a distance.

"Elizabeth...?"

Mac's heightening anxiety forced open her eyes. She smiled sleepily into his before she took in the two tense figures.

"Tracy's fine," she said at once. "The baby's fine. We have a little girl. Seven pounds, twelve ounces. She should be on view in the nursery by now."

Just then Allen came out of the doors, looking spent but deliriously happy. Accepting congratulations all around, he announced, "Tracy's awake. She's already gotten to hold Mary Katherine."

He beamed foolishly. "Mary Katherine is what we've decided to name her. She's so beautiful. Come down to the nursery. She's just had her bath."

Evan followed Allen out of the room. Mac lingered to stare down into Elizabeth's tear-stained face.

"Are you okay?"

"You mean these?" She brushed at her cheek. "I was just relieved and happy. Without any sleep, I got carried away."

"But you were crying in your sleep."

"I must have drifted off and started dreaming."

"What about?"

"An old story." She evaded his look. "Nothing that concerns anybody."

"It concerns me." His gaze was very intense.

By now Elizabeth was fully awake. "Come on, Mac," she urged him while changing the subject, "call your mother. But hurry. I want to see the baby."

In the end, she couldn't wait and left him by the phone. She found Evan and Allen with their faces pressed against the window of the infant nursery. The object of their scrutiny was a small bundled blanket with a button nose sticking out. Even the baby's head had been covered with a knitted pink cap.

Wisps of blond hair curled out from the knitting. A heart-shaped mouth puckered in a sucking motion. Eyelids flickered open. Dark blue eyes looked around, unfocused.

"She is beautiful, Allen," Elizabeth crooned.

"She is?" Evan asked dubiously, obviously inexperienced in his avuncular role.

"All babies are perfect, Evan, didn't you know? Allen, was Mary aware she might have a namesake?"

"No. Tracy wants to tell her tomorrow." Allen turned to Elizabeth suddenly. "I hope Mac hasn't given away the surprise. I'd better catch him before he does."

After he'd taken off, Evan stood staring another moment at the baby. "I don't know," he said in a thin sounding voice. "I thought I wanted kids, but I don't think I could put someone through these last twenty-four hours."

Elizabeth examined several responses before she found one to offer. "Tracy wanted Mary Katherine as much as

Allen," she reminded him. "I think if you asked, she'd say it was all worthwhile."

"Yeah, but you can't tell me she knew what she was getting into."

"Evan—" she cupped his shoulder "—how many of us ever know what we're heading into? And aren't we glad we don't?"

At last she managed to elicit a grin. But he obviously continued to struggle with the matter. "Still, times like this make you stop and wonder. Seems like the more you know, the more courage it takes."

"How did you get to be so wise?" she asked him half-teasingly.

"I didn't always ask for it."

"We seldom do."

He ducked his head before meeting her look. "Does any of this have to do with you and Dad? Last night, I could tell things still weren't right between you." He shook his head in self-disgust. "Hell, I'm getting as bad as Tracy. But I just wanted to say—I wanted to make sure you knew... I won't be in the way much longer."

"Evan." She looked straight into his eyes, willing him to listen. "You'll never be in the way. Ever. Don't you know, two of Mac's biggest assets with me are his children."

"Yeah, well, I just wanted to say it to you. Just in case." His face was fiery.

"And you have. Now don't worry about it again. That's an order." She hugged him briefly. "Go find out what's holding up your father. I want him to see his first grandchild."

Relieved, Evan wandered off to see what was keeping Mac.

For a moment, Elizabeth stood alone at the window. As she gazed down at the tiny bundle of life and pictured her in Tracy's arms, she waited anxiously for the dreaded envy. When it didn't come, she leaned against the glass, dizzy with relief.

She could barely wait to see Tracy holding her baby.

Elizabeth smiled mistily. "You don't know it yet, Mary Katherine, but you are one lucky kid. You're gonna have so many people in your life to love you—"

Mac's arm went around her shoulders. "Which one is she?"

"The prettiest one, of course."

Elizabeth pointed to the identifying information.

"Of course," Mac said, peering through the window. "She looks just like me."

"She does not. The only thing you have in common is a probable bald spot."

Mac lifted his hand to his hair. "I am not balding. I've just thinned a little." He glared down at her, and his expression stilled.

"What? Again?" he asked, and caught a tear on his finger.

"She's just so small and beautiful. I can't get over the wonder of life."

"If I don't get you home, where you can rest," he said gruffly, "you'll be wondering if you're still alive."

"I know. And Tracy probably won't be up to seeing anyone but Allen and the baby till tomorrow."

She lingered another moment, gazing down at Mary Katherine, before Mac took her arm and guided her away.

"I've sent Evan home to bed," he said while they waited for an elevator.

"Good. I could tell he'd had about all he could stand of hospital routine."

"So have I," Mac muttered. He studied her closely. "It was good of you to stay."

"Tracy asked me to," she said simply.

He acknowledged her explanation with a single nod.

Moments later, as he led her through the parking garage, Elizabeth felt the full weight of exhaustion drag at her body. She stumbled. Mac caught her. And when they reached his car, he carefully tucked her in.

She must have dozed during the ride, because the next thing she knew, Mac was opening the car door where he'd parked beside her house.

While he rummaged through her purse for the door key, she leaned against him heavily, not sure she had the coordination to stand alone.

When the couple entered the darkened house, three vociferous cats greeted them.

"They haven't been fed," Elizabeth mumbled.

"I'll do it." Mac took her directly to the bedroom. "Undress and climb into bed. I'll be back in a minute."

She stepped out of her clothes and slipped between the covers, leaving various garments strewn around the floor. Stretching luxuriously, she reveled in the texture of the sheets as they caressed her skin, the give of the mattress as it cradled her weary muscles.

So tired. So relieved. So at peace.

Damn... the light was still on.

In a minute.

In just a minute she'd get up to switch it off.

Hearing a faint click, she felt darkness dust her eyelids. The bed sagged, the covers shifted, and Mac's hands pulled her surely into the bow of his body.

Elizabeth burrowed close with an inarticulate murmur.

Seconds later, she was fast asleep. . . .

SHE WAS SITTING in the turret room, part of a circle of women. Warmth and light sifted in through the windows, with patterns of leaves drifting over the floor. A quilt stretched in front of her; in her hand was a needle. Meticulously she began to stitch.

In the center of the quilt a flowering tree had been sewn, with birds and a squirrel decorating its branches. In each of the squares that surrounded the tree, a wildflower bloomed with a splash of color.

Elizabeth stopped for a moment to admire the bluebonnet she was outlining with fine stitchery. Looking up, she found Carol and Hope to her right and Tracy and Mary to her left. All were bent to their squares of cloth.

When Elizabeth glanced across the quilt, she discovered her mother looking well and happy, as she'd been before her illness. She was chatting and laughing with Sarah Elizabeth. The two women smiled as she caught their attention.

She smiled back serenely and again took up her needle.

The door opened and a nurse entered, carrying a newborn baby girl. First the nurse offered the infant to Mary, who cradled her lovingly and after a moment passed her to Sarah Elizabeth.

One by one each of the women held her. When Elizabeth's turn came, the babe cooed and clutched at one of Elizabeth's fingers.

Then the baby's face puckered into a hungry whimper. Elizabeth turned to Tracy, who took the infant to her waiting breast. As the other women began to sew once more, Tracy nursed and rocked contentedly.

The scene changed....

Elizabeth lay on a pallet in a spring meadow. The scent of bluebonnets sweetened the air. A sound of a bee droned close to her ear. Warm sunlight streamed over her naked body.

When the warmth changed texture, she opened her eyes and found Mac kneeling beside her, his nude body shadowing the sun.

As he watched her lie there, a butterfly fluttered near, and after hovering for a moment, lighted on a breast.

The butterfly became Mac's fingers, flickering over her.

With a languid stretch she invited his touch, and he molded her body to fit his pleasure.

This time when Elizabeth opened her eyes, heat and darkness surrounded her senses. Mac had found her breasts with his mouth and was teasing her nipples. One of his hands had insinuated itself between her legs.

She moaned and arched to his stroking.

He lifted his head to move up over her. Her fingers delved into his hair, urging him down to meet her lips.

Elizabeth's acknowledging gesture was all Mac needed. As his mouth sought hers and their tongues tangled, he moved urgently between her thighs.

She met him and they joined.

In the darkness and heat they fused their passion. Wordlessly. Yet with murmuring sounds of delight.

She came with a cry and he came with her.

Then he laid his head against her heart.

WHEN ELIZABETH AWAKENED the next day, she sensed she was alone. Her hands searched for Mac beside her, but she found only his imprint. Her bedside clock informed her it was close to noon.

Grumbling to herself, she scrambled out of bed and threw on a robe.

"Mac?"

She followed the scent of coffee into the kitchen. He'd brewed a pot and placed his dirty cup in the sink. Outside of that, he'd left no traces of his stay. When she went to the side door, his BMW was gone.

Thoroughly out of sorts, she wandered back to the kitchen and discovered the message he'd left on the table.

Elizabeth,
I had to run by my office to check an order for a job that starts tomorrow. Should be back by twelve or one at the latest. In the meantime, have some decent coffee for a change and take your time dressing. We'll go to the hospital this afternoon.

                                                              Mac

Hope you had a good night's sleep. Parts of mine were excellent.

As a love note, his directive left something to be desired. And if he thought she'd be content to sit around waiting for him, he didn't know her as well as he imagined. She had important activities planned for today.

She did condescend to pour a cup of his coffee. Sipping from it slowly, she sighed in bliss. It was nice to love a man who was multitalented, even if his nature was sometimes less than romantic.

Of course, she was presuming quite a bit, Elizabeth realized belatedly. Still, last night hadn't been a dream, at least not those "excellent" parts of it.

Mac's body had spoken to hers though no words had been uttered. And when next they met, she knew what she wanted to say.

After an invigorating shower, Elizabeth dressed and called the hospital.

Mary answered the phone in Tracy's room.

"How's everyone doing?" Elizabeth asked.

"Tracy's in better shape than Allen. Poor boy, he collapsed sometime early this morning, and I sent him home to get some sleep. Elizabeth, they've named the baby after me. I got to hold her after Tracy nursed her this morning."

The half-forgotten dream flickered through Elizabeth's mind.

She asked smilingly, "Did you tell her she had to get used to being passed around?"

"I should have. Allen's parents fly in this afternoon. She's their first grandchild. Which reminds me, where's my son this fine Sunday morning?"

"He had to run by his office." She recognized too late what her answer implied.

"How's Grandpa taking his change in status?" Mary asked slyly.

Elizabeth remembered their lovemaking. "I'd say he's holding up pretty well."

"Tracy wants to know when you'll be up here."

"I'm leaving right away."

Twenty minutes later, she walked into Tracy's room. Mary was there along with a woman. A pretty woman, petite and delicate, who looked to Elizabeth like a youthful thirty-five.

"Darling," the woman was saying, "I don't know why you dragged it out so long. We just aren't equipped to have children the hard way. I wish you'd listened to me."

"What's done is done, Karen," Tracy said patiently. She saw Elizabeth and her face lit up.

"Karen, I'd like you to meet Elizabeth Waite. Elizabeth, this is my mother, Karen."

Karen smiled charmingly at the newcomer, then turned back to her daughter. "I'm just glad you didn't call me until this morning, when everything was over. I don't think I could have stood seeing my little girl in pain."

"I know," Tracy said evenly. "That's why I waited."

Karen beamed at the other two occupants of the room. "Isn't she thoughtful? But much too young to have babies."

"You mean," Mary said, "you're not ready to be a grandmother."

Karen looked at her with a hurt expression before she decided laughter was a more becoming response. "Actually, I've decided Tracy and I are more like sisters. We look enough alike, don't you think?"

Elizabeth realized Karen was asking this of her. "Yes," she agreed dutifully. "The resemblance is striking."

And it was. Elizabeth had always thought Mac's daughter took after Mary. Now she understood where Tracy got her gaminelike features and slight figure.

When she saw Karen's pleased expression, she realized she'd answered correctly.

"Well, I have to go." Karen stood gracefully. "Darling, do take care of yourself. I'm afraid I won't be in town the next few weeks. Of course, I can change my plans, if you need me. Although I'm not much good at a sickbed...." Her voice trailed off. She said the last with a certain distaste.

"Go on with your trip," Tracy said soothingly. "I have more than enough nurses."

Elizabeth could sense Karen heave an inner sigh of relief.

"I was sure you did." She aimed a kiss near Tracy's forehead. "Give Evan and your father my love. It was delightful meeting you . . ." She faltered.

"Elizabeth," Tracy supplied.

"Elizabeth," Karen repeated. "And Mary, so good to see you."

She bussed Mary's cheek and sailed out of the room, trailing a cloud of Giorgio perfume.

As soon as she was gone, Tracy rolled her eyes and broke the tension, but when Elizabeth leaned over to offer a proper hello, she clung for an extra moment.

Settling down beside her, Elizabeth said conversationally, "Now you can tell me all about Mary Katherine."

A SHORT TIME LATER, Dr. Cable interrupted their cozy chat. He'd come to give Tracy her afternoon checkup, and the other two women left them to stroll down the hall.

"I'm pleased to say my son's taste has improved," Mary said without preamble, as soon as they were safely out of the new mother's earshot.

Elizabeth didn't pretend to misunderstand. "Karen's quite beautiful. I see where Tracy gets her looks."

"Fortunately, she inherited the Reynolds backbone. Although I must say in Mac's defense, Karen wasn't always this insipid. Some people grow through adversity, some people shrivel. You can see what happened to poor Karen. And now you understand why I feel protective of the children."

"Yes."

"And why I'm so glad to see the three of you grow close. Karen never knew how to parent. She always reminds me of the depressing fact that being a biological mother doesn't guarantee a woman a maternal instinct."

No more than being childless prevents a woman from understanding how to nurture.

As if mirroring her thoughts, Mary went on, "I was hoping you'd provide Tracy and Evan with some mothering. Although I have to warn you, grown children are the hardest to raise."

Elizabeth laughed. "I'll keep that in mind."

Mary sent her a direct look. "Karen should be a lesson to us both."

"Oh?"

"Not to run away from whatever life plans for us."

"Well, I'm glad to see you stopped running." She smiled. "Herb's a lucky man."

"No," Mary said, her look softening. "I'm the lucky one."

"You're both very fortunate. And I'm delighted for you. I have to go now. Tell Tracy I'll be back this evening."

"But where are you going? You just arrived."

"I have to go visit an old, dear friend."

"What about Mac? He called earlier, asked if you were here and said he was on his way. What will I tell him?"

"That I'll be back soon."

"But...?"

Elizabeth had no prior experience with future mothers-in-law, but she knew already she'd have to set limits on this one.

"Mary." She took hold of the older woman's shoulders and kissed both her cheeks. "Go keep Tracy company and stop being so nosy."

Mary's delighted chuckle followed her down the hall.

ELIZABETH WAS GLAD to find the CCE premises deserted, as she didn't want to explain the reason she was there. After she unlocked the front door, she didn't bother to go by her office. Instead, she headed directly for the flight of stairs.

Her footfalls echoed hollowly in the empty hallway, yet she didn't feel alone. Others hovered near, blessing her presence.

When she arrived at the appointed place, Sarah Elizabeth was waiting as though she were expected.

For a moment, Elizabeth didn't know how to begin. So much had happened within herself.

At last she said quietly, "Thank you for being with me the other evening. For appearing to me as you have. You've taught me so much. Now I want to find a way to help you."

She gazed at Sarah Elizabeth, searching her expression, and saw the same beseeching look of that first gloomy night.

"I know how Johnny died," she said in a rush. "I found the clipping in your book of sonnets."

As soon as she spoke, a swell of sadness washed over her. She struggled through it to find words to say.

"I feel like I know him. I see why you loved him. I wish . . . I wish you could have had a life together. I wish

I knew how to comfort you at his loss. I wish I could bring you peace at last.''

As Elizabeth watched Sarah Elizabeth for a sign or direction, she seemed to cry out and sink to the floor.

Her silent sobs tore at Elizabeth's heart.

''Is the returned letter the key?'' she asked urgently. ''Was it sent to him too late?''

And this time, the same ineffable sadness she'd felt from the first became at last the answer to her questions.

''I think,'' she whispered, ''I'm beginning to understand. You know, I've often wanted to open and read what you wrote, but I admit I was afraid of what I would find. And I couldn't break the seal you'd left for a lifetime without coming first to ask your permission.''

Elizabeth moved closer and held out her hand. ''I'm not afraid anymore. I feel I can help you.''

Sarah Elizabeth raised her face in profound entreaty.

''Will the letter free you? Do you want me to read it?''

Yes . . . yes. . . .

The plea whispered like a murmuring wind.

Carrying Sarah Elizabeth away.

Leaving only a trace of her shadow on the wooden veranda.

ELIZABETH DIDN'T REMEMBER much of the drive home. When she arrived, she hurried in and retrieved Sarah Elizabeth's belongings, her mind and heart intent on her task.

Carefully, lovingly, she arranged them on her kitchen table. The shawl, the diaries, the brass letter opener, Johnny's articles, his letters, the books he'd given her. The final clipping. And the still-sealed letter.

Elizabeth's hand shook slightly as she picked up the letter opener and gently tore open the envelope flap.

The stationery was thin and crinkled as she unfolded it, and Elizabeth pressed flat the pages of script.

And after ninety years of being trapped in darkness, the words Sarah Elizabeth had written were freed to be read and revealed to the light.

August 26, 1900

My Dearest Johnny;

I must write it once more! My dearest, dearest Johnny. Indeed, I feel the urge to shout it from the rooftops. I wish everyone could know the joy in my heart.

"How do I love thee? Let me count the ways...." The poets say it best. Yet what I write must be in my own words.

You were right, dearest. Everything you said that day was true. We do not need to ask God to forgive us. The God I believe in is not a vengeful Being. I know He will bless our imminent union. I have come to understand my feelings these last weeks as I have seen more clearly. We need only ask forgiveness of ourselves, dearest love.

When we spoke, you had made peace with yourself. Now I have done so.

The first half of my life was given to your father. I was the best wife and companion I knew how to be. Perhaps I should feel guilty his life was prolonged through my efforts. I only know I did what I must through the years. As we all must.

Now it is over. He rests in peace.

And I am free to give my love to you.

Oh, Johnny, it wasn't so much guilt that bound me and made me turn away from your proposal. It was fear.

I see that now. I have lived a circumscribed existence. You have tasted of the world. I was not sure I could be the wife you truly needed. I could not believe that you would want me as I am. I still cannot believe it.

But I must! Because you spoke it. Just as you promised I would write this letter. Your trust was greater than mine. You kept the faith I'd lost, dearest.

Thank you for believing in my love.

I love you, Johnny. I will love you forever.

Come to me! This instant! I am impatient, my love, to feel your touch. I ache with longing. Only you can assuage my desire.

Will the newspaper still grant you immediate leave to take your bride on her honeymoon? If not, insist upon it! I can think of no greater pleasure than to see New York City from the midst of your arms.

Read no further. I want to whisper my love words to you. I want to hold thy heart in mine.

Come to me, Johnny. Claim me as your own.

CHAPTER SEVENTEEN

THE RING OF THE KITCHEN phone broke Elizabeth's reverie. Dropping Sarah Elizabeth's letter to the table and wiping her eyes, she reached for the receiver.

"Where the hell have you been?" Mac asked as soon as she answered. "Mother said you left the hospital on a mysterious errand, and I've been calling you every twenty minutes for the last hour."

"Mac, I love you." She took a deep breath and let it out raggedly. "I love you."

After a long moment of silence, he asked, "Is there a qualifier attached to that declaration?"

"No. Just—I love you. I wanted to be sure you knew."

"I love you, too," he answered. "Elizabeth, about the other night—"

"No. Not over the telephone. Come to me, Mac. I want us to speak face-to-face. I want to whisper my love words to you. I want to hold you to my heart."

She heard a muttered exclamation, then, "I'm on my way."

"Mac!"

"What?"

"Don't...don't have a wreck. Don't let anything happen to you."

"Elizabeth, *nothing* is going to come between us. Hold on, sweetheart, I'll be right there."

The twenty minutes Mac took seemed like a lifetime. When he arrived, she flew out the door and into his arms.

"Hey! What's going on?" he asked as she clung to him fervently.

"Just shut up and let me kiss you," she directed, and proceeded to do so in a thorough fashion.

Mac lifted her bodily and went inside.

When she started to unbutton his shirt, however, he halted her progress, set her away from him and held up a hand.

"Wait. We'll get to that later."

Before he spoke again, he took time to study her.

"I don't know what brought this on," he said at last, "but I'm ready to take advantage of it. Will you marry me?"

"Yes."

"Elizabeth, I wanted to say how wrong I—"

"No, let me say it. I apologize for what happened. I said and did some hurtful things."

"I was an insensitive clod."

"No. You were stunned, and I don't blame you. You couldn't possibly know that the woman you loved looked on you as a means to an end."

"Because it wasn't true. I knew you loved me, too."

"Then you had more faith in me than I did. It's taken me a while, but I've finally worked through this. Much of what you said that evening was true. I was so consumed by my own needs, I couldn't see what you'd been through. I understand better now."

"I understand, too. Listen—"

She covered his lips with her fingers. "Just—just please don't believe I'd ever look on another person as a possession. I'd hate for you to think that of me."

"No! God, no, Elizabeth. Just the opposite." He claimed her hands with his. "I've been doing a lot of thinking, as well. These last two days have been a revelation. Do you know what Tracy called you?"

She shook her head.

"A nurturing woman. A woman made to have children. She was right. And I've been selfish to want you all to myself."

"No, Mac—"

But he wouldn't let her speak. "You make me happy, Elizabeth. I want to make you happy. And if having a baby will accomplish that, we'll have one. Someway or other."

Elizabeth searched his face. He was utterly sincere.

"You're not selfish," she said. "You are a very generous man."

"I can afford to be. If I have you."

"But as it turns out," she said, smiling, "I don't need to have a baby."

"Don't lie to me," he came back sternly. "I saw you crying at the nursery window."

"Oh, Mac, you idiot. I explained those tears. When I looked at Mary Katherine, what I felt was peace and joy and a newfound freedom."

"But you also felt sorrow at relinquishing your dream. I don't want you to sacrifice anything to be my wife."

She stood back, looked him over leisurely and wiggled her eyebrows. "Some sacrifice."

"You have just changed the subject." The stern tone reentered his voice.

"Not entirely." She reached out to stroke his cheek ever so lightly. "Mac, you once pointed out that life wasn't tidy or simple. We also know it's all about compromise and accommodation. I've sacrificed in the past.

And so have you. We will again. But we are so very lucky to have found each other. Our love gives meaning to both our pasts and our future. And I want you to understand that my relationship with you will always be the most important thing in my life."

"Yes, but I want to give you motherhood, a child to cherish. What the hell, I've gotten pretty good at this fatherhood business."

"You're a wonderful father. The only child I'd ever want would be yours. And since you already have two, I thought we could share."

"Oh, Elizabeth," he murmured, and took her into his arms. "I only want your fulfillment."

"Then listen to me carefully. You know that engagement of mine Mary told you about?"

"Yes."

"It wasn't what you'd call a passionate attachment. Steven was a good, kind man. But frankly, I was marrying him so I could raise a family. I've never been passionately in love before. And when I imagined having someone to care for, I thought only a child could fulfill me."

She stroked back his hair with her fingers. "But I am desperately in love with you. And being your wife and partner and friend and bedmate sounds like a full-time occupation." Elizabeth smiled at him tenderly. "Did I miss any of the job requirements?"

"I don't think so," he answered gruffly. But she could still see a question lingering in his eyes.

"Mac, dearest...." She cupped his face between her hands. "My dearest, dearest Mac. You must believe me when I say—the only fulfillment I need is being a wife to the man I love."

He gave a shuddering sigh before he pressed her lips with his. His arms convulsed around her. "I do believe you. And I want you to know...loving you completes me."

They stood for a timeless moment fused by the joy in their hearts.

Finally, Elizabeth leaned back and grinned, lightening the moment. "Now, about those two children..."

"They've already claimed you."

"I'd also like to put in my application for the post of Grandma."

"You're the sexiest grandmother I've ever made love to."

She pushed her hands against his chest. "Just how large is your sampling?"

"You're the only grandmother," he clarified, "I've ever made love to."

"Be sure and keep it that way."

"I would like to negotiate a similar arrangement."

She chuckled as she wrapped her arms around his neck. "I promise not to proposition any other grannies."

"You know what I mean," he growled, and pulled away slightly to gaze down at her. "Marry me now."

"Today?"

"Within the week," he compromised grudgingly.

Elizabeth thought of Johnny and Sarah Elizabeth.

"Handling the logistics would be difficult...." she began.

"To hell with logistics. Or better yet, we'll let Mother deal with them."

"I'd hoped Tracy could be my matron of honor."

"And I'll ask Evan to be my best man. Okay. We wait till Tracy and the baby are home from the hospital and she's had a chance to recover. That's my final offer."

"I'll take it," she said.

ON A FRIDAY EVENING three weeks later, Mac and Elizabeth were married in Tracy and Allen's home.

The intervening period had been hectic. Elizabeth's work hadn't diminished in consideration of her upcoming nuptials. She, Herb and Carol wrote grants to be submitted to the city and county. And as a result of the publicity from the gala, Elizabeth had received several requests to speak on CCE's behalf. She'd had little time to call her own.

Away from work, Mac was an ardent and persistent lover. Elizabeth understood why he claimed her evenings and nights. The period of estrangement had frightened both of them. But because of his attentions, never once did she get the chance to pay a call on her friend. Yet she sensed Sarah Elizabeth had found peace at last. She'd felt it from the moment she'd read the letter.

One evening while Mac was in her kitchen puttering over supper, Elizabeth had opened the door to a long-closed room. Taking a key from her mother's jewelry case, she unlocked the chest at the foot of her parents' bed.

Inside was her mother's wedding dress and veil. Baby clothes Elizabeth had worn. Bootees and a cap her mother had crocheted for her hope chest.

Elizabeth retrieved the handmade baby quilt, the bootees and cap and her own tiny christening dress. They were to be a gift to Tracy and her newborn daughter. In their place, she put Sarah Elizabeth's possessions. Gently she closed the chest and put away the key.

Fortunately, considering the tight schedule for the wedding, Mary came through on the arrangements in her usual fashion, and all the happy couple needed to do was show up on time.

Mary had even procured a dress for the bride. An ivory silk sheath topped by a long-sleeved jacket with a mandarin collar.

When, at Mary's insistence, Elizabeth had modeled the outfit, she'd had to admit that the simple lines complemented her lithe figure and lent her an air of elegance.

On the day of the wedding, she decided that Mac was exceedingly handsome in his dark suit and tie.

Present for the ceremony were Mac's two brothers and their wives, Herb and Mary and assorted other members of the Reynolds clan. Elizabeth's brother and sister-in-law. Carol and Lane. Joe Beasley and his granddaughter. Hope and Suzanne.

Tracy, though still a little fragile, was blooming nonetheless and openly smug as she stood next to Elizabeth. Evan was preternaturally solemn. But when he handed his father the simple gold bands, she recognized his gleam of satisfaction.

When she and Mac exchanged the time-honored vows, Elizabeth felt a great well of love bubbling within her. They had been given so much. They had so much to share.

As the ritual unfolded, she understood that their joy was the joy of all lovers, and she knew they weren't saying their vows for themselves alone. Next to Mac she could almost make out a shadowy figure. And she felt Sarah Elizabeth's presence deep within.

Afterward, everyone agreed the wedding was beautiful.

"So when are you and Herb going to take the plunge?" Carol asked Mary.

"Actually," Mary said, drawing everyone's attention, "there's a charming chapel outside of Dunedin, New Zealand. We thought while we were in the neighborhood, we'd helicopter ski the New Zealand Alps."

"Do you ever get the feeling," Mac said close to Elizabeth's ear, "that we'd have a hard time keeping up with them?"

"Mmm-hmm." She leaned against his chest, enjoying the feel of him along the length of her back.

"You're living dangerously," he told her.

"I hope so," she said, but straightened when Joe's granddaughter came to offer congratulations.

"I just wanted to tell you how excited Joe was when you invited us to the wedding. He said your getting married would make everything right." The young woman looked at Elizabeth curiously. "Do you have any idea what he meant by that?"

Elizabeth glanced over where Joe and Herb were deep in conversation.

"Your grandfather is a very dear man," she said. "Visiting him and his garden helped me get through the spring."

She was saved further explanation when Hope and Suzanne took the granddaughter's place in the impromptu receiving line.

"I knew CCE had developed a number of programs," Suzanne said, "but I didn't realize we ran a matrimonial bureau."

"I think," Hope said, "it's one of our most innovative projects."

"Do you suppose we could find any grant money for it?" Carol had joined them and added this quip.

"I don't know," Hope responded. "But I bet we'd get a whole passel of volunteers."

Everyone laughed as Elizabeth offered her cheek for the requisite kisses.

"Please tell us," Suzanne said with just a hint of distress, "that we aren't losing you as well as Mac."

"Don't worry," she assured them. "I'll be in bright and early Monday morning."

"Not too bright and early," Mac contradicted dryly.

"But I'll be there," she said, fighting a becoming blush. "The coalition still has a few battles to fight."

Herb and Mary took the place of the three women.

"Welcome to the family," Mary said as she embraced Elizabeth. "And congratulations, son." She hugged Mac, too. "With a little help from me, you did quite well for yourself."

"Wait a minute," Evan said from just behind them. "Tracy and I should get the credit. Elizabeth told me we were Dad's chief assets."

"Well, at least I know you're not marrying me for my money," Mac murmured for her ears alone.

Turning she kissed him and whispered, "There are a few other assets that captured my attention."

"Okay, okay," Evan complained. "You have time for that later."

He freed Elizabeth from Mac's clutches and slung an arm casually around her neck. "Yes, I'd say we got ourselves a fine little stepmom." He grinned down at her, and for just a moment they shared a private look.

Evan turned to the others. "I thought for a while Dad had bungled the job and we were going to have to call in reinforcements."

"What's this about reinforcements?" Tracy had arrived, carrying the youngest member of the family. "Mary Kate wants to say hello to Grandma Elizabeth."

Elizabeth immediately cradled her and moved to a chair to enjoy the greeting. Mac and Tracy followed them.

"Hello, sweetheart," Elizabeth said softly. "Are you happy with your grandma?" Mary Katherine stared up with a wondering expression.

Holding her close, Elizabeth stroked one rosy cheek and was rewarded with a contented burp.

"Be careful," Tracy warned, draping a blanket over Elizabeth's silk-clad shoulder. "She's just had supper."

"I don't care about the dress," Elizabeth said dismissively. She nuzzled the soft skin of Mary Katherine's neck.

"I can tell," Tracy moaned, "you're going to spoil her rotten."

"Well, of course. That's what grandmas are for." She kissed a button nose. "Aren't they, sweet thing?"

Mary Katherine gurgled her agreement.

Seeing herself outnumbered, Tracy threw up her hands and left them in peace.

Dropping to a crouch beside the chair, Mac looked deep into Elizabeth's eyes.

"Are you sure you don't want a comparable model?" he asked. "You'd make a beautiful mother. I never realized just how beautiful until seeing you like this."

"Thank you, Mac, for a lovely compliment." She smiled and leaned to kiss him. "I have a feeling you'll find me in this pose rather often. Tracy plans for us to do our share of baby-sitting, in case you haven't realized it yet."

"She does?" He looked disconcerted.

Elizabeth laughed and nodded. "I thought we'd fix up your spare bedroom as a nursery."

She directed him into the chair and handed the baby over. "Here. You might as well get used to it."

Mac took his granddaughter with a surprisingly sure touch. As Elizabeth watched him grin into the miniature features, she felt a shimmering surge of excitement.

Lord, how she did adore this man!

Mac glanced up, caught the look and returned it. Then he stared solemnly down at Mary Katherine. "Little one, as much as I'd like to stay and get better acquainted, there's this older woman making goo-goo eyes at me. I think," he went on confidingly, "she wants to drag me off so she can make mad, passionate love to me. And, the truth of the matter is, I'm putty in her hands."

"Mac, behave! Mary Kate's ears are innocent."

"Well, she might as well get used to goings-on among her relatives, because I don't intend—"

"I know, dear," Elizabeth said hurriedly, taking the baby from him. "You've already told me."

Tracy, seeing the commotion, sent Allen over to rescue their offspring.

Soon afterward, the newlyweds made their escape. In the nick of time, Elizabeth decided. Mac's behavior had become unruly.

When he'd patted her backside in plain sight of a just introduced sister-in-law, she knew it was his way of saying he was ready to embark on their own private celebration.

"Alone at last," Mac said as soon as they reached his car. He pulled her to him for several lingering kisses. "Mmm...I may just take you home. We'll drive to Kerrville later."

They were spending their first weekend as man and wife in a charming Texas hill-country inn.

"Mac..." she said breathlessly when she had time to speak, "before we make the trip down, I need to go by the office."

"What?" He drew away from her, frowning.

"I... I need to go by the office, for just a minute."

"We have little enough honeymoon as it is," he grumbled. "If you think I'm going to share you with a computer printout..."

"That's not why I need to run by," she assured him, and ran her hands up under his suit coat. "Just fifteen minutes. I have a small errand to do. Then I'm all yours."

"Are you trying to get around me with your womanly wiles?" he asked suspiciously, fighting a grin.

"Do you think I could?" Her hands wandered lower. "It's a distinct possibility."

He groaned. "You win. I'll give you fifteen minutes."

Pleased with her efforts, she settled back in her seat. Having womanly wiles was an intoxicating feeling.

"I've created a monster," Mac mumbled as he started the car.

Several minutes later, in transit, he glanced her way. "Okay. What's this errand you have that's so urgent? You know—" his look was speculative "—you're occasionally a mysterious lady."

"Do you know what I believe?" she said, ignoring his comment. "I believe this love we share isn't ours, not really."

"Oh?" His expression, this time, was arrested by her tone.

"Yes. I think it was just entrusted to us. To use wisely and then pass on."

"A lovely thought, but I'm not sure what you mean by it."

She smiled. "Maybe I didn't intend to be understood. You're always saying you know me so well. Perhaps I should be more enigmatic. To hold your interest."

He pulled up in front of the main entrance to the old building.

"Lady." He turned to her and grinned. "I expect you'll hold my interest for the next forty years—without much trouble."

"Mac—" her voice was suddenly urgent "—are you sure?"

"Now what's bothering you?" He took her face in his hands.

"It's too late to back out," she said.

"Who wants to?" he asked. "What on earth has got you obsessing?"

"Nothing. I just feel we've been specially blessed. And we have the responsibility to be very very happy. To make up for..."

"For what?"

She shook her head. "Don't mind me. I'm bewitched by the day. Do you realize we're actually married?"

"And do you realize we're wasting our honeymoon sitting in a car in front of your office?"

She opened the door. "I'll be right back."

"I'll go in with you."

"No." She held up a palm. "You stay here. I'll just be a minute."

He looked at her oddly but did as she asked.

Elizabeth hurried into the building. When she reached the turret room, she unlocked the door and went in. For a moment she stood silently, looking around, remembering.

Then opening the door to the porch, she took a peek down at the street, where Mac was parked. She could just make out his head through the back windshield of his car. He wouldn't be able to see her from where he sat.

Smiling, she continued out on the veranda.

No one was waiting to meet her. But she felt there was one last appointment to keep.

"I don't know if you're still here, Sarah Elizabeth. I understand how opening the letter freed you. How having another person read your words of love somehow made up for Johnny never seeing them."

Elizabeth looked around and saw no one, yet serenity enveloped her. She closed her eyes for a moment, letting that serenity settle in her being.

"I wanted you to know," she said finally, "that Mac and I are married. And we're going to lead a full and happy life together. I want to thank you again for all you've given me. It's so much more than I could give you. But I promise the love Mac and I share will somehow make up for all you and Johnny were denied."

She opened her eyes slowly, and Sarah Elizabeth stood smiling at the far end of the porch. Just beyond her hovered the figure of a man.

Come to me! This instant!

Johnny had obeyed the summons and returned at last.

As Elizabeth watched, speechless, the two figures embraced, kissed and slowly dissolved.

A strangled sound caused her to turn around.

Mac stood rooted behind her, the most peculiar expression on his face.

"Elizabeth . . . ?"

He stared at her for a long moment before his look was drawn back to the spot where the ghostly couple had made their farewell appearance.

"Who—" he cleared his throat "—who were you talking to? Did I just see...?"

He shook his head in bemusement and couldn't seem to finish, then he blurted out his fear. "What the hell is going on here? You took too long. I was worried!"

"And impatient."

"Damned right. And when I found you..." Again he wasn't able to complete the thought.

Taking pity on him, she wrapped her arms around his waist and laid her cheek against his shirt.

"Do you really want me to explain what you saw just now?"

He pulled away to stare at her, his look a combination of amusement, speculation and sheer astonishment.

"Yes. Although I have a feeling I'd better be sitting down."

She hugged him briefly before tugging at his hand. "Let's go, then. You can lie down if you want to. I'll tell you a bedtime story. About two sets of lovers."

"How does the story end?" His lips quirked upward.

"Happily." She kissed him. "The best ones always do."

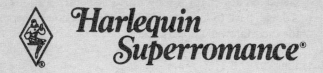

Harlequin Superromance®

COMING NEXT MONTH

#474 ALL THE RIGHT MOVES • Brenna Todd
New principal Lesley Tyler wanted everything done by the book. Football coach Gil Fielden wanted a winning team. When Lesley enforced the no-pass, no-play rule at Warren High School in West Texas, Gil knew it could cost him the state championship. Which was more important? Winning the title or winning Lesley?

#475 NIGHTSHADES AND ORCHIDS • Kelly Walsh
If only they'd met under different circumstances, Sharon McClure knew she and Steve Nordstrom could have had a future. But Steve's brother had been murdered, and Sharon was the only suspect.

#476 MADE TO ORDER • Risa Kirk
Kay Stockwell wanted no part of Del Rafferty's plan to improve her company's image. She was an engineer who built robots and, as she was fond of saying, she dealt in substance, not style. But Del was a man with a style all his own. It was something Kay was finding hard to resist.

#477 MOON SHADOW • Dawn Stewardson
In 1887, the West was wild—and dangerous. Schoolmarm Emma McCully had to save her brother from being hanged as a horse thief in Tombstone, Arizona. Luckily, her brother's childhood friend, Will Lockhart, showed up to help her. Only one thing about Will had Emma worried. He seemed to believe he was from the future—from the twenty-first century, to be exact....